DOWNFALL'S ECHO

THE KYONA CHRONICLES BOOK SIX

DEBORAH GRACE WHITE

LUMINANT PUBLICATIONS

DOWNFALL'S ECHO

By Deborah Grace White

Downfall's Echo

The Kyona Chronicles Book Six

ISBN: 978-1-925898-38-5

Luminant Publications
PO Box 201
Burnside, South Australia 5066

http://www.deborahgracewhite.com

Cover Design by Karri Klawiter
Map illustration by Rebecca E. Paavo

For my brother Stephen
Knights may not be a thing anymore, but honor and valor still are.

Forest of Rune
Dragon Real
VAS
Kynton
Kerr
Montego
Pravat
GREAT RIVER
KYONA
Nerita
Argath
Alezae
MARSHLANDS
NORTH L
SOUTH L
BALENOL
BASE TREE

North Wilds
ELISA
VALORIA
DRAGONCAVE
LOCH ARINE
Arinton
Basal Headlands
Wyvern Islands
Bryford
ANDS
ANDS
Razad's Bastion
Nohl
Jeweled Peaks
Thirk
THORANIA
Logging Camp
SPICE FIELDS

CHAPTER ONE

Henrik drew in a deep breath, satisfaction coursing through him as he inhaled the clean Valorian air. Not that there was anything wrong with Kyona's air, of course. He was just happy to be home.

"I love this view." His best friend's voice interrupted Henrik's thoughts. "It's my favorite part of the journey."

"I can see why," Henrik responded, turning. He smiled as Kincaid climbed awkwardly onto the rock next to him, hampered by the small child on his shoulders.

And Henrik really could see why. He may not be a prince like Kincaid, but Valoria was just as deeply in his blood. He'd never thought of himself as sentimental, but after two and a half months away, the vista before him certainly warmed his heart.

The rocky slopes descended steadily beneath his feet, and he had an excellent view of the Great River that separated the Kyonan mountains from the Valorian pastureland beyond. Even from this distance, he could see the morning sunlight dancing off the spray from the enormous waterfall that sat so close to Bryford. A bridge ran across the river, not far upstream from the falls, and beyond he could see the Valorian capital.

Bryford looked like a miniature city from this height, and Henrik was fascinated by the sight. It was the first time he'd seen it from a bird's eye view—his previous visit to Kyona, a few years before, had taken him by way of the main highway, further south, rather than through the mountains. Having spent most of his life there, Henrik had never really thought much about his home city. But seeing it from this vantage point gave him a rush of pride.

The walls were thick gray stone, strong and unyielding. The castle rose impressively from the center of the city, its pennants fluttering wildly in many bright colors. It was every bit as grand as the castle where Henrik had spent the last few months, at the Kyonan capital of Kynton.

"I wanna horsey-ride!" declared Kincaid's passenger imperiously.

Henrik chuckled at the sight of the almost-three-year-old perched on his royal father's shoulders, clutching the prince's hair like reins.

"You and me both, kid," muttered Kincaid. He threw Henrik a rueful look. "Sorry about all the trekking. I should've warned you that Jocelyn always insists on going through Montego, every time."

"I don't mind," Henrik chuckled. "I'm not a tired old man, like you."

"You're two years younger than I am," Kincaid protested.

"Yes, but becoming a father ages you by at least a decade," Henrik pointed out, shooting a wink at the toddler still mounted on his noble steed.

The little boy surely didn't understand the joke, but he giggled anyway.

"I thought you liked visiting the mountain people," Henrik pressed.

"Oh, I do," said Kincaid. "And as much as I don't want to

prove your point, I have to admit," he jerked his head toward his son, "this is the first year I've been bothered by having to send the horses around by the highway with the rest of the group, and make the crossing on foot."

"Horsey-ride!" the toddler insisted, losing patience with the adults' conversation. Kincaid grimaced as he started forward obediently, and Henrik laughed again.

"Old man," he repeated. But his chuckle disappeared at the child's next words.

"No, no, no! Uncle Henwik give me a horsey-ride!"

"I'm sure Uncle Henrik would *love* to give you a horsey-ride, Norik," Kincaid encouraged his son wickedly. He shot an un-princely smirk at his friend. "Being so young and full of energy."

Henrik barely restrained a groan as he eyed the rocky descent ahead. He was very fond of his godson, but the boy was heavy for a two-year-old, and he shuddered to think what the king and queen would say if he dropped their only grandchild onto his head by accident.

"Uncle Henwik, Uncle Henwik, horsey-ride!" Norik declared jubilantly.

"What's all the shouting about, Norik?" Princess Jocelyn appeared alongside her husband, reaching her arms toward her son commandingly. "It's too steep for a horsey-ride here. You can walk like the rest of us."

"No, no, I want a ride!" the toddler insisted, his voice threatening tears as his mother removed him from his lofty saddle.

"I'll hold your hand," Jocelyn offered, her tone brooking no argument.

Norik was showing signs of digging in his heels, so Henrik crouched down next to him. "Or, if you like, you can walk with us men."

Norik's tears ceased instantly, his eyes wide as he gave a solemn nod. "Because I'm a big boy."

"That's right," agreed Henrik.

Jocelyn shot him a look that was half-grateful, half-apologetic, and he grinned. He had become inured to the intensity with which the toddler experienced emotion during his months staying with the royal couple. Prince Norik was an engaging child really, and had borne the journey through the mountains better than Henrik had expected. Better than some of the adults in the retinue, he reflected, glancing back at the half dozen guards and the two maidservants who were following them, looking disgruntled at the terrain.

The three adults started down the slope at a leisurely pace, allowing the toddler to keep up with them. He was sticking so close to Henrik's legs that the fortunate favorite could barely avoid tripping over him.

"Oh, Kincaid," said Jocelyn suddenly, turning to her husband. "In all the chaos of departure, I think I forgot to tell you I got a letter from Lavinia just before we left Kynton."

"Did you?" asked Kincaid comfortably. "How is Lavvy? Still wreaking havoc with Mother's family?"

"No, actually," said Jocelyn, keeping her eyes on Norik as he negotiated a large rock. "She's coming home now the summer's over. She'll probably beat us there."

"Really?" Kincaid gave his wife a shrewd look. "Is it really because summer's over, or is she being sent home in disgrace for flirting with every eligible—and ineligible—scoundrel between the age of fifteen and thirty?"

"Kincaid," scolded Jocelyn. "That's not fair. She's been there for six months—there's no reason to think she's being exiled just because she doesn't want to extend her seaside holiday into winter."

"Mother's holiday, you mean," Kincaid chuckled. "She claims Lavinia's turning her hair gray, but after Lavinia left, Mother wandered around aimlessly for a week. I don't think she knew what to do with herself without Lavvy to keep an eye on."

Henrik remained silent through this conversation. He and Kincaid had been close since childhood, and fond as the prince was of his incorrigible little sister, he'd never been reluctant to laugh with his best friend over her antics. When they'd been younger, Henrik had laughed along, finding the young firebrand as entertaining and as unpredictable as her family did. But in recent years he had begun to be uncomfortable when included in such conversations, and he had no idea how to explain that.

So he didn't try, either to his friend or to himself.

"Norik, don't climb that," Jocelyn called, suddenly losing interest in the conversation. Henrik started guiltily. He hadn't even noticed how far the toddler had strayed from his side, but he saw now that the little boy was attempting to scale a steep and unstable boulder.

As the princess hurried after her son, Kincaid turned to Henrik, his voice dropping conspiratorially.

"Speaking of flirting, I don't know whether to be impressed or disappointed, Henrik."

"What do you mean?" Henrik asked warily, feeling guilty for no discernible reason.

"Well, when we invited you to join us for our stay in Kyona this summer, I wasn't sure you'd be able to help yourself from mooning over the famously beautiful crown princess. I seem to remember you falling all over yourself trying to charm her when she came to Valoria for our wedding."

Henrik snorted. "That was before she married Prince Eamon, if you recall. He would have my head if I tried to charm her now."

"Precisely the source of my disappointment," Kincaid said. "I thoroughly expected to be entertained by a jealous duel between the two of you, at the very least."

Henrik shook his head, smiling indulgently at what he knew to be a joke. "To be fair to Princess Luciana," he said, "I don't think it would have done me any good if I tried to flirt with her. I'm too smart to try to compete with her prince. In fact," he added cheerfully, "even back at your wedding, I'm pretty certain she only gave me any encouragement because she was trying to make Prince Eamon jealous."

Kincaid raised an eyebrow. "You don't seem bothered by the discovery."

Henrik flashed his friend a grin. "It's not news to me. You don't get to be this charming with the ladies," he gestured flippantly at himself, "without knowing how to read them."

Kincaid chuckled. "You're a scoundrel," he said without malice.

"Well, what else is there for the lowly third son of a viscount to do in court than flirt with all the pretty girls?" asked Henrik lightly. "But even I have my boundaries. And princesses are well and truly across the other side of them."

"So now that she's married Prince Eamon, Princess Lucy is forever safe from your compliments," Kincaid finished humorously.

"What?" Henrik looked over at his friend, confused for a moment. "Oh, yes. Precisely."

"Are you sure it wasn't more because she was the size of a wild boar when we arrived?" Kincaid muttered, dropping his voice as Jocelyn approached.

Henrik stifled a laugh. Kincaid didn't realize it, but such jokes about royalty were another of the lines the prince could cross without even thinking about it, but Henrik couldn't approach.

"She was blooming with health when we left," he said properly, "and the baby seems healthy and strong."

"Yes, she's a cute little thing," Kincaid agreed fondly. He

shook his head as Jocelyn joined them, a reluctant Norik now holding her hand.

"Baby Violet is my cousin!" Norik announced, clearly proud to know what they were talking about.

"Yes, she is," Kincaid agreed. He exchanged a look with Jocelyn. "It's ridiculous that we have a niece through Eamon, who's what—twenty-two?—before we have any nieces or nephews on my side. Ormond is thirty! When's he going to hurry up and get married?"

"It's hard to imagine what's making him delay," Henrik agreed. "You'd think it would be enough to terrify anyone, having you as their heir."

Kincaid grinned, unperturbed by the insult. "Exactly. And since I have absolutely no desire to inherit the crown one day, he'd better get a move on."

"That wouldn't actually happen, would it?" Jocelyn asked anxiously. "Surely he knows he can't just...not get married?"

Henrik chuckled internally at the princess's alarm. No one would ever accuse Kincaid and Jocelyn of scheming for the throne. They were clearly both very satisfied with their lot as the second child in their respective royal families.

"Of course he knows," said Kincaid reassuringly. "He has too strong a sense of duty not to ensure the succession. He just has to rally himself to actually woo someone. Poor guy thought he would be saved the task when my parents started making noise about settling the matter nicely with a marriage alliance with a certain neighboring kingdom. It was really a mean trick for me to cut him out."

"I can see how remorseful you are," said Henrik, grinning as he observed the cheerful bounce in Kincaid's step.

Jocelyn rolled her eyes. "I don't think anyone would be fool enough to imagine Ormond is pining for me. That was over three years ago, anyway. I doubt he even remembers that your parents initially intended for him to marry me, and if he does, it's probably only with gratitude for the lucky escape."

"His loss," said Kincaid comfortably. His face brightened as he looked ahead. "Oh good! Our horses are waiting for us at the bottom of the slope."

"Old man," said Henrik cheekily.

"Horsies!" Norik cried, attempting to pull free of his mother's grip so as to race down the slope more quickly.

Jocelyn let out a long breath, even as she wrestled with him. "That is a relief. I'll be glad to ride for the last stretch. I swear the mountain pass gets steeper every year."

Kincaid looked at his wife in concern. "I didn't like to mention it, but it did seem like you struggled a little more with the climb up this time. Are you all right?"

"Of course I am," said Jocelyn dismissively.

"No you're not, Mama," interrupted Norik unexpectedly. "You're sick."

"What are you talking about, Norik?" laughed Jocelyn, although she looked a little flustered. "Mama's not sick, don't worry. I'm just a little tired." She sighed, returning her gaze to her husband. "I'll be glad to sleep in my own bed again."

There was still a slight crease between Kincaid's eyebrows as he looked at her, but he spoke lightly. "Yes, I'm looking forward to being home again, too. I'm glad we decided to come back a couple of weeks early this year."

"It was the right decision," said Jocelyn, with a wistful note to her voice. "Although I'm sad to miss Violet's first few months. Babies grow so quickly."

"Yes they do," agreed Kincaid, scooping up his still-struggling son. "Come on, little man. I'll give you a horsey-ride to the real horsies."

Norik squealed with delight at the victory, and Kincaid

charged off down the slope, leaving the other two to follow at a more sedate pace.

"I'm so pleased you were able to come along this summer," said Jocelyn, turning to Henrik with a smile. "I know my parents enjoyed hosting you. I hope it will be the first of many visits."

"Thank you," said Henrik, gratified. "Kyona is a beautiful kingdom."

"You know," Jocelyn added slyly, "it wasn't very sporting of us to tease Ormond for dragging his heels when he's not here to defend himself. Unlike you. From what I saw, there were plenty of girls in the Kyonan court who would have been very happy to be swept off their feet by the dashing Valorian knight. But I hardly saw you flirt with a single one."

Henrik smiled self-consciously. He was well aware of the reaction he had evoked among some of Kyona's noble girls. A year ago he would have been only too happy to have passed the time with a stream of harmless flirtations, but somehow he hadn't had the heart for it.

He hoped Jocelyn didn't imagine his restraint was a sign that he was pining after the beautiful but unavailable Luciana. He suspected Kincaid's teasing might have indicated such a suspicion. It was one thing from Kincaid, but it would be mortifying if Jocelyn thought he was mooning over the lovely Lucy. In addition to being married to Kyona's crown prince—and therefore being Jocelyn's sister-in-law—she was also the princess's best friend.

"No, as lovely as your homeland is," he said smoothly, "I'm too attached to Valoria at heart to leave permanently. As only a younger son, I won't inherit anything of note, you know. Without an estate in Valoria, a Kyonan bride might expect me to settle in her kingdom. I'll have to look for a wife in my own country."

"Hm," was Jocelyn's only reply. She was watching him with an uncomfortably shrewd expression, and Henrik was glad when one of the maidservants caught up to them, claiming the princess's attention.

For all his teasing of Kincaid, even Henrik was glad to reach the rest of the delegation, who were waiting at the highest point of the mountain pass that was passable for horses. The journey back from the Kyonan capital of Kynton had felt much longer than the journey there, somehow.

Norik was determined to ride in front of his father, and it was only at Jocelyn's patient but firm intervention that the little boy's nursemaid was prevailed upon to release him to Kincaid so soon after being reunited with him. The nursemaid—a grandmotherly woman who had been Kincaid's nurse as well, and was too old to trek through the mountains—absolutely doted on the boy.

Henrik had been interested to observe during his time with the family that while Jocelyn was always very gracious, there was a surprising undercurrent of steel in her dealings with the woman. The princess was clearly determined to exert her authority when it came to the raising of her son. It had occurred to Henrik to wonder if the more intimate family group was part of the reason Jocelyn was always adamant about spending a few days in Montego on the passage to and from Kyona.

It was a relief to give their mounts their heads once they finally reached flat ground. The sentries at the border greeted the royals and their retinue with a formal salute, and they galloped across the broad wooden bridge like returning victors.

Kincaid challenged Henrik to a race as soon as they reached the flat pastureland on the other side of the river, forgetting that he was hampered by his small passenger. Henrik streaked easily ahead, his heart soaring at the sight of the city's walls rising up in front of him. He didn't slow when Kincaid fell behind, pushing his mount faster for the sheer joy of it.

He was still some distance from Bryford when a cry caught

his ears, and drew his attention to the southern highway that was about to intersect with the road he was taking down from the mountains.

He slowed his horse, frowning in confusion as he tried to make out the scene before him. A carriage was stopped by the side of the road. At a glance it looked like a common mishap, perhaps a broken wheel. But from what he could see, all of the people milling around the stationary vehicle—and there were at least half a dozen—were men, whereas the cry had certainly been made by a woman.

Henrik spurred his horse toward the vehicle, calling out as he approached.

"Hey there! Do you need assistance?"

One of the men turned at his voice, and Henrik realized with a jolt of surprise that he was wearing a mask. For a moment he just stared, too astonished to believe his eyes. A robbery in the middle of the morning? And on the main highway, so close to the capital? But the man's gruff shout and the ensuing flurry of activity seemed to confirm it. Henrik pushed his horse faster, drawing his weapon as he rode.

The men turned toward him, their own weapons raised. But before Henrik reached them, one of them raised an arm, pointing behind him with another shout. Presumably they had spotted the larger party accompanying the royals, some distance behind Henrik.

He didn't turn to confirm his guess. The men were fleeing, those on foot leaping onto their mounts with all speed. Henrik increased his pace, hoping to catch at least one of them. To Henrik's satisfaction, the one who had called out wasn't quick enough to reach his horse before the knight descended on him with ruthless force.

Scorning the advantage of his mounted position, Henrik threw himself from the saddle to fight man to man. Not for nothing was Henrik a member of Valoria's royal guard, one of the elite among the king's knights. His blade flashed with deadly speed as he advanced, and the other man was hard pressed to defend.

The masked stranger was bigger than Henrik, and probably older, although it was hard to tell with the mask on. And he was a skilled fighter.

But so was Henrik. The knight pressed his opponent backward, trying to trap him between the blade and the carriage he had been waylaying. He was determined to capture the man alive, for questioning as to what group would be so bold as to mount such a brazen attack.

Henrik was vaguely aware of a young woman leaning precariously out of the window of the carriage, watching the fight with wide eyes. He didn't pause to take a good look at her, his attention fully focused on his fight. He had pressed the man back almost against the vehicle now, and was beginning to be confident of the outcome.

But just as Henrik thought the other man was faltering, the woman leaned too far in her attempt to see what was happening. The door of the carriage flew open, and she tumbled out onto the road, between the two fighters.

Henrik drew his sword up hastily, afraid of accidentally hurting her. Her eyes, wide and terrified, passed between the two men, and following her gaze, Henrik saw that the masked man had wasted no time in making use of the knight's distraction.

By the time Henrik darted around the woman, who was still on the ground, the stranger had reached his horse. Henrik lunged forward, thrusting his blade out heedlessly. He caught the man's side as the stranger swung up into the saddle, but he was a moment too slow. Instead of inflicting an injury that might have slowed the other fighter's escape, he managed only to slash a long cut in his tunic.

The fabric flapped open as the man found his seat, and Henrik caught a glimpse of scarred and mangled flesh that made him wonder for a moment whether his blade had made contact after all. But the steel showed no blood, and he was sure he hadn't felt his sword connect. He had no time to examine the wound, because the man had already spurred his horse forward, reaching a gallop within seconds.

CHAPTER TWO

"Oh thank you! You saved me!"

Henrik turned to the woman, who was picking herself up off the ground. He felt anything but chivalrous—if her accident hadn't hampered him, he was sure he would have bested the other man.

But his irritation fell away as he took in the face looking up into his. She was lovely, and clearly still afraid. Her caramel skin—which identified her as a South Lander—glowed in the morning sun, and her eyes were wide with shock.

And no wonder, he thought indignantly, sheathing his sword and hurrying forward to help her up. For anyone to be robbed on the king's highway was scandalous, let alone a foreigner who might be newly arrived in their kingdom. What a poor impression she must be forming of Valoria.

"It was my honor, My Lady," said Henrik. He had no idea if the title was accurate, of course, but she was dressed finely enough to be a noblewoman. "I hope you are unharmed?"

"Oh yes," she said earnestly. "Just a little shaken." But she didn't look shaken, and Henrik found himself admiring her evident resilience as she turned toward the carriage. "It's all right, Ginny. You can come out now. We're safe." Another young woman, looking like a maidservant, poked her head out of the window cautiously. "The poor carriage driver fared worse," the first woman added.

Following her gaze, Henrik saw a man tied up and gagged at the rear of the carriage. He hastened to free the man, who was looking dazed.

"They hit him on the head," said the young woman regretfully. "I do hope he'll be all right."

Henrik spoke quietly to the man, who responded in monosyllables, still seeming disoriented. Henrik helped him up, encouraging him to sit for a minute inside the coach before he turned back to the women.

"I think he'll be all right, but we should get him to the castle physician." His eyes passed over the beautiful young woman. She really did seem to be unharmed. "Did they rob you?" he asked, and she nodded, annoyance darkening her pleasant features.

"They took my jewelry and my cases," she confirmed. "But," her tone took on a hint of satisfaction, "they didn't find my reticule."

Henrik saw that she was indeed clutching a small reticule in the folds of her skirts. Clumsy thieves, he thought, to take the jewelry off her person but miss such a promising item. Again, he was full of admiration for the young woman's defiance and good humor in the face of her misadventure.

"Henrik! What's going on?"

Henrik turned his head at the sound of his friend's voice, beckoning with a hand for the royal couple to join him. "Kincaid, Jocelyn, over here!"

He heard a sharp intake of breath from the woman whose name he still didn't know. "Did you say...is that the prince and princess?"

"That's right," said Henrik, noting that she knew their names. Perhaps she wasn't a new arrival after all. "They'll assist in getting you safely to the castle."

"Oh no," said the woman, putting a hand to her heart. "I wouldn't wish to impose on Their Highnesses."

"Nonsense," said Henrik dismissively. "They'll be delighted to help. They're not at all formal, you'll see."

The woman still looked nervous, exchanging a glance with her maidservant, but she nodded tentatively. She slipped her reticule into a pocket of her voluminous skirts, resting her hands on the folds, presumably in readiness for a curtsy.

"Is anything amiss?" Kincaid asked as he reached them, his eyes passing between Henrik and the young woman.

"Actually, it is," Henrik said grimly. "I can hardly believe it myself, but these ladies were set upon by bandits. They were robbed, and unfortunately I wasn't able to detain any of their attackers. They all got away."

"Bandits, here?" Jocelyn asked in astonishment, pulling up beside her husband. "In the middle of the day?"

Kincaid's pleasant face had creased into a frown. He passed his son off to Jocelyn, slipping from the saddle to approach Henrik and his new acquaintance.

"Please allow me to offer you my apologies..." He trailed off, looking inquiringly to Henrik.

"I am Lady Claudette, Your Highness," said the young woman breathlessly, dipping into the anticipated curtsy. "And I'm honored by your concern."

"Not at all," said Kincaid, waving a hand vaguely. "What can you tell me about these bandits?"

Henrik frowned slightly at his friend. The prince could show a little more chivalry—he was clearly more concerned with the activities of the bandits than with Lady Claudette's well-being.

Perhaps being happily married had the effect of blinding him to the charms of other young ladies.

Although, as Henrik glanced back at Lady Claudette, he was surprised to realize that she wasn't as pretty as he had at first thought her. He scolded himself mentally for his own lack of chivalry. Of course her attractiveness was irrelevant to his responsibility as a knight to assist her when she was being waylaid by robbers. Perhaps it was just her nerves about speaking with the prince that made the lines of her face seem less soft and pleasant, somehow.

"Very little, I'm afraid, Your Highness," Lady Claudette was saying, her accent marking her once again as a South Lander. "They were masked, and they didn't say much, just demanded that we hand over anything of value."

"It was terrifying," chipped in the maid, Ginny, with a shudder.

"I'm very sorry for your ordeal," said Kincaid, but he still sounded distracted, clearly wrestling with the mystery of the bandits' boldness.

"Have you just arrived in Valoria?" Jocelyn asked Lady Claudette kindly. "Are you on your way to Bryford?"

"Yes, Your Highness," said Lady Claudette, keeping her eyes lowered. "I've only just arrived from Thorania." She seemed even more in awe of Jocelyn than of Kincaid, and Henrik wondered fleetingly if rumors of the princess's magic abilities had spread to the South Lands.

"Thorania?" Jocelyn's face brightened. "Are you part of Cody and Yasmin's delegation? I thought they weren't coming for at least another month. Have they moved their visit forward?"

"No, Your Highness," said Lady Claudette quickly. "I'm afraid they're not here. I was supposed to be part of their visit. But..." She hesitated, casting her eyes down again. "I recently lost my parents, and I wanted to get out of Thorania without delay. I paid my own way over on a trading vessel, intending to meet up with the rest of the group when they arrived." She looked up nervously. "I'm realizing it was foolish of me to be so impetuous. But Lord Cody led me to believe that I would be welcome here."

"Of course you're welcome," said Henrik chivalrously, to cover Jocelyn's evident confusion. He could only imagine she was wondering why Cody, a close friend of Lucy's family who had become a friend of Jocelyn and Kincaid's as well, would send a visitor to Valoria instead of to his native Kyona.

Henrik wouldn't say it to Jocelyn, of course, but he suspected it was because Kyonans tended to be a little more suspicious of South Landers than Valorians. Understandable, given Kyona's history of being exploited by Thorania's neighboring kingdom of Balenol. But still...it might make someone like Lady Claudette nervous to arrive in Kynton unannounced.

"Indeed," Jocelyn added politely. "And I'm very sorry to hear of your loss."

"Why we stopping?" Norik whined from his perch in front of his mother. He scowled at the new arrivals. "They don't *need* help."

"Norik!" scolded Jocelyn, throwing an apologetic look at Lady Claudette and her maid.

"But I'm tired," Norik complained. "I wanna go home."

"Yes," Kincaid said briskly, throwing one last glance up the road, as though hoping the bandits would still be lurking within sight. "We should all be heading for the castle without delay. My father will want to know about the attack. And," he added hastily at a pointed look from Jocelyn, "to welcome you, of course." He looked between the two women, once again frowning in confusion. "Is it just the two of you?"

"Yes, Your Highness," said Lady Claudette. "A guard accompanied us, but unfortunately he was vilely ill on the crossing, and hasn't yet recovered. My manservant stayed at the port with him to look after him. We hired a carriage to come on to the capital, leaving them to join us once the guard is restored to full health." She gave a rueful glance at the carriage, and the poor bludgeoned coachman, who was touching a spot on his head, wincing as he did so. "Another impetuous decision that has proved to be very foolish."

"Nonsense," said Henrik, frowning. "Of course you wouldn't expect such trouble on the main highway. A guard shouldn't be necessary to make the trip from the port to the capital in broad daylight."

The rest of the group that had traveled from Kynton had joined them by this point. At a word from Kincaid, a groom hastened to the carriage, seeing to the horses, and taking command of the vehicle. Lady Claudette accepted the offer of the man's mount, but her maid opted to ride in the carriage with the injured coachman.

Kincaid was at the front, clearly impatient to speak with his father. Henrik stayed with the ladies, thinking that Lady Claudette might feel more secure between him and Jocelyn after her astonishing attack.

"How are Cody and Yasmin?" Jocelyn asked the Thoranian girl as they started toward Bryford.

"They're very well, Your Highness," said Lady Claudette formally. "They are looking forward to their upcoming visit."

"As are we," said Jocelyn brightly. "I'm delighted they'll be bringing their daughter with them." She laughed. "Although it's still hard for me to picture Cody as a father. I'm sure she's gorgeous—does he dote on her?"

"She's a very sweet child," said Lady Claudette. "Not much younger than your son, I believe."

She cast a glance at Norik, still seated in front of his mother. Henrik thought she looked a little wary, but he couldn't imagine why. The toddler was being unusually quiet and well-behaved, now that his demand to continue to Bryford was being obeyed.

Their progress was slowed by the carriage, but they reached the city gates at last. A shout went up from the guards on duty, and a moment later a trumpet was blown from the ramparts.

"Was that an alarm?" Lady Claudette asked nervously. "What was it for?"

"No, no," laughed Jocelyn. "It's a signal announcing that a member of the royal family has returned. They do it every time Kincaid rides through the gates."

"Or you," Henrik added pointedly.

Jocelyn laughed again, a little self-consciously. "Yes, or me. Even for little Norik here." She tousled the toddler's hair fondly, eliciting a loud protest. "I'm still not quite used to it—I come from Kyona, you know, and they don't greet us with fanfare every time we ride through the gates at Kynton."

"Fanfare every time you ride through?" Lady Claudette repeated as they rode under the gate. Henrik couldn't quite identify the look in her eyes as she stared up at the herald. She was probably feeling awed.

"They claim it's for the prince," he joked. "But I'm with him most of the time, so who's to say it's not for me?"

He winked at the Thoranian, and she rewarded him with an engaging smile and a giggle. Henrik concluded that he must be right that she was overwhelmed—she certainly seemed more comfortable talking to him than to either the prince or princess.

Jocelyn gave him a speaking look, but he just grinned, unrepentant. A bit of flirting was exactly what this Lady Claudette needed to cheer her up. Besides, there was some truth behind his joke. He had always loved entering the city with Kincaid. He wasn't jealous of his friend's position—not by a long stretch. Even as the younger prince, Kincaid had so much less freedom than his friend. But there was no denying that there was a certain rush in having your arrival announced triumphantly, and having passersby line the streets as the prince and his knights rode past, cheering for their safe return.

Today's entry was no different. In fact, the residents of Bryford were more enthusiastic than ever. The younger prince was considerably more dashing—and therefore more popular with the common folk—than his brother. His marriage to the beautiful Kyonan princess had made him even more of a favorite, and the arrival of a cute little son had set the final seal on the popularity of the young royal family. People might have become used to the fact that the couple always spent the summer as guests at the castle in Kynton, but their return was invariably the cause of great excitement. And the fact that they had cut their trip a couple of weeks short this year clearly met with the crowd's approval.

Henrik and Lady Claudette were naturally included in the cheers. The knight waved merrily to the people who gathered along the main road, giving the ladies his most charming smile, and winking at the children, to their great delight. Little girls giggled as they pointed at him, and a number of boys produced wooden swords, dueling fiercely with one another, clearly dreaming of how glorious it must be to be one of the king's knights.

As much as he enjoyed the homecoming of entering the city, Henrik's heart sank a little as the party reached the castle, and it became clear that Kincaid was determined to go straight to the king and queen. Henrik would have preferred to slip away to his own home first, but Kincaid wanted him to describe what he'd witnessed to King Malcolm.

They were informed that the king was in his study, meeting with his steward, but he came promptly in response to his son's message. Kincaid had led the group into the throne room. Henrik supposed he had chosen the location in light of the presence of a noble visitor from a foreign kingdom. Certainly the formality would not have been observed for Henrik's sake.

The king greeted his son and daughter-in-law warmly, and he was listening to his grandson's barely coherent description of the journey with a serious expression that clearly delighted the boy, when Queen Marguerite entered. She embraced Kincaid and Jocelyn, giving Henrik a polite but more restrained welcome, then turning to Lady Claudette and her maid, who hung nervously behind her.

Jocelyn performed the necessary introductions, Kincaid already deep in conversation with his father about the bandit attack. King Malcolm's brow was deeply furrowed, clearly as surprised and concerned by the incident as his son had been. When asked, Henrik described his part in the little adventure succinctly, keeping his face emotionless even as Lady Claudette expressed her great gratitude to him for coming to her rescue. The king and queen were no audience for his charm.

Lady Claudette seemed to have overcome her awe a little. She conversed more easily with the king and queen than she had with their son and daughter-in-law. The reason for her satisfaction at the survival of her reticule was explained when she produced from it a letter of introduction from Lady Yasmin's father—Cody's father-in-law—sealed with the noble family's personal seal.

Queen Marguerite was expressing her concern, and discussing appropriate arrangements for Lady Claudette's accommodation, when a joyful cry from Norik heralded a new arrival to the little group.

"Auntie Vinya, Auntie Vinya!"

CHAPTER THREE

Henrik tried to keep his eyes on the queen, who was still speaking, but his head seemed to move without his permission.

Princess Lavinia burst into the room with her usual flamboyance, exclaiming with delight at the sight of her brother and his family.

"You're back! Come here, you little scamp!"

At her invitation, Norik broke free of his mother and threw himself at his aunt, shrieking with laughter.

"Lavinia," chided Queen Marguerite, in a voice of long-suffering. "We have guests."

Henrik glanced back at Lady Claudette and her maid, and barely restrained a smile at the Thoranian noblewoman's expression. She looked stunned, whether by the young princess's exuberance in spinning her nephew around in her arms, or by the child's continued high-pitched squeal, Henrik couldn't guess. His eyes didn't linger on the visiting pair for long, drawn irresistibly back to the Valorian princess.

"I beg your pardon," Lavinia was saying, her eyes dancing with a mischief that belied her polite words. "Welcome."

Queen Marguerite performed the introductions, and Lavinia greeted the two foreign women cheerfully, before turning to her brother.

"I'm so glad you're back, Kincaid!" She gave the prince a one-armed embrace, hampered by Norik, who had succeeded in getting her to hoist him up onto her hip. "But not nearly as glad as I am to see you, Joss." She turned to her sister-in-law.

Kincaid shot Henrik an amused look, his eyes sparkling as he laughed off his sister's unflattering honesty. Henrik knew that Lavinia had always been a favorite with Kincaid, who had generally been entertained by her antics rather than scandalized like their older brother Ormond.

But Henrik didn't have any attention to spare for his friend. Despite his best efforts, he couldn't seem to tear his eyes from the vivacious young woman who was now interrogating Jocelyn about their trip. It was a little bit of a shock to realize just how much of a young woman Princess Lavinia had become. It had been six months since he'd seen her. And although he had realized before then that she had ceased to be a child—somewhere around the time he'd discovered it no longer felt appropriate to call her Lavvy, as Kincaid did—he couldn't help but be struck by how much she had changed in her absence.

Not that her features had changed dramatically. As seemed to be its natural state, her face was alight with laughter, the expression softening the strong lines of her straight nose and defined chin. But her hair was longer, he was fairly certain. Like its owner, it seemed determined to burst free of its bounds, cascading in thick auburn waves from the princess's headdress. Henrik knew that the queen had often been frustrated by the unruly nature of her daughter's hair—again much like its owner—but personally Henrik thought the picture was pleasant.

A little too pleasant, he thought ruefully. His thoughts about the queen had made him glance self-consciously at her, and it was all he could do not to fidget when he found her eyes on him. She always made him feel like she could read his thoughts, and it wasn't a comfortable sensation.

"Welcome back, Henrik."

Henrik's head whipped back around. He hadn't noticed the pause in Lavinia's conversation with Jocelyn, and he was glad that she'd chosen the few moments when he wasn't watching her to address him.

"Thank you, Your Highness."

She raised an eyebrow, looking irritated by the formal mode of address. Henrik's eyes flicked briefly to Lady Claudette, whom he noticed was watching with great interest. Lavinia followed his gaze, and her expression softened slightly. He thought she barely refrained from rolling her eyes—after all, she'd made it clear she felt no need to stand on ceremony in front of the strangers—but at least she didn't seem to be angry with him.

"Was your time in Kyona...pleasant?" Something in her tone made Henrik wonder if she was a little annoyed with him after all, although he couldn't imagine why she would be. But he responded as cheerfully as he could under the queen's continued watchful gaze.

"Ah yes," Queen Marguerite interrupted suddenly, motioning to someone behind Henrik. He turned to see that the head housekeeper had entered the room. "Have accommodations been prepared for our guests?"

"Yes, Your Majesty," said the middle aged woman, bobbing a curtsy to her queen before turning to the two Thoranians. "If you'll come along with me, My Lady?"

Lady Claudette took a gracious leave of all the royals before turning to Henrik. "Thank you again for coming to my rescue," she said, smiling up at him through her eyelashes. "You were amazingly gallant to take on the bandits like that."

"It was my honor," said Henrik with a bow. He hoped he had

been appropriately chivalrous. His mind was still on his interrupted conversation with Princess Lavinia, and Lady Claudette's attempts at flirtation seemed faintly ridiculous. He was having trouble remembering why he had thought her so attractive when they met.

As the pair left the room, he returned his gaze to Lavinia, noting that she once again looked far from impressed.

"What were you saying, *My Lord*?" she said waspishly. "Something about how charming the Kyonan court is?"

"Uh..." Henrik floundered, distracted from her words by the storminess of her gaze. How had he already managed to offend her? "I think I was saying that the Kyonan countryside is charming, actually."

"You're mad at Uncle Henwik. Why?" Norik asked curiously, gazing up into his aunt's eyes from his position in her arms.

Lavinia flushed at the toddler's unexpected contribution to the conversation, and Henrik hardly knew where to look himself.

"Lavinia," cut in the queen sternly, for all the world as though her adult daughter and not her infant grandson had made the embarrassing comment. "I'm sure Lord Henrik would like to return home after his journey, not stay to be interrogated about his impressions of Kyona."

Henrik bowed quickly, mainly to hide his frown. He had sometimes thought the queen was severe on her youngest child, but she seemed unusually critical of her daughter today.

"Indeed, Your Majesty, I should rejoin my own family. My parents will wish to know that I have returned safely."

He said a quick farewell to the others, making rapidly for the door. But not quickly enough to avoid overhearing Lavinia's sulky rejoinder.

"Well, maybe if you'd allowed me to go to Kynton with Joss and Kincaid for the summer instead of banishing me to the coast, I would have been able to form my own impressions, and wouldn't need to *interrogate* anyone."

Henrik slowed his steps slightly in spite of himself. He hadn't been aware that Lavinia had asked and been denied permission to go to Kyona with her brother.

"We've been over this, Lavinia," interjected King Malcolm, in a tone that precluded further discussion. "You can go next year."

"Where are you going, Uncle Henwik?"

The protest caused Henrik, almost at the doorway of the throne room, to turn. Norik had wriggled free of Lavinia and was toddling toward the knight on his plump little legs.

"I need to go see my family, little man," said Henrik, kneeling down to ruffle the boy's hair.

"No." Norik scowled. "You stay. You're in *our* family."

Henrik chuckled self-consciously, glancing up at the royals. Queen Marguerite's lips were pursed, and Lavinia's expression was difficult to read. Kincaid looked amused, but when Henrik met his eye, he started forward in response to his friend's silent request.

"Come on, little rogue. Release your prisoner." He strode toward the pair, scooping the protesting child into his arms.

Henrik made good his escape the moment the toddler was no longer clinging to his tunic. But he wasn't quite quick enough to avoid hearing the queen's quiet chastisement to her son and daughter-in-law.

"You really shouldn't encourage him to call a friend— however close—'uncle'. It's confusing for the poor child."

Henrik winced. He knew the queen didn't altogether approve of her younger son's best friend. Henrik was fairly certain she thought him irresponsible, and therefore a bad influence on the already less than serious prince.

He supposed he should be flattered that she thought he, at two years younger than Kincaid, had the ability to be any influence on the prince at all. But instead he was more rattled than ever before by her disapproval. It was unusual for her to make it so obvious. Perhaps she had thought her comment would be covered by the loud protests still emanating from the "poor child" at Henrik's departure.

Henrik strode quickly through the familiar halls of the castle, his earlier elation at his homecoming to Bryford soured by the uncomfortable interaction. He'd been gone for almost three months. How he had managed to fall further from the queen's favor while not even present, he couldn't imagine.

He returned the smiles of passing courtiers mechanically, breathing a sigh of relief when he exited the castle. Although he had spent so much of his childhood haunting the corridors with Kincaid that it felt sometimes like he lived there, his family didn't actually have rooms within the building as some other nobles did. His father's estate was close to the capital, allowing him to oversee much of its management from Bryford. As a result, the family usually lived in the city, and had a handsome manor house for the purpose.

Henrik's horse had already been taken away by a helpful groom, but the manor wasn't far from the castle, and he was more than happy to walk. He drew in a deep breath as he traversed the familiar route. The sun was shining, and the city really was beautiful.

"Welcome back, Lord Henrik!"

He looked up at the salutation, flashing his most charming smile at the trio of giggling noble girls who were heading into the castle.

"Thank you, ladies." He paused, resting his hand on the hilt of his sword in an almost unconscious posture of rest as he turned to talk to them. "I won't ask if you're all well, because I can see that you're blooming."

One of the girls giggled again, and the one who had

spoken looked up at him coquettishly. "I'm glad to see you've returned safely. I hope you didn't find the Kyonan court *too* pleasant."

Her comment tickled something in Henrik's memory, something about his conversation with Princess Lavinia, but he couldn't quite chase the thought down. After a moment he realized that the noble girl was looking at him expectantly, and he gave himself a mental shake. He wasn't sure when he had become so absent-minded, but for the second time that morning he was distracted from the attempted flirtation of the girl in front of him by thoughts about a girl not currently in his sight. Given the identity of the girl in question, it was a worrying trend.

"My time in Kynton was very pleasant," he said smoothly. "But it could never be pleasant enough to displace Bryford from my heart, with such lovely ladies as yourselves to make it the most beautiful city in the North Lands."

The girls giggled again, but the words tasted bitter to Henrik as they came out. Perhaps he was getting too old for such games, because instead of enjoying the obvious success of his charm, Henrik felt ridiculous. He took his leave quickly, directing his steps once again toward his own home.

He had almost reached the manor when his attention was caught by a group of riders approaching from the city's main gate. They were moving a little too quickly for politeness over the cobbled streets, and it was clear from their faces that they weren't happy. Neither of these things would have held Henrik's attention, but he and everyone else in the vicinity stopped and watched with interest as a trio of royal guards moved to intercept the group.

"Whoa, slow down there," called the guard in front, stepping out into the road.

The riders were forced to slow to a halt in order to avoid

trampling the guards, but their impatience was clear on their faces.

"Let us pass," grunted the man in front gruffly. "We're sick of being passed off. We insist on being heard!"

"And so you will be," said the guard sternly. "But you can save your complaints for your audience with the king. There's no rush, and there's no need to crush every pedestrian in your path."

The man grumbled something unintelligible, and the guard's frown deepened.

"And I'd recommend you to speak with a bit more respect when you meet with His Majesty."

The rider's snort said more clearly than words what he thought of the guard's recommendation, but he held his peace. The guards stepped aside, and the group continued toward the castle, at a more sedate pace.

"Henrik! You're back! We weren't expecting you for a couple more weeks."

Henrik turned with a smile at the familiar voice. "Winton," he said brightly, acknowledging his brother with a nod. "Princess Jocelyn wished to return a little early. I've just come from the castle this minute." He gestured back toward the street with his head. "Any idea what that was about?"

Winton followed his gaze inquiringly, understanding lighting his face as he took in the disappearing forms of the riders. "Ah, the little spat between the guard and the farmers, you mean?"

"Farmers?" Henrik echoed.

Winton nodded. "There's been a bit of tension in the last few weeks over the upcoming harvest. We had some freak storms that damaged a lot of crops in the southeastern region, and there are concerns that the yield will be much smaller than last year. Some of the farmers from the area feel the crown isn't doing enough to help them, and they're not shy about letting everyone know it."

"Oh," said Henrik, dismissing the matter from his mind. It was just the sort of routine problem the royals had to deal with on a regular basis.

"Come on in," Winton said, turning toward the manor. "Mother will be delighted to see you."

"And Father will tolerate my return?" Henrik joked, and his brother grinned.

"You'll never get him to admit it, but I think he missed you. Every time he commented about how quiet and peaceful it is without you around, he had a look in his eye that made me think he really meant it was boring."

Henrik laughed lightly as he followed his brother through the elaborately wrought metal gates around their manor. "That I would have to see to believe." He shook his head with a smile. "I'll be glad to see the old fellow, though."

"From the disrespectful form of address, I gather that my youngest son has returned." Henrik turned quickly, trying to keep a straight face at his father's long-suffering expression.

"Father," he said, his tone more respectful. "Yes, I'm back, and I'm pleased to see you in your usual good health."

His father looked him over, a hint of fondness hidden behind his measuring gaze. "You seem well enough yourself. I hope your early return doesn't mean you were sent home by the Kyonans."

Even as he reassured his father good-naturedly, Henrik couldn't help but be struck by the similarity between this accusation and Kincaid's suspicion about Lavinia's return from her own extended visit. His thoughts turned rueful as the comparison made him think of the encounter in the throne room. His father shared the queen's view about Henrik's lack of responsibility, but unlike Her Majesty he had no hesitation about saying it openly.

"In any event," he finished cheerfully, "King Calinnae and Queen Elnora invited me to come back next summer if I wish, so I don't think I can have disgraced the family name too drastically."

"Well, well, it's good you're back home at any rate, where you can't cause too much mischief," said his father gruffly.

Henrik thanked him solemnly, a twinkle in his eye. He bore his father no malice for his strictures, any more than he resented Winton's evident amusement at Henrik's expense. Winton was a little more steady, but there was no doubt that he enjoyed the freedom of not being the heir as much as Henrik did. Their oldest brother was serious and humorless enough to satisfy even their father. Perhaps it was the responsibility that made him that way. It would certainly be consistent with the personalities of the princes, Ormond and Kincaid.

"Come on then," their father was saying. "Your mother will no doubt want to make a fuss."

"No doubt," Henrik agreed cheerfully. "I'll try not to let it go to my head." With a last glance toward the castle, he followed his father and brother inside.

CHAPTER FOUR

Henrik strolled into the castle with a spring in his step. A day with his own family and a solid night's sleep in his own bed had done a lot to restore his usual confidence. Surely whatever had been irking the queen the day before had passed. It likely had nothing to do with him.

It was early, and not many people were up and about yet in the castle. Well, not many of the nobles, that was. The servants were already busy about their chores, probably having been up an hour or two earlier even than Henrik.

But compared to most of his peers among the court, Henrik was certainly an early riser. Perhaps it was because at heart, he was much more knight than courtier. He had joked to Kincaid that there wasn't much for the younger son of a viscount to do in court beyond charming the ladies, and it was true. But that didn't mean that Henrik had nothing better to do with his time. Like Kincaid, he had always avoided the stiff formality of court circles as much as possible. It was one of the shared passions that had sparked their friendship, and it was certainly the reason Henrik had pursued a position in the royal guard.

It was toward the training yard of the royal guard that he

directed his steps now. When he had finally reached his bed the night before, he had not been able to fall asleep immediately, his thoughts returning to the strange bandit attack he'd thwarted the day before. He had never seen such a brazen attack before, at least not anywhere outside the North Wilds.

No one had called on him to discuss the matter further after his report to the king, but he wouldn't be quite easy until he had reported the incident to his commander as well. It had also occurred to him that he should make the commander aware of his early return. He had been granted the full season of leave in light of his invitation to join the prince and princess on their trip, but he had no desire to prolong his inactivity now that he was back in Bryford.

As he knew he would, he found the commander of his squadron in the training yard. The man seemed to live there when not on an active patrol. Henrik sometimes wondered if he even had a home.

The commander seemed to be drilling some new recruits, and Henrik hung back for a moment, watching with interest. As always, he had to admire the unmatched skill of his commander. Henrik knew he was lucky to be in the man's squadron.

He had formerly been under Kincaid's command. When his friend was given the honor of leading his first squadron, Henrik had been very ready to volunteer for a place, to support the prince. But it had been a relief when Kincaid moved up in his intended vocation not long after his marriage, taking on a broader oversight role in training the knights. It freed Henrik to pursue his own goal, which was to be accepted into the commander's elite.

That goal was clearly shared by the group now training with the commander. The aspiring knights looked so young, but Henrik could well remember being in their position. An eager young stripling who'd never been much good for anything in the life of privilege he'd been born into, and who was determined to prove his prowess in a role he considered more manly than the position of influence his older brother would inherit.

Henrik smiled, shaking his head indulgently at his former self. As physically demanding as a position in the royal guard could be, he had come to realize that his oldest brother was in line for a harder role.

"Enough, Ginny. Relax."

The voice pulled Henrik's focus from the training in front of him. It was unusual for women to hang around the training yard, especially this early in the morning, and he scanned the area curiously for the source of the conversation.

"I don't like it. We should have put off our trip when we were delayed, or even canceled it. We didn't bargain on having—"

"Nonsense."

Henrik finally located the two women, partially hidden by a pillar several yards away, also watching the training. But he had realized their identities before he saw them. Their accents marked them as the new arrivals, and he frowned as he tried to make sense of Lady Claudette's chastisement of her maid.

"You are overreacting. It's a setback, but nothing we can't handle. We just need to adapt, as we always do."

Henrik shifted slightly to the side, trying to make out Lady Claudette's expression. Her tone surprised him. He could still remember her wide, frightened expression when she'd been under attack from the bandits the day before. But she was speaking now with great determination.

The same couldn't be said for her maid.

"But you heard them! They're calling the attack a shocking—"

"Yes, it seems we were most unlucky to have fallen afoul of those rogues." Lady Claudette cut the other girl off flatly.

Henrik's eyes jumped to the Thoranian noblewoman, and he

realized with a jolt that she was looking right at him. His earlier movement must have drawn her attention. He bowed quickly, wincing internally at being caught eavesdropping.

"Good morning, My Lady," he said as brightly as he could, his nod encompassing the maid as well. "What an unexpected pleasure to see you here."

Lady Claudette acknowledged the greeting with a smile, and Henrik was once again struck with how appealing her features were. She really was a beautiful young woman, and he couldn't for the life of him remember why he had found her faintly irritating the day before.

"I was going to say the same, My Lord, but that would be foolish, I suppose. Since you're one of the king's elite knights, the royal training yard is exactly where I should expect to find you."

Henrik paused for a moment, surprised by her comment. He was fairly sure he hadn't mentioned his title or his position the day before. It wouldn't be difficult for her to discover that information, of course. It was just surprising that she would spend the effort to do so. Perhaps she found him attractive as well. He couldn't deny the hint of smugness he felt at the thought. It seemed he wasn't getting too old for this game, after all, if a good night's sleep had restored his charm as much as his energy.

"It's not where I expected to find you, however," he said smoothly. "I trust that nothing is amiss?"

"Oh no," Lady Claudette assured him quickly. She glanced at her maid. "That is...the truth is that I dragged Ginny along here to prove to her how safe and well-guarded we are in the castle. We still don't know for certain how soon our own guard will be able to join us, you know. And I'm afraid yesterday's attack has rattled poor Ginny a great deal."

"Most understandable," said Henrik sympathetically,

inclining his head toward Ginny, who looked less than impressed by her mistress's candid discussion of her concerns.

"We were just speaking of it, actually," Lady Claudette went on. "You see, we were delayed in setting out from Thorania, and Ginny was of the view that we should wait and just come over with the rest of the delegation, as originally planned." Lady Claudette sighed. "Most likely you were right, Ginny. But how were we to know the timing would be so unlucky?"

"How indeed?" said Henrik staunchly. "And as unchivalrous as it is for me to say it, I can't be entirely sorry for the unfortunate timing. If you hadn't been coming along the road at just that moment, I might not have had the honor to intervene on your behalf."

He flashed her his most charming smile, and she giggled coquettishly. Yes, Henrik thought. He hadn't entirely outgrown this particular pastime.

Any further attempts to captivate the pretty foreigner were cut short as his commander caught sight of him.

"Henrik," the man called across the training yard. "Reporting back for duty already?"

"Excuse me, ladies," said Henrik regretfully, giving them a bow before striding across the yard.

"Yes, sir," he said, saluting the commander as he approached. "Their Highnesses cut their visit to Kyona short, so here I am."

"Glad you're here," said the commander briskly. "With this bandit attack, I want everyone on duty. It might have been an isolated incident, but I don't plan to take any chances. We're increasing our patrols."

"Yes, sir," Henrik repeated, his hand resting on his hilt again. "I'm ready for service."

"Yes, well..." The commander glanced out at the young trainees, who were sparring in pairs. "As I said, I'm glad you're back, but you're not needed at this moment. I'll be tied up with this useless lot all morning, and His Majesty wishes for a full report on our capacity this afternoon." The older man wasn't much given to smiling, but his face softened slightly as he looked back at Henrik. "Take the rest of the day, and report in tomorrow morning."

"Yes, sir," said Henrik, surprised. "Thank you."

He stayed for a few minutes more to greet some of his fellow members of the royal guard. Naturally they all wanted to hear the story of his heroic rescue the day before, and he repeated it with considerably more flourish than the version he had given to the king and queen. There was much hilarity over the fact that the dashing Lord Henrik, lady-slayer, would of course be the one to swoop in to save the day when a lady was in distress.

It was clear that Lady Claudette had already made quite an impression among the young men of Bryford. Remembering her lovely features and sweetness of expression, Henrik could easily understand why, and he was only too delighted to rub it in that he had stolen a march on the rest of the squadron in being introduced to her.

Henrik was still grinning in good-natured acknowledgment of their jokes an hour later, when he left the training yard. With the unexpected free day, he thought he might check in with his traveling companions, and see how they were faring after the tiring journey.

Accordingly, he turned his steps toward the royals' wing of the castle, nodding pleasantly in response to the friendly greetings of the guards and servants he passed. Everyone was well used to him haunting the halls, making himself at home while running amok with Kincaid.

His boldness stopped short of actually entering the private dining hall where the royal family broke their fast, but timing favored him on the day. He was just strolling down the adjoining corridor when the door up ahead opened, and a familiar figure emerged.

"Kincaid!" he called, increasing his pace.

The prince turned, his face lighting up as he saw his friend approach. "Hello, Henrik. I thought you'd forgotten all about us—haven't seen a hint of you since we got home!" He gestured back toward the dining hall, as Jocelyn wandered out behind him. "You've just missed breakfast. Want me to have the servants bring something back out for you?"

"No, you lazy layabout, I ate hours ago," Henrik said cheerfully.

He didn't comment on how inappropriate it would be for him to join the royal family for their meal. With his usual obliviousness, Kincaid made the offer regularly, seeming not to notice that Henrik never once accepted. Not that the knight minded. For all the jokes about his irresponsibility, he was well used to being the only one in his friendship with the prince who kept an eye on the boundaries inevitably created by Kincaid's royal status.

"Good morning," he said, turning to Jocelyn with a smile. "Did you sleep well?"

"I did, thank you," she said warmly, although to Henrik's eye she still looked very tired.

"Where's my little tyrant?" Henrik demanded, looking around for Norik.

"He's still in there." Kincaid jerked his head back toward the dining hall. "Hoodwinking his nurse into giving him three times what he should be eating for breakfast."

Henrik chuckled. "I'm guessing you had her just as wrapped around your finger at that age."

"Oh, if not more," said Kincaid cheerfully. "He gets his charm from me, you know."

Jocelyn sighed, lowering her voice as she glanced at the

guards standing by the door. "Does he also get his outrageous bluntness from you?" She started to walk, and the two men followed her absently. Only once they were out of earshot of anyone else did she continue. "I could've sunk through the floor when your mother said she was happy to have all her children home again, and he contradicted her to her face." She glanced at Henrik, adding by way of explanation, "He said, 'You're not happy to have Auntie Vinya home.'"

Henrik winced sympathetically. The child was a little too forthright, there was no denying it.

"Well, I know he doesn't get it from you," said Kincaid, giving his wife an apologetic look. "You're always painfully careful with your words." He shook his head. "I'll admit I don't have much experience of other small children, but aren't all toddlers uncomfortably honest? I seem to remember Lavinia being that way."

"Wait for me, you two—oh. I mean, three. Hi, Henrik." As if summoned by her brother's mention of her, the princess appeared in the doorway they had just left.

CHAPTER FIVE

The three of them paused, turning back to look at the princess, and she hurried toward them.

"Please, for the love of my sanity, let me join you," Lavinia said, not bothering to lower her voice as her sister-in-law had done.

"Join us for what?" Kincaid asked blankly.

"Whatever you're doing," said Lavinia firmly. "I don't care. Just don't leave me to another lecture from Mother, if you have any love for me at all."

Kincaid frowned slightly. "What's going on with you two, Lavvy?" he asked as he resumed walking, speaking in a more moderate tone than his sister. "She seems a little...put out with you since we got back."

Henrik remained respectfully silent, aware that he shouldn't really be overhearing this conversation about the royal family, but undeniably curious. It seemed he hadn't imagined it the day before.

Lavinia sighed, tossing her unruly hair over her shoulder. "Apparently six months of exile wasn't long enough. She was hoping I'd stay with her family at the coast forever."

"That's not true, Lavinia," said Jocelyn quickly.

"Your son thinks it is," Lavinia retorted dryly.

"Norik is hardly a reliable authority," said Jocelyn, exasperated. Her face softened as she looked at her sister-in-law. "I know the two of you don't always see eye to eye, but your mother doesn't want you to disappear."

"No, I know that," Lavinia acknowledged with another sigh. "When I said she wanted me to stay with her family forever, I wasn't actually trying to say that she doesn't want me around. I just mean that I didn't quite fulfill her expectations while I was away."

"Hah," said Kincaid, shooting a triumphant look at Jocelyn. "I knew it. I said you were sent home for causing a ruckus." He grinned. "What did you do, Lavvy? Flirt with the guards?"

But his sister clearly didn't share his amusement. "I wasn't sent home!" she protested, looking unusually flustered by the accusation. "And I wasn't *flirting* with anyone." Her voice turned dry, dropping almost to a mutter. "Quite the opposite, actually."

"Where are you off to, Henrik?" Kincaid said suddenly. "Aren't you coming in?" They'd reached the door of Kincaid's private receiving room, and the knight had been trying to discreetly slip away as the royal trio entered.

Henrik cleared his throat uncomfortably. "No, no, I don't want to intrude."

"Intrude?" Kincaid repeated, staring at Henrik as though he was mad. "What are you talking about? Didn't you come looking for us? Come on, stop hanging about in the doorway."

Unable to politely refuse, Henrik followed his friend into the room. Usually he found it easy to talk to Kincaid about anything. But for some reason it was as impossible as ever to explain to the prince why Henrik didn't want to be included in a conversation about the young princess's flirtatious ways.

"So what were you going on about, Lavvy?" Kincaid asked

his sister once they were all inside. "You were sent home for *not* flirting?"

"Basically," said Lavinia, raising a challenging eyebrow at her brother's clearly unconvinced expression. She had thrown herself onto a settle with all the unceremonious ease of being tucked away from the public eye. Henrik thought ruefully of Norik's claim that he was part of the royal family—if only that were true, he wouldn't be the only uncomfortable one in the room.

"What do you mean, Lavinia?" Jocelyn asked with a frown. "What went on with your mother's family over there? You've hardly told us anything about your visit."

Lavinia shrugged a shoulder. "They were nice enough. I did enjoy being so close to the ocean, but six months was more than long enough for the novelty of that to wear off. Everyone was very friendly, and there were lots of galas and things to keep all us young people entertained."

"But?" Kincaid pressed, stretching his long legs out before him as he joined his wife on another settle.

Henrik, left standing awkwardly, elected to perch on a wooden chest rather than sit beside Lavinia.

"But...toward the end of my stay," Lavinia continued dryly, "it became obvious that there was another reason for my enforced visit, one Mother hadn't seen fit to mention to me." She saw that all three of her listeners were watching her expectantly, and she flicked her auburn waves back over her shoulder in a defiant motion. "They were all scheming for me to marry Rodney, our cousin. And Mother is still sour that I didn't go along with that plan like the docile daughter she wishes I was."

"Ah," said Jocelyn. For some inscrutable reason she glanced right at Henrik, who tried not to fidget. "I see."

"Rodney?" Kincaid repeated vaguely. "We don't have a cousin called Rodney."

Lavinia shrugged impatiently. "Second cousin, third cousin, I don't know. You've probably never even met him. He's the darling of Mother's family, and he's an unutterable bore. Can't wait to take over the estate and spend his life overseeing tenants and managing the farmland."

"And Mother thought he would be a good match for you?" Kincaid asked disbelievingly.

Lavinia sighed. "I think she hoped he would be a sobering influence." The princess looked uncharacteristically subdued as she ran her hand along the curves of the settle, not meeting anyone's eye. "Since I got back, she's been at some pains to remind me that I'm almost nineteen, and she was married with Ormond on the way by that age."

She looked up at her sister-in-law, a spark of her usual vivacity returning as her nose crinkled in a mock pout. "And you don't help my cause, Joss, married to Kincaid at barely eighteen." She sighed. "It's not fair. No one seems to think it's relevant that Kincaid was twenty-one before you even met, or that Father was in his mid-twenties when he married Mother."

Jocelyn laughed. "You're right, it's not at all fair. But I wouldn't worry too much, Lavinia. I don't think anyone really believes you're in danger of becoming a spinster."

"No," Lavinia agreed, a dimple appearing on one cheek as she flashed a mischievous grin at the other princess. "But I do think Mother is terrified I'm going to run off with some adventurer." She sighed mournfully. "And I probably would, if only one would present himself."

"Careful what you wish for," Jocelyn chuckled, throwing a sideways glance at her husband. "I fell for a dashing, carefree adventurer, and he turned out to be a prince after all, with all the responsibilities and restrictions of a royal role."

"That is a sobering thought." Lavinia laughed musically, and for some reason Henrik felt a weight lift from his own heart.

There was something inherently wrong about seeing the outrageous princess serious and downcast. Laughter was a much more natural state for her. If only that twinkle in her eye wasn't so dangerously attractive.

"Poor old Cousin Rodney," he said, before he could stop himself. "After a failure like that, he's probably in as much trouble with his family as you are with yours."

Lavinia turned to him, a humorous look on her face. "I did feel a little sorry for him when he made his offer," she acknowledged. "I don't think he wanted to marry me any more than I wanted to marry him, but he was shouldering his duty very manfully. It certainly hadn't occurred to him that I might refuse. The poor soul didn't know what to do with himself."

Henrik shook his head, trying to picture the scene. "Every man's nightmare," he joked, with a dramatic shudder.

Lavinia rolled her eyes. "Well, we all know you don't have any experience of rejection," she said, her voice suddenly dry again. "I daresay it's impossible for you to imagine any woman not falling prey to your charms."

"Not entirely impossible," Henrik muttered. He obviously hadn't spoken quite as low as he'd intended, however, because Jocelyn once again shot him a shrewd look.

"No need to rip up at Henrik," Kincaid said, coming to his friend's defense. "It's not his fault that Mother tried to marry you off to some boring distant cousin."

Henrik couldn't quite stop himself from fidgeting this time. For some reason, Jocelyn was still watching him with uncomfortable intensity, whereas Lavinia suddenly seemed to be at great pains not to look in his direction.

"But you're not wrong that it's a bit unfair for Mother to be hassling you just because you're a girl," Kincaid went on, clearly oblivious to the silent communication going on around him. "I mean, Ormond is so much older than you, *and* he's the one who needs to father an heir. Why aren't they hassling him?"

"But they are!" said Lavinia, straightening up in her seat, her eyes bright with gossip. "Haven't you heard? That's why he wasn't here to greet you when you arrived yesterday. He was meeting with Lord Thornton at his estate, in the southeast."

"What's that got to do with—"

"I'm getting to that," Lavinia cut her brother off impatiently. "The official reason he was there was to discuss the harvest concerns for those of Lord Thornton's tenants affected by those storms. His land was the hardest hit, you know."

Henrik leaned forward, his interest caught as he remembered the confrontation he'd witnessed the day before.

"But the real reason," Lavinia went on mischievously, "was to pay another visit to Lord Thornton's oldest daughter, the lovely Lady Brielle."

"Is that so?" asked Kincaid, a mischievous grin spreading across his face. "Don't tell me Ormond has finally noticed a girl!"

"I don't know if I'd go that far," said Lavinia, kicking her slippers off so she could curl her legs up under her, clearly ready for a comfortable gossip about her oldest brother.

Henrik noticed that Jocelyn, far from settling in for a comfortable chat, looked uncharacteristically ill at ease as she shifted around on her settle. Perhaps he wasn't the only one who realized that his presence wasn't entirely appropriate.

"Mother and Father are basically arranging the whole thing," Lavinia was continuing cheerfully. "They think it's about time Ormond settled down, and the Thorntons are a very loyal, very influential family. But I don't get the sense that Ormond's against the idea. Honestly, I think it's a relief to him."

"Yes, I can imagine," grinned Kincaid. He glanced at his friend.

Henrik smiled absently at the unspoken reference to their

earlier conversation about Ormond being cut out of his last arranged marriage by his little brother. Jocelyn still looked uneasy, and Henrik was distracted from the conversation by his attempts to find a suitable reason to excuse himself.

"What's Lady Brielle like?" Jocelyn asked, her voice quieter than normal.

"I haven't actually met her," said Lavinia. "At least, not recently. I believe she's been to Bryford a number of times, but I don't remember her. She's several years older than me, so we probably didn't have much to do with each other. I asked Ormond what she's like, but you know how he is. He gave me such a bloodless answer I couldn't get any sense of her at all."

"I wonder why she's not married yet, if she's so much older than you," mused Kincaid. He raised a teasing eyebrow at his sister. "Since you're basically on the shelf. Maybe she's ugly."

"Kincaid," Jocelyn scolded, without much conviction.

But Lavinia chuckled. "I wondered the same thing, but I don't think that's it. Apparently her mother was very unwell for a long time, and Lady Brielle cared for her, as well as shouldering a lot of her mother's responsibilities on the estate. But her mother has passed away now, and Lord Thornton seems to have realized he's left it a little late to look for a husband for his daughter. As you can imagine, he's very eager about the whole idea."

"Poor thing," said Jocelyn softly. "Sounds like she's had a difficult time."

"Yes," said Lavinia, with a dramatic shudder. "And then to be landed with a cold fish like Ormond for a husband on top of it all..."

Henrik hid his smile as Kincaid chuckled. He knew that the pair were both fond of their brother at heart, for all their jokes. But however much Ormond's overly serious formality might invite the mirth of his less responsible siblings, Henrik knew he shouldn't be privy to their teasing. Even Jocelyn, who was now a sister-in-law to Ormond, wasn't laughing along.

"Well," said Henrik, standing up quickly. "I'd better be off. My commander has given me orders to report back for duty tomorrow, so I'd better let my mother know. She had all sorts of plans for my last two weeks of leave, so she won't be too happy with me."

"You won't be on patrol tomorrow night, will you?" asked Lavinia quickly.

"I don't know," Henrik said, turning to her. "Why?"

Lavinia looked down, sounding a little too casual. "Oh, the welcome banquet, you know. For your return."

"Ah, of course," said Henrik. He had forgotten about the customary gala hosted by the king and queen to welcome back their younger son and his family after each summer's visit to Kyona. He gave a forced chuckle. "It's hardly for my return, though, is it?"

"Sure it is," said Kincaid cheerfully. "It's a welcome feast in honor of the whole delegation, and you were on the delegation this year, weren't you? Don't think you can leave me to face the bowing and scraping on my own."

"You don't have to twist his arm, Kincaid," said Lavinia dryly. "Henrik has never shared your distaste for flattering and being flattered by every girl in Father's court."

"That's because he didn't spend his whole youth being constantly hounded by girls who were only after his title," said Kincaid darkly.

"Too true, sadly," said Henrik. He tried to speak lightly, not wanting to show how irritated he was by Lavinia's openly poor opinion of him, but there was a bite in his voice nonetheless. "With no title whatsoever to inherit, I've never had anything but my natural appeal to work with."

Kincaid snorted. "And yet you seem to do all right. Lady Claudette already seems quite taken with you, for example."

Henrik didn't immediately answer, distracted for a moment by the memory of his conversation with the visiting noble-woman that morning. He was quite taken with her as well, there was no point denying it to himself. His gaze passed absently to Lavinia, and he saw that her eyes were narrowed as she looked at him.

He straightened his shoulders, sick of her criticism. After all, she wasn't one to talk. She'd been scandalizing her parents with her flirtatious ways since she was fourteen. He well remembered her entertainingly childish attempts to flirt with him at that age. Being some five years older, he'd found no difficulty in laughing it off, and thankfully she'd grown out of that habit quickly. Or at least, shifted her attention to more responsive targets.

"Well," he said at last, a barb hidden beneath his polite words, "since Princess Lavinia assures me that every girl in the court will be there, I don't see how I can resist."

CHAPTER SIX

It was with relief that Henrik reported to his commander the following morning. Between his mother's disappointment that he was resuming his duties immediately, and his rankling annoyance over Lavinia's jabs, he had worked himself into a surly state by the end of the previous day, and he was more than ready to have something active to do with himself.

He would have been even more relieved if he had been needed for patrol that night, but he had no such luck. Without Henrik even bringing it up, the commander informed him that he would of course release Henrik to attend the banquet, as a member of the returning delegation.

Henrik barely suppressed a groan. Whatever Lavinia might think, he felt no enthusiasm at the prospect of an evening surrounded by admiring courtiers' daughters, who would expect him to turn on the charm for them. Of course, he had created those expectations over years of being overly liberal with his flirtatious compliments, but that knowledge did nothing to improve his mood.

Even the certainty that Lady Claudette would be there

created mixed emotions. Henrik had gone back over the previous day's interaction with the Thoranian woman in his mind several times, and it puzzled him. He remembered that at the time he had been drawn to her for her confidence and determination. But when he reflected on what he had actually heard, he struggled to recall what he had admired in her words. If anything, the whole conversation seemed...suspicious.

But he was sure that couldn't be right. He was left feeling disoriented and confused, and was only too glad to put the matter from his mind as he spent the morning in training exercises with others from his squadron.

Having been away from duty for so long, he counted himself fortunate to be given a patrol to lead on his first afternoon back. Even if it was a low priority patrol. He tried to remain watchful as he led his group northward, but he had little expectation of seeing any action. Valoria's North Wilds were well known for their lawlessness, but the squadron wouldn't be going anywhere near that far north.

He was inclined to think the strange bandit attack had been an isolated incident, anyway, but even if not, there would be no real reason for thieves to be raiding the highway north from Bryford. The route to the southern coast, where goods from trade ships made their way to the city, would be a much more logical target. Or even a patrol heading east toward the suffering farmland might see some unrest, given the open displeasure of some of the farmers. But the northern patrol was nothing more than a chance to stretch the horses' legs.

Which was why Henrik was absolutely astonished when, several hours into the patrol, he saw the unmistakable signs of a wagon being held up on the road ahead. They had turned off the highway some time before, and were on their way back toward Bryford by way of a smaller road. They were less than an hour's ride from the city, and the road was just passing through a small copse of trees.

"What the blazes?" muttered one of his knights, a young man around his own age, as he took in the masked men surrounding the cart. "Who would hold up a produce wagon?"

"Took the words out of my mouth," agreed Henrik grimly. But there was no time to discuss the ineptitude of the bandits. He raised his voice, calling the patrol to action, and half a dozen of the king's best horses sprang forward.

The thieves turned at his cry, and Henrik saw that just as during his last encounter with bandits, the men's faces were completely swathed in dark fabric. They must have slits for their eyes, but from a distance, Henrik couldn't make out a single feature. This time they were quicker to respond to the arrival of the knights. They were all mounted and riding into the trees before the squadron was upon them.

Without breaking stride, Henrik directed his men, leaving two to assist the waylaid travelers, and taking the others with him as he plunged into the copse. The bandits didn't have much of a head start, and he expected to catch them without difficulty, but he soon realized his error. The trees were thicker than he'd expected, and when the little grove ended, it gave way not to smooth grassland, like much of the area, but to an uneven slope strewn with massive boulders.

Visibility was poor, and after a few fruitless minutes of searching, Henrik was forced to acknowledge that he had no idea which direction the masked men had taken. With barely contained frustration, he called his men together, returning to the road to see what the travelers could tell them.

Very little, it turned out. The owners of the cart, a farmer and his son, seemed more bewildered than alarmed. They said that the bandits had come from nowhere only scant minutes before Henrik's group had arrived. Thankfully no one had been bludgeoned this time, but the armed men had quickly overpowered the pair, and tied them up. Just as with the attack on Lady Claudette, the thieves had said nothing beyond a curt demand that the travelers hand over anything of value.

"Which, o' course, we couldn't do," said the farmer reasonably, flexing his freed wrists, "seeing as how we don't have anything of value." He shrugged. "I told 'em all we had were the vegetables, an' since I didn't see how they planned to make off with a cartload o' them, it seemed as how we weren't no use to them."

"And how did they respond?" Henrik asked, frowning at the absurdity of it all.

The farmer shrugged again. "They didn' respond. You fellas rode up, and they took off."

Henrik's frown deepened as his eyes followed the direction the bandits had taken.

"Beats me why armed thieves would try to rob a farmer on the way to market," said one of the other knights, a middle aged man. He chuckled. "Unless they were just after a snack."

"Well, what else were they expecting to find, raiding a north-ward road at this time?" said another member of the squadron, perplexed. "Quite apart from how it's the stupidest spot for such a robbery—how do you get such cumbersome goods through all those trees?—anyone with anything worth stealing lives east or south of the capital." He nodded to the farmer. "No offense."

"None taken, none taken," said the farmer amicably, his attention on his horse, who seemed more spooked by the encounter than its human companions. "Nonsensical robbery, my boy and I said as much ourselves."

"Yes, there's not much sense in it, is there?" Henrik mused, his eyes still on the trees, and his thoughts on the rocky slopes beyond.

"They might be useless thieves," said the knight who had

been riding beside Henrik when they had approached the hold up. He spoke quietly, his gaze following Henrik's. "But they must be good horsemen to get over that terrain so quickly, and without leaving any trail."

"Yes," said Henrik, his mind passing methodically over every aspect of the incident. He said nothing further, saving it for his report to the commander. But it hadn't escaped him that while the spot had been poorly chosen for a successful robbery, it had been very well chosen for a clean getaway.

Leaving two men to follow at the wagon's slower pace, to ensure the harassed farmer encountered no further mishaps on his way to Bryford, Henrik made straight for the capital. His surprise at this second bandit attack was laced with unease, and he was eager to discuss what had happened with his commander.

It was therefore with impatience that he heard someone hailing him as he relinquished his horse to a groom in the castle yard.

"My Lord Henrik!"

Henrik turned, and his annoyance melted away at the sight of Lady Claudette hurrying toward him. She was already dressed for the evening's event, by the look of her, and she was more attractive than ever.

"My Lady," he said, with a slight bow. "You're looking well."

"Thank you," she said, smiling up at him. But a moment later, her face creased in a frown. "Do you know if the rumors are true? Was there really another bandit attack?"

For a moment Henrik just stared at her, confused. He knew as well as anyone how quickly news traveled in a castle, but there was no way that word of his patrol's activities could have reached Lady Claudette already.

"You know about the bandit attack?"

"Just the rumors," said Lady Claudette. "Apparently a

merchant was waylaid on his way out of the city this morning, on the eastern road." She took in Henrik's surprise, and raised an eyebrow. "You hadn't heard?"

"No," he said grimly, glancing toward the training yard. Some part of his mind was more eager than ever to make his report to the commander, but he made no move to leave. There was something magnetic about Lady Claudette's presence, and it was strangely hard to pull himself away. He looked over her magnificent gown appreciatively.

"Did I tell you that you look lovely?" he asked.

She rewarded him with a bright smile. "You'll be at the gala tonight, I hope?"

"Of course," Henrik said promptly. "I trust I'll see you there? This latest attack hasn't made you uneasy, has it?"

"I certainly will be there," said Lady Claudette, raising her chin slightly. "It would take more than a bandit attack to make me hide myself away."

Henrik smiled in approval at this display of defiance and determination. He had never had much patience with girls who imagined themselves to be fragile.

"Henrik!"

He didn't need to turn this time to know who addressed him —his best friend's voice was too familiar to mistake. But while he might be as comfortable in Kincaid's presence as he was with his own brothers, Lady Claudette clearly didn't feel the same way. She had been very poised a moment before, but she fidgeted uneasily at the prince's approach, her movements a little jerky. She had the wary look of a hunted rabbit, and it made the lines of her face less pleasant in a way that was diffi-cult to define.

In fact, not for the first time, Henrik found himself appraising her features with some confusion, unable for the moment to find the beauty that had just been enchanting him.

He had a sudden flash of memory to his private musings the day before, when he had acknowledged to himself that her behavior had been suspicious. The memory made him feel disoriented, and the feeling was only intensified by Lady Claudette's altered demeanor as she curtsied, her eyes on the newcomers behind Henrik.

"Your Highnesses."

Henrik pulled his eyes away from the Thoranian at last, turning to greet Kincaid. His friend seemed baffled by Henrik's delayed response, but the knight barely spared the prince a glance.

He had assumed from Lady Claudette's greeting that Jocelyn was with Kincaid, but in fact it was Lavinia who stood beside her brother. And, like the prince, she had also clearly noticed Henrik's abstraction. Her eyes—so strikingly blue—were shooting sparks, and she flicked her untamed auburn waves behind her shoulder in a characteristic gesture. Speaking of girls who radiated defiance and determination...

Henrik looked between the two women, feeling slightly dazed. He had a sinking feeling that the princess's undeniable vibrancy might be the cause of Lady Claudette's sudden drop in appeal. The thought suddenly struck him that not many women could stand up to comparison with the princess, and he had a vague sense that the realization wasn't good news for him. But no...he hadn't even realized Lavinia was there when he had noted Lady Claudette's strange behavior.

"Did you just get back from patrol, Henrik?" Kincaid was saying, having greeted Lady Claudette politely. "Is your commander releasing you for the gala tonight?"

"He is," said Henrik, pulling himself out of his confusion with an effort. "But I need to make my report first." He pushed other thoughts aside as he met his friend's eye seriously. "My patrol came upon another bandit attack, on the north road. The men got away again. And apparently there was another one this morning, east of here."

"What?" Kincaid instantly matched his friend's frown. "Do you mind if I come with you to speak to your commander? I'd like to hear the report myself." He didn't wait for an answer, turning instead to his sister. "Lavvy, can you let Joss know? Tell her I'll look in on her before I go to the gala."

Lavinia nodded, but Kincaid was already looking at Henrik again. The knight nodded as well, inclining his head in farewell to the Valorian princess and the Thoranian noblewoman. He was only too glad to push the enigma of his varied reactions to the two young women to one side as he led the way toward the practice yard.

His commander received his report with a deepening frown. He grilled Henrik about the details, seeming particularly interested in the unique location of the attack, and Henrik's reflections on the bizarre nature of the attempted theft. Henrik's own concern grew when the commander confirmed the rumors mentioned by Lady Claudette. Apparently the report of the morning's attack had come in not long after Henrik's patrol had left the city.

"Do you think it's the same group?" Kincaid asked Henrik, as the two of them made their way back toward the castle's entrance. "I know such attacks aren't unheard of, but they're unusual so close to the city."

"Yes, they are," Henrik agreed. "I'm inclined to think it's the same group. One attack south of here, one east, one north...it suggests a larger network, but the attacks all sound so similar. I would have no difficulty believing that the two I've seen were the exact same men." He sighed. "Not that I can be sure. I didn't see anyone's faces."

Kincaid ran a hand through his hair, his expression troubled. "The whole thing is exactly the sort of irritation we don't need right now, with Father deep in negotiations with the worst-hit of the farmers."

"They wouldn't be behind it, would they?" Henrik asked. "The farmers?"

Kincaid looked at him in surprise. "Why would you think that? What would the farmers have to gain from such attacks?"

Henrik shook his head slowly. "Nothing that I can think of. It just strikes me that the attacks aren't very effective robberies. The one this afternoon was absurd. Half a dozen armed men waylaying a farmer's wagon? What was the point of that?"

Kincaid frowned. "You think the bandits' aim is to stir up trouble rather than actually steal anything?"

"I don't know," said Henrik, shrugging. "I just know that something doesn't quite add up."

Kincaid looked more thoughtful than ever as they parted ways at the castle's entrance. Henrik turned the matter over and over in his mind as he walked the short distance to his own family's home.

But no new insights occurred to him, and as he changed out of his knight's livery into attire more suitable for the evening's gala, he found his thoughts drawn to the ordeal ahead. His short encounter with Lavinia earlier had demonstrated that the princess was still irritated with him, although he had yet to figure out the reason. Nevertheless, some instinct warned him that an evening of being enthusiastically welcomed home by every young lady present at the gala wasn't going to make Lavinia warm to him. If only his commander had sent him out on an evening patrol. He had less patience than he'd ever had before with the vapid flirtations of the court.

He was too practiced in his role as a dashing knight to allow any of this to show on his face when he made his way into the royal ballroom a short time later. As a member of the returning delegation—and a close friend of the younger prince—he was part of the more select group invited to dine with the royals before the gala's formal opening. Although, with some four dozen people included in this smaller gathering, it was barely distinguishable from the event itself.

The long tables were lined with guests, talking and laughing in the golden light of the summer evening, thrown so generously across the room by the arched windows that stretched from the floor almost to the ceiling. The glass sparkled with the reflection of a multitude of candles, and flowers floated in bowls of water on every table.

But it wasn't the richly-decorated room that brought the event to life. It was the guests—the bright colors of the ladies' gowns, the frequent flashes of silver as the orange light caught the blades of the men's ceremonial swords. The dancing wouldn't come until later in the evening, but the swish of fabric could already be heard throughout the space as the dinner guests mingled with one another.

Henrik cast his eyes across the room as he wondered whether Lady Claudette had arrived. He hardly knew whether he would be glad or sorry to see her. But the thought didn't occupy his mind for long. Just like every other guest, he made his way toward the royals on arrival, in order to be formally greeted by his hosts. And as soon as he caught sight of the royal family, all other considerations disappeared.

He was vaguely aware that Queen Marguerite was still slightly distant in her greeting, whereas Ormond—whom Henrik hadn't actually spoken to since his return—welcomed him warmly. He also noted in a detached way that while Kincaid stood beside his brother, Jocelyn wasn't present. But he didn't stop to consider how unusual that was, because the young woman who was instead standing on Kincaid's other side captivated his whole mind as soon as he laid eyes on her.

CHAPTER SEVEN

As familiar as her features were, the Princess Lavinia who greeted him with her best hostess manners bore very little resemblance to the headstrong girl who had always followed Kincaid and Henrik around with maddening persistence.

In fact, in her sweeping emerald green gown, with her hair elegantly dressed on top of her head, adorned by a delicate golden circlet that seemed to bring out the glints of gold in her auburn hair, she seemed astoundingly different even from the girl he had spoken with a mere two hours before.

Henrik could barely marshal his thoughts enough to respond appropriately to her greeting, and long after he had been swept along, replaced by the next guest in line, he had difficulty keeping his eyes from straying back to her graceful form. Where had this young woman come from?

Because there was no doubt that she was a woman now. Henrik had thought he was fully aware of the changes in Lavinia. But somehow, as he saw her standing beside her family, looking every inch the eligible princess, it hit him with such force that he realized he had never fully comprehended it before.

As he watched, Kincaid took advantage of a lull in the arrivals to lean over and mutter some private joke to his sister. Lavinia's familiar laughter gurgled up before she could stop it, and the mischievous dimple that appeared on one cheek helped Henrik to shake off some of his stupor. The Lavinia he knew was there, under all those unnerving changes.

But that reality did nothing to reduce the discomfort of Henrik's realization about what Lavinia had become. He wished he could go back to five minutes before, when he hadn't grasped how beautiful she was. Or at least, hadn't said it to himself in so many words. Because he had an unpleasant feeling the realization wasn't going to make his life easier.

As if to confirm his thoughts, the queen suddenly looked over at him with a piercing gaze, and Henrik forced himself to pull his eyes from the princess. He frowned slightly as he once again noted Jocelyn's absence. The welcome feast was in her honor as much as Kincaid's, and there must be a very particular reason for her not to attend. He hoped nothing was amiss with little Norik.

To Henrik's equal disappointment and relief, he wasn't seated with the royals for the meal. Instead he was placed with the few other young members of the nobility who had been invited to join the Kyonan delegation. They chattered merrily around him, but he had little attention to spare either for their conversation or for the sumptuous feast laid before them. He felt acutely uncomfortable, as if he'd accidentally sat on the hilt of his sword.

Lady Claudette had arrived shortly after him, and was sitting with some of the local nobles further down the long table. She threw him the occasional smile, but he barely saw her, his eyes drawn constantly to the table where the royals sat.

An unfamiliar young woman was seated near them, and Henrik looked her over with interest. His best guess was that she must be Lady Brielle, the noblewoman picked out by the king and queen for their oldest son. She looked poised and calm, the quiet reserve of her manner a sharp contrast to the spirited young princess who was attempting to engage her in conversation over the top of the senior nobleman seated between them.

Henrik smiled as he returned his gaze to his plate. If Lady Brielle was the opposite to Lavinia, she would probably suit Prince Ormond very well.

The meal had barely finished when additional guests began to arrive for the gala. Like all the guests, Henrik and his companions stood the moment the monarchs did, regardless of whether or not they had actually finished their food. The tables were cleared and rearranged against the wall in an astonishingly short time. Henrik didn't waste any regret on his uneaten scraps —he knew that the tables would be kept well stocked with an endless supply of delicacies for the whole duration of the gala.

King Malcolm gave a formal welcome to all the new guests, marking the return of his second son and family, without any specific reference to Jocelyn's absence. He briefly welcomed Lady Claudette as well, and she received the mention with a gracious dip of her head. Henrik raised an eyebrow, and he heard a barely audible mutter pass around the room at her failure to curtsy to the king as expected. He wouldn't be surprised to learn that Thoranian ways were different, of course. But he was a little surprised that she hadn't been fully briefed on the customs in Valoria, given she was intended to be part of the formal delegation due to arrive in a matter of weeks.

As soon as the king had finished speaking, the musicians struck up, and Lady Claudette's omission was instantly forgotten. Henrik evaded a group of hopeful-looking girls as dexterously as he could, making his way toward the royal family.

Princess Lavinia had of course been swept instantly into the dance by an eager young courtier, and he assumed that Prince Ormond would open the dancing with Lady Brielle. But with Jocelyn not present, Henrik thought Kincaid might be as hopeful of avoiding dancing as Henrik was.

He was therefore surprised when he managed to push his way through the room to discover no trace of his best friend. The king and queen had retired to elaborately carved wooden seats at one end of the room, but Ormond and the young lady Henrik assumed to be Lady Brielle still stood against the wall near where they had been seated.

"Lord Henrik," the crown prince greeted him pleasantly, as he drew near. Henrik gave a slight bow. "I'm glad to see you here this evening. Let me introduce you to Lady Brielle."

Henrik bowed politely to the young woman, saying all the appropriate things.

"I imagine you're looking for Kincaid," Ormond said, once Lady Brielle had responded in kind. He turned to her. "Lord Henrik is my younger brother's oldest friend, you know." He looked back at Henrik. "He's gone up to his rooms for a moment, but he'll be back shortly."

Henrik thanked him. He was confused, but he knew better than to ask Ormond for an explanation. The older prince was friendly enough to Henrik, but he never slipped into the level of informality Henrik was used to from the prince's younger siblings.

"Well," said Ormond, his eyes straying across the room. "I mustn't neglect my duty in opening the dancing. I wouldn't wish to offend our foreign visitor."

With a final half-bow, he disappeared into the crowd. Astonished, Henrik followed the prince with his eyes. Ormond made directly through the throng toward Lady Claudette, bowing over her hand in a clear invitation.

Henrik could understand why the prince wanted to dance with the Thoranian. It had somehow not shown when she was seated at the table. But framed in the glowing light of the sunset, her elaborate gown cascading down from her form, she looked more beautiful than Henrik had ever seen her. He watched from across the room as she cast her eyes down demurely, placing her hand in Ormond's. A crowd of hopeful young men dropped back a step, their expressions disappointed but resigned. No one could hope to compete with the crown prince.

Henrik tore his gaze from the sight, turning back to the young woman beside him. He gave her a winning smile, trying to muster all his charm as he debated how best to soften Ormond's most uncharacteristic rudeness.

"I have the luxury of no title, Lady Brielle. And therefore I'm free to ask you for the honor of a dance."

Lady Brielle smiled, casting her eyes down in a self-conscious gesture. "You are very kind, Lord Henrik," she said quietly. "But I must give you the same answer I gave His Highness. I'm still in half-mourning for my mother, who passed away recently. This gala is the first event I have attended since her death, and it wouldn't be appropriate for me to dance."

Henrik felt a stirring of sympathy for the quiet young woman, mingled with his relief at the discovery that Ormond had at least asked Lady Brielle to dance first. Still, he couldn't help but consider the prince's speedy abandonment to be a slight on his first companion.

"I am sorry to hear of your loss," he said earnestly, seeing the traces of real pain behind her reserve.

"Thank you," she said calmly. "My father and I miss her terribly."

"Is your father here tonight?" Henrik asked, casting his eyes around the room. His gaze lingered for a moment on Lady Claudette, swirling through the room with Ormond, and for an even longer moment on Princess Lavinia, who was laughing as she twirled in the arms of an attractive young nobleman. Henrik pulled his eyes back to Lady Brielle with an effort as she answered.

"No, he isn't, I'm afraid. Their Majesties were gracious enough to invite him, and he would have liked to be here to welcome the prince and princess back from Kyona. But he was detained on our estate by pressing business."

"Ah yes, I've heard about the difficulties being faced by many of your father's tenants," Henrik said, willing his attention to remain politely on the woman in front of him. She had a pleasant enough face, her rather precise features framed by carefully controlled brown curls. But while the gaze of her blue eyes was clear and intelligent, they lacked a certain sparkle of mischief, and there was certainly no dimple to be seen.

"It hasn't been an easy time," Lady Brielle acknowledged, her voice as calm as ever. "But my father is very capable of navigating the difficult season to come. It's understandable that some of the farmers are feeling afraid. I don't blame them—I'm sure I would be too, if I was uncertain whether I would be able to feed my family come winter. But the truth is that my father is an excellent master, and he'll see them through it. He's been meeting with each one, individually, to discuss what help he can offer, and what efforts he expects from them. Most of them come out of those discussions much reassured, but of course the whole process takes time."

Her gaze strayed over to the king and queen, seated some distance away.

"Their Majesties have been incredibly generous with the assistance they've offered. I know how grateful my father has been for their support and advice."

Henrik hid a smile. He had no doubt that Lord Thornton was wholehearted in singing his monarchs' praises. He must be overjoyed at their interest in his daughter on the crown prince's behalf.

But Henrik could see why she had caught the sovereigns' eye. She had all the quiet grace that the queen had tried so unsuccessfully to cultivate in her own daughter, and she seemed to be kind-hearted as well as intelligent. Henrik could imagine her suiting Ormond very well, and being just the sort of well-brought up young woman the current rulers would wish to see as queen one day. It seemed to be a good choice.

Not that Henrik's opinion on the matter was of any relevance, of course. And unfortunately, the young man whose opinion was most important, seemed to have forgotten all about his guest. Henrik gladly stayed by Lady Brielle's side for the duration of the first dance, talking over her father's plans to bolster the weak harvest, and her impressions of Bryford. But when the dance ended, he was dismayed that Prince Ormond, instead of returning to the noblewoman's side, swept Lady Claudette into a second dance.

Henrik glanced involuntarily at the king and queen, and saw Queen Marguerite frowning at her oldest son. She must be as surprised by Ormond's lapse in etiquette as Henrik was, but short of making a scene, there was nothing she could do about it. Henrik returned his attention quickly to Lady Brielle, hoping to again smooth over the awkward moment, but the look on her face only increased his discomfort. She didn't look angry, or even offended. But again, he thought he saw pain behind her calm front, and he was at a loss for what to say.

"Ah Henrik, I see you've met Lady Brielle."

Henrik turned eagerly at his friend's familiar voice, grateful for the distraction.

"Yes, we've just been—hello! What's this?" Henrik's astonished gaze passed from Kincaid to his miniature companion and back, hardly knowing whether to laugh or stare.

Kincaid grimaced slightly at him as his son replied on his behalf.

"Dada said I can come!"

"Only for a minute," Kincaid reminded the boy sternly, but Norik just grinned, clearly secure in his victory.

"Is that so?" Henrik asked, bobbing down to the little boy's level. "And what would you want to come to a gala for, little man?"

Norik grinned endearingly, his voice lowered to a conspiratorial whisper. "Auntie Vinya said there are sweets."

"Did she now?" Henrik repeated impressively, unable to hold back a grin as he looked up at Kincaid.

"Yes, yes, I'll wring her neck later," Kincaid muttered, a long-suffering look on his face. He turned to Lady Brielle. "This is my son, My Lady. Norik."

"Yes, I gathered as much," said Lady Brielle. Henrik thought she had looked taken aback at the appearance of the pair, but she smiled at the toddler now in her quiet way. "Is this your first gala, Prince Norik?"

The little boy puffed out his chest as he acknowledged it, and Henrik used the cover of the child's excited chatter to draw close to his friend.

"Your mother is going to have your hide," he said with a grin.

Kincaid shot him a look. "I know, I know, he shouldn't be here, especially not this late. But with the days so long, it's hard to convince him that it's bedtime."

Henrik's grin broadened at the prince's pleading tone, and Kincaid grimaced. "The trouble is, Joss had promised him a brief visit to the gala, right at the start, you know, to see the family all dressed up before the guests started to arrive, and no doubt to steal some sweets from the kitchens on the way past, the little scamp."

"Where *is* Jocelyn?" Henrik asked, glancing behind the prince as if his wife might materialize.

"Unwell," said Kincaid briefly.

Henrik raised an eyebrow. "Is she going to be all right? She must be pretty sick to miss a welcome feast in her honor."

"Oh yes," Kincaid said airily. "She'll be fine." He saw that Henrik looked unconvinced, and he suddenly gave a mischievous grin. "Oh, what does it matter? It'll be all over the city in a week, there's no keeping secrets in a castle. The truth is she's expecting again."

"What?" Henrik glanced at the little boy still bombarding a patient Lady Brielle with his conversation. The idea of two such miniature firebrands was overwhelming. But Kincaid seemed pleased, so Henrik hastened to give all the proper congratulations.

"Sly little thing never said a word to me until we got home, but apparently she suspected as much before we left Kyona," Kincaid said. "That's why she wanted to leave early. She was hoping to be settled back in Bryford well before the sickness hit." He frowned. "But for some reason it seems to have come earlier this time, and to be much worse. It's been building over the last few days, but this afternoon it just took over. Poor Joss. She doesn't complain much, but...Well, you said it yourself. She wouldn't miss an event like this unless she really wasn't capable of being here."

Henrik felt a pang of sympathy for the absent princess, along with a powerful surge of gratitude that he would never have to experience the awkward discomfort that seemed to be pregnancy.

"So she was in no state to exert parental authority over the little warrior," Henrik finished, inclining his head toward Norik. "Leaving you in sole charge of the battle."

Kincaid sighed in resignation. "And I caved immediately, yes."

Henrik gave a snort of laughter that he tried to conceal as a cough. "I'm surprised his nurse allowed him out this late."

Kincaid shook his head woefully. "She was too busy fussing over Joss to be any use to me. If there's anything that can distract Nurse from the antics of a royal child, it's the prospect of another one coming."

"Uncle Henwik!" Norik's demand for attention drew Henrik's eyes down to knee height, where a pair of brown eyes were staring up at him with great determination. "Where are the sweets?"

"None of that now, it's time to go," said Kincaid firmly. "I said a minute, and it's been several."

"But—"

Kincaid cut off the toddler's protests. "We'll get you something from the kitchen on the way back to the nursery." The prince shot Lady Brielle a rueful look. "The cook is as unable to stand up to this little tyrant as I am. Thank you for your patience, My Lady."

"Not at all," said Lady Brielle, smiling gently at Norik as she swept him a small curtsy. "Thank you for the conversation, Your Highness."

"But Auntie Vinya said the sweets are at the gala," Norik complained, his eyes searching the swirling figures. "Where's Auntie Vinya?"

In spite of himself, Henrik felt his eyes leap right to Lavinia, although he couldn't explain how he had known exactly where to find her. The whole group followed his gaze.

The princess was dancing with another young man, but she looked up suddenly, seeming to feel their collective scrutiny. At sight of Norik, her face broke into a dimpled grin, and she excused herself from her partner with the impetuousness that was the despair of her mother.

She hurried across the room toward them, her eyes glowing and her cheeks flushed from the dancing. A few of her unruly auburn curls had already escaped her elegant hairstyle, but the look suited her even better, the runaways curling around her face with a careless freedom that matched her mischievous expression.

"Norik!" she exclaimed when she reached them. "You made it!"

"Yep!" the little boy announced, but his face quickly darkened in a scowl. "But I didn't find the sweets, and Dada says I have to go."

"Ah yes," said Lavinia reminiscently, greeting Lady Brielle in a friendly way before returning her attention to the little boy. "I understand your pain. I used to be denied access to all the delights of galas too."

"He's two, Lavinia, not thirteen," said Kincaid, unimpressed.

His sister just grinned up at him. "I had to let him in on the secret, Kincaid. How else could he know that his favorite auntie has his back?"

"I dunno if you're my favorite," said Norik in a thoughtful tone.

He glanced up at Henrik, who had remained silent, torn between the desire to laugh at Kincaid's predicament and the hope that no one noticed how difficult he was finding it not to stare at Lavinia.

"I think Uncle Henwik is my favorite."

"What?" Lavinia's mock outrage made Henrik chuckle in spite of himself. She shot him a glare that was somehow still full of laughter. "But he's not even a real uncle!"

"He's real!" Norik protested. "And he's more fun than Uncle Ormond."

"Where is Ormond?" Lavinia asked, glancing up at Lady Brielle in confusion before scanning the room. "I thought he was over here with…" Her voice trailed off and her eyebrows shot up as she caught sight of her oldest brother, fetching a drink for Lady Claudette at one of the heavily laden refreshment tables.

"He's been making sure our Thoranian guest is comfortable," said Henrik blandly.

"What's he thinking?" Kincaid muttered to Henrik, clearly not intending the ladies to hear. "I'll admit Lady Claudette looks unusually beautiful tonight, but—"

"She's not beautiful!"

CHAPTER EIGHT

Norik's loud interjection made them both look down, Kincaid's horrified expression confirming that he hadn't intended anyone but Henrik to hear his comment.

Lavinia and Lady Brielle both looked over at the trio, the princess's eyes dancing with laughter and the noblewoman looking uncomfortable.

"Norik," said Kincaid firmly.

His son looked up at him out of innocent eyes. "The lady with Uncle Ormond isn't beautiful," he insisted. "Her face is mean, and she looks silly."

"That's enough." Kincaid's voice had become uncharacteristically sharp, and Norik fell silent, seeming to sense that his easygoing father had reached some kind of limit. "Time to go," the prince added, and this time Norik didn't argue. After a hasty farewell, Kincaid hauled his son toward the ornate door, leaving the other three standing in awkward silence.

Lavinia didn't seem to feel the awkwardness too acutely. She was clearly still attempting to hold back laughter, making only a halfhearted effort to conceal her delight at her nephew's blunt description of Lady Claudette. Lady Brielle was looking determinedly away from Ormond and his companion, trying unsuccessfully to look as though she hadn't heard the little boy's comments.

Henrik, on the other hand, couldn't tear his eyes from the Thoranian woman across the room. He stared at her, rooted to the spot, as the truth of Norik's words hit him with bizarre force.

Because the two-year-old had been absolutely right. Well, Henrik wasn't sure he'd describe the visiting noblewoman's face as "mean"—although there was a certain hardness to her expression that he'd never noticed before—but the rest of it had been right on target.

Lady Claudette wasn't beautiful. She just wasn't.

As he scrutinized her features from across the room, Henrik was baffled as to how he had ever been struck by her.

It wasn't that she was hideously ugly. But describing her as beautiful was a painful stretch. She was ordinary—her figure lacked any particular elegance, and her face was sharp, and too angular for beauty.

And Henrik had to agree with Norik's other comment as well. Lady Claudette did look silly. Not because of any of her physical features, but because of her demeanor. Henrik had been admiring her determination and resilience mere hours before, but it was impossible even from across the room to miss her air of demure hesitance as she spoke with Prince Ormond. Henrik found himself wondering how he had ever been led into admiring her strength and confidence. It seemed embarrassingly obvious as he watched her now, not only that she was making no attempt to show Prince Ormond a confident front, but that her docile manner was forced and intentional. Simpering was the best word for it, and Norik couldn't have been more accurate with his childish observation that it made her look, well, silly.

Henrik blinked in confusion as he watched her. He distinctly remembered admiring her striking beauty more than once, but it was hard to believe that any trick of the light or unlucky choice of gown could produce the contrast he saw before him now.

He felt irritation rising within him alongside the bewilderment as he remembered his own flirtatious behavior toward the noblewoman. He didn't mind mistaking his own opinion of her appearance so much—it was perplexing, but it didn't really matter.

However, it maddened him that he had allowed himself to be attracted to someone whose behavior was so artificial. He had never before struggled to recognize scheming young women for what they were—they had tended to hang around Kincaid in abundance when the pair had been younger. And yet, he hadn't until this moment recognized the familiar calculating gleam in Lady Claudette's eyes. How had he allowed himself to be blinded to it by a pretty face, one that in brutal honesty wasn't even all that pretty. He must be as irresponsible and foolish a flirt as Queen Marguerite believed him to be.

Henrik shook his head, trying to clear away the whole strange and humiliating episode. But as he turned his attention from the woman across the room to the two women beside him, his thoughts became only barely more coherent. Lavinia's beauty, which had struck him so uncomfortably earlier in the evening, now seemed almost blinding when compared with the false charm of the near-stranger currently hanging on Ormond's arm.

Henrik turned to Lady Brielle, summoning up a polite question about her home with great effort. His usual charm may have fled him completely at the evening's confusing series of revelations, but basic good manners could still come to his rescue.

Lavinia showed no inclination to return to her abandoned partner, lingering to listen to Lady Brielle's answer, and asking her own questions with good-natured interest. Her presence was like a constant discomfort to Henrik, who was determined to keep his attention on the young woman who had been all but spurned by the crown prince. And yet, he couldn't quite bring himself to wish that she would leave.

After a few minutes, a courtier from Lady Brielle's southeastern region approached the group, inquiring politely after her father. With the noblewoman's attention captured, Henrik had no more excuse not to look at the princess. Her eyes were still on the other two, but she seemed to feel his gaze immediately, looking up at him with an engaging smile.

"I like her," she said quietly, inclining her head toward Lady Brielle and her companion. "She would be excellent for Ormond, don't you think?"

Henrik nodded stupidly, still uncharacteristically tongue-tied.

Lavinia didn't seem to notice, her face creasing into a small frown as she glanced across the room at her oldest brother. "And I'm pretty sure that this morning he thought so too."

Henrik followed her gaze, and for a moment the two of them watched in silence as Ormond led Lady Claudette into yet another dance. The musicians had been taking a quick break, but they were starting up again, and couples were returning eagerly toward the cleared space in the center of the ballroom.

"Mother's furious, look," said Lavinia.

Henrik followed her gaze again to see Queen Marguerite watching her oldest son with an impassive face but unwavering focus.

"I know she looks calm, but trust me, I know that expression better than anyone," Lavinia continued. Lady Brielle was still deep in conversation with her other acquaintance, and Lavinia's voice was lowered conspiratorially. Henrik had to lean his head close to hers to make out her words as she went on. "She's ready to murder Ormond. He's going to be in serious trouble once no one else is around." The princess gave a dry chuckle. "Probably for the first time in his life."

Henrik looked down at Lavinia, trying not to laugh at the poorly concealed glee in her voice. "I can see you're full of sympathy."

Lavinia grinned responsively, meeting his gaze with dancing eyes. "I should be, shouldn't I? I'm the expert on receiving Mother's lectures." She glanced over at Lady Brielle, and her expression became more subdued for a moment. "I'm not glad Ormond is neglecting Lady Brielle, I'm really not."

She shot another look at her mother. When she returned her gaze to Henrik, she was no longer attempting to hold back her delight, her natural vivacity bubbling instantly to the surface. "It's just so entertaining to think of Ormond getting scolded. It makes a nice change for it to be someone else for once."

Henrik grinned back, unable to resist either the sparkle in her eye or the dimple that emerged as she smiled mischievously over her normally serious brother's lapse.

She was utterly enchanting. Her candor might be a constant source of frustration to her mother, but Henrik could never consider it a fault. Not when Lavinia was so incapable of the kind of false behavior that Henrik had always despised in the scheming young women who used to pursue Kincaid for his title. Behavior he had apparently failed to recognize in Lady Claudette. His eyes fell on the Thoranian once again, now swirling through the room with the crown prince.

"Dance with me?" The words were out before he'd thought them through, but Henrik had no desire to pull them back in.

Lavinia's grin disappeared, replaced with a look of astonishment. "Did you just ask me to dance?"

"Is it so surprising?" Henrik asked.

Lavinia raised an eyebrow. "Uh, yes, it is."

"Why?" Henrik pushed. "Why wouldn't I want to dance with you?" An internal voice was scolding Henrik as sternly as Queen Marguerite was apparently going to scold Ormond, reminding him what he had said to Kincaid, about princesses and boundaries. He ignored it recklessly.

"How should I know?" Lavinia asked dryly. "But I can only assume that you don't want to, because the last time you asked me to dance was at Joss and Kincaid's wedding. Four years ago."

"Well," said Henrik, "apparently I want to now. So all that remains to be seen is whether you want to dance with me." He held out his hand in a silent question.

Lavinia didn't look at it, her eyes burning into Henrik's in unabashed assessment. He held her gaze steadily, forcing his expression to remain calm as he tried not to glance toward the queen, to make sure she wasn't watching him with her eagle stare.

Then all of a sudden Lavinia's face dimpled into a smile, her hand slipping into his as comfortably as if they did this all the time. "Oh, why not?" she said, her words laced with the same recklessness that was still coursing through Henrik.

Henrik could think of a couple of reasons, but he didn't mention them as he led her into the dance. Her hand felt small, and unnaturally warm in his. Everything about her was warm, from the glinting red strands in her auburn hair to the fiery exuberance of her personality.

Even her cheeks were flushed again, although they hadn't yet actually started the dance. She didn't meet his eye as they walked through the room, and Henrik was feeling a little less poised than usual himself. For some reason, it was the swish of her skirts as he swept the two of them into position that suddenly woke him up to what he was doing. He was dancing with Lavinia—how had that happened? He hadn't been aware of any such intention when he'd entered the room. In fact, he'd been very intentional for years about *not* doing anything of the kind.

He was suddenly very grateful that Kincaid wasn't in the ballroom—not to mention his alarmingly perceptive wife—and it was harder than ever to avoid looking at the queen. But it was too late to back out now.

He forced himself to come out of his stupor as they joined the movement of the dance. Lavinia had been unusually quiet since accepting his invitation, and he only hoped it wasn't because she noticed how awkward he had become. He smiled down at her mechanically, his mind searching for something charming to say. It had never been difficult to find glib compliments before.

"How am I doing this time?" Lavinia asked.

Henrik blinked. "What?"

She chuckled. She seemed to be a step ahead of him in recovering herself, and the mischievous twinkle was back in her eyes.

"Do I dance well enough now to meet the Lord Henrik standard of charming young women?" she asked, her tone unconvincingly innocent. "I don't remember stepping on your feet last time, but I thought I must have. I'm sure you've danced with every other girl in the court twenty times since then, so I can only assume my performance last time was absolutely woeful in order to earn me a four year ban."

Henrik couldn't help his grin, even though a part of him was wincing. His decision not to dance with Lavinia had been intentional of course, but he hadn't realized how conspicuous it had been.

"Consider the ban lifted," he said lightly. "You dance beautifully."

"I'm so relieved to hear you say that, My Lord," Lavinia responded, batting her eyelashes at him in mock bashfulness. "I've been working so very hard at my dancing lessons ever since."

Henrik laughed aloud. "That's hard to believe. I didn't think you'd ever worked hard at any of your lessons, Your Highness."

Lavinia's expression became mournful. "You wrong me, My Lord. Where is the famous charm and chivalry we ladies have come to expect from the dashing Lord Henrik?"

Henrik shook his head, remaining silent but unable to keep the smile from his face as the steps of the dance separated them temporarily. He watched Lavinia swirl across the space. He wasn't sure how her every movement could display this mysterious new elegance while still retaining the vivacious impulsiveness that had always characterized her. Yet somehow, that's just how it was.

Henrik linked arms with another woman as the dance required, and it brought him momentarily out of himself. He barely even took in the identity of his temporary partner, smiling vaguely in response to her coquettish comment in the hope that he would escape being considered rude. His attention drawn from the princess, he glanced around the room. He still pointedly avoided looking toward the sovereigns, but he caught sight of Prince Ormond and Lady Claudette, further up the group of dancers, also separated by the flow of the steps.

His eyes were quickly drawn back to Lavinia as she made her way down the row. The vibrant green of her skirts seemed to him the brightest spot in the room, and he realized with a shot of displeasure that he wasn't the only one to have noticed. Lots of the other young men in the ballroom were watching the princess appreciatively, and Henrik refrained from scowling only with an effort.

It was enough of a shock for him to realize that Lavinia had grown up. The fact that many others were clearly also having the same realization was even more alarming.

He tried not to let any of that show as she finally rejoined him. As before, her hands seemed to burn with warmth as they linked with his. He had danced with a lot of beautiful young women over the years. But dancing with Lavinia was nothing like those experiences. There was something both natural and exhilarating about the way she fit into his arms as he swung her across the floor that he couldn't remember ever noting before.

He found he liked the sensation immensely.

"So," he said quickly, wanting to reclaim her attention without a moment's delay. The man who had most recently passed her off in the dance was still smiling flirtatiously at her, ignoring his own partner. Henrik resisted the urge to elbow the man in the gut as he swirled Lavinia away more forcefully than the dance required. "What were you saying? Accusing me of a lack of charm, I believe?"

"Actually," said Lavinia humorously, "I think you were accusing me of not applying myself in my studies." She looked up at him from beneath her lashes in an excellent imitation of the kind of girls Henrik had flirted with more times than he could count. "But there's only so much you can learn from books, you know, My Lord."

"Princess Lavinia," said Henrik, torn between the desire to laugh and the distracting realization of just how long her eyelashes were, "are you trying to flirt with me? Because that's something *you* haven't done in about as many years as it's been since we last danced."

"Well, you said you wanted to dance with me now," Lavinia reasoned, abandoning the coquettish posture in favor of a more natural grin. "Doesn't that mean you want to flirt with me as well?"

For a moment Henrik just stared at her, his mind completely

empty of anything charming or witty. "No," he said at last, his tone unintentionally blunt. "I don't want to flirt with you."

Lavinia's smile faltered, but Henrik barely noticed. He was locked in some unnameable internal struggle. She pulled back slightly, but Henrik tightened his hold, his arms determined to keep her close while his mind attempted to untangle whatever was happening inside him.

He knew he hadn't been polite, but he also knew that he had spoken the truth. Flirtation was light, pointless, completely lacking in substance. He didn't want that from Lavinia. He wanted something more substantial—he just wasn't sure what that was.

"Well," Lavinia said, her voice flat. "I can't complain that you're not honest, at any rate."

She flicked her head in her characteristic gesture of defiance, apparently forgetting that her hair was confined on top of her head rather than cascading over her shoulders as usual. The movement distracted Henrik from his thoughts, and he almost smiled at the defiant sparkle in her eyes. Her mother might think the princess lacked poise, but by Henrik's observation, few women took rejection with as much grace as she was showing.

Lavinia was silent for a moment, but when she looked up at him again, her face was set in determined lines. That unquenchable determination, like her defiance, was something Henrik had always admired about her, even when she was a frustrating child. He remembered, with another flash of confusion, admiring those same qualities in Lady Claudette not long ago. It was strange that he had so inaccurately endowed the foreign visitor with those traits. Compared to Lavinia, she was entirely lacking in them.

"Henrik." Lavinia's unusually serious tone recalled his mind to their conversation. "Why haven't you wanted to dance with me all this time? Was it really such an unpleasant prospect?"

"Of course not," said Henrik quickly, but Lavinia cut him off, her expression still earnest. Clearly she was tired of playing games, and determined to get a straight answer.

"I mean it. I've seen you dance with girls who are plain, girls who are so dull I can only feel sorry for them, girls who are downright nasty in temperament. Maybe I shouldn't say it, but it's true. And I've never seen your charm falter with any of them. Would it really have been so hard to swallow whatever reluctance you have and just give me a dance here or there? The omission has been so obvious, it's humiliating."

Henrik swallowed. "Nonsense," he said weakly. "I doubt anyone else has even noticed we haven't danced in so long."

Lavinia raised an eyebrow, unimpressed. "Well, I've noticed. And you didn't answer my question. Why?"

"You were fourteen when we danced at your brother's wedding," said Henrik shortly.

"So?" Lavinia pressed, after a prolonged pause.

"You're not fourteen anymore."

Lavinia was silent for a moment, thinking this over. "Is that why you didn't want to dance with me before? Or why you do want to dance with me now?"

"I..." Henrik hesitated, unsure how to put any of his thoughts into words.

It wasn't that Lavinia was wrong. The omission had definitely been intentional. And there were very specific reasons why he hadn't asked her to dance since Kincaid's wedding. But he didn't want to tell Lavinia that while she hadn't stepped on his foot on that occasion, she had driven him away just as effectively with her blatant attempts to flirt with him. As childish as they had been, Henrik had been wise enough to know that if he didn't want to encourage such behavior—and deal with all the consequences from those who didn't approve of her conduct, most obviously her parents—his safest course was to distance himself from the volatile young princess. To be fair, she had stopped the attempts not long afterward, but Henrik had still deemed it best to hold her at arm's length.

Except, his honesty as much as his good manners prevented him from using that answer to Lavinia's question. It had been years since she had given him that particular reason to avoid dancing with her. As much as she had flirted outrageously with most of the court, she hadn't attempted it with him in a long time. The trouble was, by the time he acknowledged that to himself, it had seemed just as unwise to cross that line with her, for reasons less clearly defined but no less compelling. Reasons that had become substantially more defined tonight, when he finally admitted to himself that Lavinia had become a very beautiful—and very much off limits—young woman.

But he couldn't exactly say as much to her.

"It's not like you've wanted for partners," he deflected lamely. "You're usually the most sought-after girl in the room. Why do you care if *one* man doesn't single you out?"

"Well, I wouldn't care," said Lavinia, a bite in her voice. "Except that when the one man is the biggest flirt in the court, it feels like a pointed snub."

"The biggest flirt in the court, am I?" Henrik shot back, rattled. "Are you sure? Because I've heard that honored title applied to someone else on more than one occasion."

Lavinia flushed, and Henrik regretted the unkind words. But she gave him no opportunity to take them back.

"It's a little hard to take an accusation of indiscretion from you," she spat. "But even if my pride is a little stung, I suppose I should be grateful to be the one girl in the court you're not determined to seduce."

"Hang on," Henrik protested, his regret swallowed by rising irritation. "I'll be the last to deny my faults, but that's not fair. Maybe your mother has reason to think I'm irresponsible, and maybe I've earned my reputation as a flirt. But I've never tried to *seduce* anyone."

Lavinia raised one eyebrow again, and Henrik scowled.

"And you know it!" he added, aggrieved. "I may not seek you out at dances, but it's not like we haven't spoken in four years. You're around half the time I'm with Kincaid and Jocelyn. You know me better than that. Or at least you should."

Lavinia was silent for a moment. "Perhaps that wasn't fair," she said at last. Her lips curved in a half-hearted version of her usual grin. "But you started it."

Henrik didn't answer, and her face once again settled into more subdued lines.

"Please, Henrik," she said softly. "Tell me what I did wrong that you've avoided me so pointedly all these years. I know I annoyed you when I was a child, following you and Kincaid around, demanding to be included in everything. But I'm not a child now, and I haven't asked anything of you, not for years."

"You haven't done anything wrong," Henrik insisted, uncomfortable.

"Then why?"

Henrik shrugged one shoulder awkwardly, the motion all the dance would allow. "I just thought it was safer not to."

"Why?" Lavinia asked again. "Why am I so dangerous?"

Henrik stared down into her eyes, and his breath caught at the expression he saw there. She had never looked at him so earnestly, and it tugged at his heart to see the real pain hidden behind her frustration. He had hurt her with his caution, and hurting her was suddenly the very last thing he wanted to do. Every chivalrous instinct arising from his role as a knight was awakened, but with a potency increased tenfold.

Lavinia created the strangest contradictions within him. He was more charmed by her than any woman he'd ever met, and yet he'd never wanted to charm any woman less. Her forthright nature would surely see his smooth words for the ridiculous facade they were.

And the desire to protect and look after her—a desire never awakened by any of the beautiful girls who'd feigned helplessness whenever around the chivalrous knight—was suddenly overpowering. Yet it was utterly wasted on Lavinia, who was as strong as she was fiery, and more than able to take care of herself.

"Is it just because I'm a princess?" Lavinia pressed, pulling his mind back to her question, and his own failure to answer.

It was on the edge of his tongue to confirm it, and take the easy answer she'd offered. But it wouldn't be true. Because while that was part of the problem, if it was just that she was a princess, she wouldn't be so dangerous to him. He'd flirted with plenty of girls above him in status, without any fear of the consequences.

The danger he'd been trying to outrun wasn't her position. It was her. And his instinct hadn't been wrong, because one reckless evening, one dance, and it had caught up with him instantly. He could no longer deny the truth that had been creeping up on him for over a year.

He was in love with Lavinia. And if acknowledging her beauty had promised to make his life uncomfortable, putting words to this realization was going to be almost impossible to live with.

Because there was no way in the kingdom that the king and queen would throw their only daughter away on the third son of a viscount, let alone one who they personally considered to be flighty and irresponsible.

"Henrik?" Lavinia's hurt was giving way to confusion at her companion's prolonged silence. He must seem like he'd lost his wits.

He shook his head slightly, wondering when they had

stopped moving. The music had ceased without him even realizing it, and another nobleman was approaching, clearly bent on asking Lavinia for the next dance.

Every instinct in Henrik wanted to snap at the man to back off, but he swallowed the impulse. He had no claim on the princess, and he needed to put some space between them if he didn't want to lose claim on his self possession as well.

"Thank you for the dance, Your Highness," he said, giving her a quick bow as the other man reached them. He tried to ignore her look of total astonishment as he retreated, leaving her standing alone.

Not for long, of course. The hopeful nobleman claimed her attention immediately, and Henrik forced himself to look away with an effort.

The room seemed overwhelmingly hot and stuffy all of a sudden, and the swirling colors he had admired on entering the ballroom were now making his head hurt. He could just make out Prince Ormond across the room, still focusing all his attention on Lady Claudette, and logically he knew that meant the queen was probably still occupied by watching her oldest son's every move. Nevertheless, Henrik could have sworn he felt the eyes not only of Queen Marguerite, but of every member of the royal family on him, as if they all somehow knew what he'd just discovered.

Jocelyn wasn't there of course, but he had a feeling she'd known before he did. The thought of the absent princess filled Henrik with sudden determination. If Jocelyn could skip the gala altogether, surely he could get away with leaving early. If he couldn't trust himself to have further conversation with Lavinia, the event held no more interest for him.

"Lord Henrik!"

Henrik turned reluctantly, wishing he'd been quicker getting out of the ballroom. The speaker was an attractive brunette, a few years younger than him, who would surely expect him to ask her to dance.

"Good evening," he managed, giving her a slight bow.

She smiled coyly, flicking her skirts in a practiced motion. "Welcome back to Bryford, My Lord. It was a dull summer without you around."

"You flatter me," said Henrik shortly, in no mood for flirtation.

The noblewoman glanced from his impassive face back toward his former partner. "I see you were cut out of your dance with the princess," she said, with a conspiratorial smile. "Her Highness enjoys a popularity we mere mortals can't dream of."

The invitation in her voice was clear, and there was no doubt in Henrik's mind that she expected him to respond with his most charming manner. They had joked before about the freedoms and limitations of their relatively low status. Like him, she belonged to the lesser ranks of the nobility. She was one of those girls he'd never hesitated to flirt with before, sure of pleasing her with the most shallow of compliments. Insubstantial, safe. The opposite of Lavinia.

He glanced back toward the princess, who was now dancing with the nobleman who had approached her. She looked up, her brows furrowed as she met his eyes, and he snatched his gaze away quickly. The girl who had approached him was watching him with a look of confusion not unlike Lavinia's. It was definitely time to go. The evening he had expected to be tedious had instead become fraught with danger, and if he stayed another minute, he was going to give himself away.

"Indeed," he said, in belated response to the girl's comment. "I'm very glad to be back home again, and I hope you've passed a pleasant summer."

With another bow, he excused himself, trying to ignore the way the girl, eyebrows raised, was looking from him back toward the princess. He made it almost to the door before he was once again hailed.

"Where are you going Henrik? Surely not leaving already?"

Henrik barely held in a groan. Ordinarily Kincaid would be the safest companion for him when trying to hide from the court. But for the moment at least, Kincaid's position as Lavinia's brother had turned him into one of the most alarming people in the room. Henrik could barely look his best friend in the eye as he turned to greet him.

"I'm afraid so. Reporting in early for patrol tomorrow," he said as naturally as he could.

Kincaid laughed, the sound slightly confused. "Who's the old man now? Morning patrol has never had you leaving a gala hours before midnight before."

Henrik just shrugged, and Kincaid's confusion grew.

"You're serious? But I only just got back here! You can't abandon me so early."

"Sorry." Henrik grimaced. "But I really do need to go."

And without so much as glancing back, he strode from the room, leaving his friend to his astonishment.

CHAPTER NINE

Henrik hadn't been entirely truthful when he said he needed to report in early. His commander had given him no such specific instruction. But he still made his way to the training yard as soon as the sun had risen. In spite of leaving the gala early, he had gotten very little sleep, and he had never needed the release of hard physical activity more.

Nothing had changed since the night before—his realization about Princess Lavinia was still hanging over him like an intoxicating but deadly cloud—but he had reached one decision in the hours of darkness.

He might not be able to do anything about the gulf between the two of them, but he wasn't going to wallow. He couldn't recall ever running away from something the way he had run the night before, and he had no intention of continuing the trend. He was one of the king's elite knights, and he didn't like feeling like a coward.

He would have to find a way to live with the discomfort, which was why dawn found him polishing his weapon in the training yard. Experience had taught him that nothing helped clear the mind from distractions or frustrations like a grueling session with a well-matched opponent.

Some of the other knights were also there early, either reporting in from an overnight patrol, or gearing up for the morning like Henrik. He warmed up with a couple of light-hearted matches with some of his peers, but none of them provided him with much of a challenge. The only time he was bested was when he discarded his sword—his preferred weapon—for a bout with the long-handled polearms. His opponent, an eternally cheerful knight about his own age, succeeded in knocking him flat with one end of the hefty wooden staff.

Henrik lay in the dirt for a moment, winded from the blow to his stomach but already analyzing how he could have better defended himself. The other knight discarded his polearm, approaching Henrik with a little too much spring in his step.

"Good fight," he said brightly, offering Henrik his hand.

Henrik accepted the help up with a dry chuckle. "You're generous. It's barely worth your while, I'm so out of practice. I have a bad feeling you were taking it easy on me, too."

The other knight chuckled as he watched Henrik rub his bruised torso. "I had an opening earlier," he admitted with a grin. "But I didn't want to go for the head, for fear of marring that pretty face of yours. We couldn't have the dashing Lord Henrik disfigured, could we? What would the ladies do?"

"All right, all right," Henrik grumbled with a half-grin, taking the sally in good part. "A pretty face, am I? Get your sword, and we'll see who ends up in the dust."

The other knight shook his head, still laughing. He had picked up his polearm again, and he retreated a step, swirling the staff expertly. "No, you clearly need more practice with this weapon. You've lost your edge, spending the whole summer flirting with all the pretty Kyonan girls."

Henrik just grunted, retrieving his own polearm with the

light of competition in his eyes. Though he might not be able to beat his opponent yet, surely he could give a better account of himself this time.

But before they actually resumed their bout, a new arrival drew both men's attention to the other side of the training yard.

"Who do you think that is?" the other knight said, as they watched the newcomer now speaking with their commander. "He looks like a South Lander, doesn't he?"

"He does," Henrik agreed, frowning thoughtfully. "Maybe Lady Claudette's guard has finally arrived."

He saw that his companion was looking at him inquiringly, and he nodded his head toward the pair across the yard as he explained.

"Lady Claudette brought a personal guard with her from Thorania. He got seasick on the voyage, apparently, and he stayed at the port town to recover. He was going to join her here once he was strong enough."

"That must be him, then," mused the other man. He flashed Henrik a grin. "Trust you to know all the details about the beautiful Lady Claudette. I forgot you were basically her personal knight."

Henrik grunted again, this time with less good humor. "I'm nothing of the kind." He looked at the other knight curiously. "Do you really think she's that beautiful?"

His companion met his look with surprise. "Of course! She's stunning. You don't think so?"

Henrik gave a one-shouldered shrug. "Not really. Well...I did when I first met her," he admitted. "But now, I don't know..." He trailed off, his mind returning to the puzzling tumult of emotions he had experienced at the gala the night before. He remembered his shock at the realization of how plain Lady Claudette really was. How much of his loss of interest in the

Thoranian had been caused by finally admitting to himself how he felt about Lavinia?

"Ah, you're a heartless scoundrel," the other knight joked. "Singing a lady's praises one day, discarding her the next."

Henrik frowned. He knew he'd been a bit of a flirt, but was his reputation really so bad? It was no wonder Queen Marguerite always looked at him with that hint of suspicion in her eyes.

"Come on," he said, thrusting the thought aside with a flicker of irritation. He'd come for an early morning sparring session to *avoid* dwelling on his nonexistent chances with Lavinia. "Let's find out what's going on."

The two knights strode across the training area, the man in question moving away from the commander before they reached the pair. Henrik greeted his commander, then watched the newcomer surreptitiously while he began warming up. The exercises he chose were unfamiliar to Henrik. Evidently guards trained quite differently in Thorania.

The commander confirmed what he had guessed, that the man was Lady Claudette's personal guard. Apparently he'd arrived in Bryford early in the morning, and had already sought and received permission to make use of the royal guards' training yard for the duration of his stay.

Henrik struggled to focus on his instructions for the day, continuing to watch the Thoranian guard. He was at least a decade older than Henrik, well built and muscular. The yard had begun to fill as more men arrived to train, and the foreigner was attracting a fair bit of attention.

Henrik spent the next hour or so assisting with the drilling of the same young recruits he'd watched the commander training a couple of days before. But his attention was divided, keeping an eye on Lady Claudette's guard, watching as he accepted several invitations to spar with some of the king's guards.

He was clearly strong, and a good fighter, although it seemed his training had been quite different from his Valorian opponents'. At times this gave him an advantage, but on a number of occasions it betrayed him, as he failed to predict maneuvers that Henrik would have expected to be obvious to any guard.

Henrik knew his fellows well, and it was no surprise to him that the novelty of a foreign challenger soon drew a crowd. The commander had temporarily left the training yard to give his daily report to the king, and his absence had its inevitable effect on the conduct of the knights. Some began to place wagers on the fight currently underway between the newcomer and a member of the royal guard close to him in age. The Thoranian man bested his opponent, to mixed cheers and complaints according to the wagers laid, and some of the more eager young knights began to look around for a more promising challenger.

"Henrik!" one cried, and others took up the call. "Henrik can beat him!"

Henrik waved them off with a dismissive hand. "I'm overseeing this lot."

"We don't mind taking a break, My Lord," said one of the new recruits enthusiastically.

"I'm sure you don't," said Henrik dryly, amused. He glanced at the Thoranian man. "But our guest is the one who deserves a break. He's been fighting with barely a pause."

Lady Claudette's guard, who had so far said nothing about the suggestion of a fight, met Henrik's gaze, his lip curling.

"No need to fight me if you're not up to it, *My Lord*," he said, speaking with a heavy accent.

Henrik raised an eyebrow. Even without the slight sneer, there was no mistaking the man's mocking tone. He thought Henrik was afraid to fight him, did he?

"On second thought," said Henrik shortly, "it is about time for you all to have a rest."

Henrik ignored the grins on the faces of his peers, as well as the cheers of those who were already beginning to place wagers on the fight. He kept his eyes on his opponent as he strode across the yard toward him.

The sun was well and truly up by this time, and it was warm. Henrik stripped off his tunic, as the knights commonly did when engaging in bouts of this kind. His Thoranian challenger was apparently less bothered by the heat, however. Not only did he keep his tunic on, but he was wearing a long-sleeved garment that covered his entire torso, an unusual choice at this time of year. At least in Valoria. Perhaps such attire was common in Thorania—Henrik had no way of knowing.

He pushed all such thoughts aside as he drew his sword, his mind running over everything he had observed about the man's fighting style over the past hour. The Thoranian seemed over-confident, perhaps because he was older and more muscled than his slim young challenger. But there was a reason the others had called on Henrik to try his hand at fighting the newcomer. He was stronger than he looked, and he had always had a natural aptitude for sword fighting. It was how he had risen so quickly in the ranks of the knights.

"I'm Henrik, by the way," he said, as he and the guard took up their positions. "I understand you're Lady Claudette's guard?"

The Thoranian grunted. "That's right. Name's Feivel."

"I hope you're fully recovered from your seasickness," said Henrik, his tone innocent.

Feivel grunted again, narrowing his eyes as he looked Henrik over, as though trying to figure out if there was a hidden meaning behind the Valorian's words. Henrik met his look squarely, trying to read the Thoranian's features. He couldn't shake the feeling that the guard was hiding something.

But a moment later, the older man raised his sword, and Henrik pushed secondary considerations from his mind as the two began to circle one another.

Feivel struck first, his movements quick in spite of his bulkier build. Henrik parried the blow deftly, continuing to circle as he took stock of his opponent. The older man lunged again, and Henrik stepped nimbly to the side, deflecting the blade with ease. He made no move to attack until he had repeated this process several times, and he could see Feivel's frustration at the younger knight's defensive approach.

When the guard lunged forward again, this time with unnecessary force, Henrik suddenly flashed out in a lightning movement, engaging his opponent's blade at last. With a tight flick, he forced the other sword to the side as he stepped neatly around the larger man, striking Feivel's hip with the flat of his blade, signifying a hit according to the normal rules of a practice bout.

The Thoranian man growled low in his throat as he spun back around, sliding his sword along Henrik's and pushing the Valorian back. Either he was too irate to acknowledge the hit, or practice sessions worked differently in Thorania. It wouldn't be surprising.

Henrik stepped back calmly, again sizing up his opponent as they commenced their circling. He had been irritated by Feivel's disparaging words earlier, allowing himself to be goaded into this fight. But beyond that passing annoyance, and his general desire to win, he felt no extraordinary investment in the outcome. Why did it feel like the Thoranian guard had something to prove?

He again hung back, allowing Feivel to make the first move. The onlookers had been calling out occasional encouragements, but they fell silent as Henrik met the guard's attack with a clash of steel, and the fighters began to spar in earnest. Both men's breaths were coming in pants now, and sweat was running down

Henrik's face. He could see the older man sweating as well, and wondered fleetingly if the guard regretted his heavy clothing.

But the thought didn't intrude for long. Henrik felt the thrill of a good fight rush through him as Feivel deflected an attack skillfully. They were quite evenly matched, it seemed. Henrik judged himself to be fitter, and capable of outlasting his opponent. But he had hopes of besting the Thoranian before that point, so as to prove his prowess as a fighter, as well as his energy.

He knew that every eye in the training yard was on him, but he wasn't rattled by the scrutiny. His sole focus was the fight, his attention fully captured by the movements of his opponent. Learning to ignore distractions was one of the most basic features of the training required to become a Valorian guard.

He was therefore surprised when he saw Feivel's attention flicker away from him some minutes into their bout. Aware that it might be a strategy, he didn't follow the Thoranian's gaze, instead keeping his eyes on the other man. But when Feivel lowered his weapon and stepped back, Henrik turned to look at last.

The commander had returned, and had joined the ranks of knights watching the match. He had a faint air of disapproval about him, as if he knew that his men had been placing bets on the fight—something he explicitly prohibited—but to Henrik's eye, he wasn't angry. A decent bout between well-matched opponents, initiated for the sheer sake of the challenge, was exactly the kind of training he encouraged.

"My apologies for distracting your men from their duties," Feivel said, with a glance toward the group of recruits Henrik had been supervising, all of whom were watching the fight with avid interest. "I won't intrude any longer."

And without another word, the Thoranian turned, still breathing heavily from the fight, and strode toward the edge of the yard. He paused at the boundary, shooting a look back at Henrik through narrowed eyes, clearly frustrated not to have beaten his opponent.

Henrik met his look blankly, too confused at first to show his own frustration at the interrupted match. Feivel had clearly been determined to beat him—Henrik couldn't understand why he had cut the bout short.

"Well," said the commander curtly, his eyes on Henrik. "I trust you're sufficiently warmed up."

Henrik wiped an arm across his brow, straightening his back as he acknowledged his commander with a curt nod. The older man looked toward the milling crowd, his eyes landing on the new recruits.

"And I trust you've had enough of a rest to continue training."

Some of the young hopefuls had been grumbling quietly about the inconclusive result of the match, but they all sprang into action at the commander's dry words, scurrying back to their places as they resumed their interrupted training exercise.

Henrik sheathed his weapon, accepting a cloth from a helpful squire, and wiping his face.

"That was odd," said the knight who had bested him with the polearm. "Why did he take off like that?"

"No idea," said Henrik, frowning. "I could have sworn he had plenty of fight left in him."

But he had lost his companion's attention. The man was looking over Henrik's shoulder, and he gave a low whistle.

"Hello, there," he said appreciatively. "It seems we have a visitor."

CHAPTER TEN

Henrik turned to follow the other man's gaze, and his heart did a strange kind of jolt up into his throat then down into his stomach at the sight of Lavinia. She was standing between two pillars on the edge of the training yard, scanning the group of guards and knights.

"It's not every day you see the princess in the royal training yard," said the other knight, his eyebrows raised. He was looking Lavinia over with far too much admiration for Henrik's liking. "She's sure grown up into an eyeful, hasn't she?" he added, as if confirming Henrik's thoughts.

Henrik just grunted, not impressed with the other man's tone. Not that he could blame him for his observation. Lavinia was of course dressed less extravagantly than she had been at the gala the night before, and her hair was cascading freely over her shoulders as normal, rather than elegantly confined on top of her head. But it made little difference. She was just as stunningly beautiful, at least to Henrik's eyes.

"What in the kingdom is she doing here?" he muttered, talking mainly to himself.

As he said the words, Lavinia's eyes fell on him, and her expression cleared. She started walking across the yard toward him with a confidence she had no business feeling in this setting. The commander didn't encourage ladies to visit the training yard, and Henrik could only assume Princess Lavinia's parents shared the sentiment.

The other knight gave another low whistle as the princess approached. "She's looking for you, is she?" He gave an incredulous chuckle. "Must be nice to be on the inside with the royal family like you are."

Henrik just grunted again, shifting his weight uneasily from one foot to the other. Lavinia was attracting plenty of notice as she crossed the yard. He wasn't sure what annoyed him more—the openly appreciative looks and mutters that greeted her passage, or the extra bounce in her step that suggested she was quite enjoying the attention.

"Lord Henrik," she said brightly, as soon as she reached them. Henrik bowed quickly, the movement a little stiff.

"Princess."

Lavinia glanced at Henrik's companion. "Good morning."

Henrik begrudgingly introduced the other knight, who hastened to bow as well. "Your Highness," he said, sounding a little awestruck. "It's an honor to see you here at our training yard."

Lavinia chuckled, casting her eyes around at the training still going on around her, albeit with a little less focus than before her arrival. "I'm a bit out of place, aren't I?"

"Not at all, Your Highness," said the knight chivalrously. "You're more than welcome. We're the king's guard, aren't we? As a member of the royal family, you have every claim on our attention."

"You're too kind," Lavinia grinned, flicking her hair slightly.

"With such a warm welcome, how could I resist coming to check on my father's elite?" She turned suddenly toward Henrik. "What do you think, Lord Henrik?" Her eyes sparkled mischievously, no hint to be seen of the vulnerability she had shown the night before. "Some people are daunted by the title, but your friend here thinks it's a princess's right to claim the attention of a knight. Isn't he chivalrous?"

"He might be chivalrous," Henrik retorted, unimpressed. "But if he really was a member of your father's elite, he'd be better trained and not so easily distracted." He shot the other knight a look. "The king's guard, are we?"

His companion chuckled, not looking repentant at being caught out in having given himself a promotion to match Henrik's status. "I was speaking in terms of aspiration, of course." He returned his attention to Lavinia, although he inclined his head in Henrik's direction. "We can't all be skilled enough to reach His Majesty's elite at such a young age."

"I'm sure you'll get there," said Lavinia, a little too flirtatiously for Henrik's liking. "You seem to me to be an exemplary knight."

"Is there something we can help you with, Your Highness?" Henrik cut in, his voice a little dry. Quite apart from his unease about Lavinia running loose in the training yard, he couldn't help but feel a little aggrieved on a more personal level. He had come here to avoid thinking about her, and it wasn't in the least helpful for her to follow him to his sanctuary in the flesh.

"Oh yes," said Lavinia brightly. "I have a message for you. But it seems I caught you at a bad time."

She glanced down at Henrik's chest, and he belatedly remembered that he hadn't donned his tunic again after his bout with Feivel. He hastened to retrieve it, his determination not to be drawn into flirting with the princess warring with satisfaction at the hint of appreciation he'd seen in Lavinia's eyes as she looked him over.

"What's the message, Your Highness?" Henrik asked, rejoining her with his tunic back on, and dismissing his companion with a curt nod.

The other knight obeyed reluctantly, after taking an unnecessarily flirtatious leave of Lavinia. Henrik scowled at his retreating back. Why couldn't he have been speaking with one of the middle aged and no nonsense knights when the princess sought him out, instead of one who was young and far too charming?

But Lavinia seemed to barely notice the other young man's departure. Her eyes were roaming over the training yard with candid interest, taking note of the many others who were now sparring shirtless, as Henrik had been.

"Don't you need chain mail on, to protect you?" she asked curiously. "Some of them are fighting with real swords."

"We don't need chain mail for this type of sparring," said Henrik shortly. "We don't use the sharp edge of the blade. Those who are too inexperienced to be trusted not to hurt anyone by accident train with blunt weapons, like the staffs."

"Interesting," mused Lavinia. "It's quite an impressive sight." She glanced again at Henrik's chest, now covered, then back at the other fighters across the yard. She showed no sign of discomfort at the sight, her usual irrepressible grin spreading across her face as she turned back to Henrik. "Some more than others, of course. I suppose this is the real reason Mother always told me not to come to the training yard."

"Did you say you have a message for me, Lavinia?" Henrik prompted, dropping the formality of titles now that they had no audience.

"Oh, yes," Lavinia said, giving him her full attention at last.

"An invitation, actually. My mother would be delighted if you would join us for a luncheon today."

Henrik blinked, unable to help the incredulity from showing on his face. "Her Majesty wants me to join the royal family for a luncheon?"

"That's right," said Lavinia comfortably. "Although it's not just the family, of course. There will be others there."

Henrik just stared at her, and she laughed.

"It's true, I promise! She invited you specifically."

"Queen Marguerite asked *you* to bring me a message, here in the training yard, that she would like me to come to lunch?" Henrik raised an eyebrow, and Lavinia grinned in acknowledgment.

"Well, no," she admitted. "She asked Kincaid to invite you, but I could see he wanted to go with Joss, so I offered to carry the message for him." Her face dropped slightly. "Joss felt so bad about missing the gala that she forced herself to come down for breakfast this morning, but it was a mistake. The poor thing looked almost green. Kincaid was only too glad to pass off the message so he could see her back to her suite."

Henrik frowned. "Is this some kind of prank? Is Kincaid punishing me for leaving the gala early last night?"

Lavinia laughed again. "You could be a little more gracious, Henrik. I'm sure any one of these other knights would receive an invitation to a royal luncheon very happily. Maybe one of them should take your place."

Her face dimpled as she smiled at someone over Henrik's shoulder. He turned slightly to see another one of the younger knights bowing to her with a look that was far too flirtatious for the difference in their stations. Henrik frowned the man down before turning back to the princess. She just grinned at him, unrepentant. There was a reason her reputation as a flirt was as bad as his.

"Of course I'll be delighted to attend," he said. "I'm just surprised." He shrugged one shoulder. "No point dancing around it. We both know I'm not Her Majesty's favorite person."

Lavinia looked at him in silence for a moment, looking surprised and a little wrong-footed. "What do you mean?" she asked at last.

Henrik was amazed to see that a small flush had appeared on her cheeks, and she was suddenly speaking more carefully, the vivacious lilt of her voice subdued. He furrowed his brow, confused by the reaction.

"Well, she's never been all that thrilled about my friendship with Kincaid, has she?" He glanced around to make sure no one was overhearing their conversation. "It's not exactly a secret that Kincaid was often in trouble for being less...responsible than Ormond." He shrugged one shoulder. "I was under the impression that both of your parents probably placed at least some of the blame for that at my door."

"Oh," said Lavinia, cocking her head to one side as she considered his answer. "Yes, you're probably right."

"Thank you," said Henrik dryly, trying not to laugh at her uncomplimentary agreement.

Lavinia, of course, laughed for him as she took in his rueful expression. "Well, you said there's no point dancing around it, didn't you?" She sighed. "If you want the candid truth, I think you're being invited to the luncheon because Lady Claudette will be there."

All desire to laugh fled, and it was Henrik's turn to be wrong-footed. "Why would you think that? What does Lady Claudette have to do with me?"

"Well," said Lavinia, not meeting his eye as she smoothed her skirts, "you seem to have taken something of a shine to her." Her voice turned dry. "Or perhaps Mother is just hoping she can rely on your generally charming ways."

She met Henrik's eyes, her expression a little more constrained. "It's supposed to be an informal luncheon to welcome Lady Brielle, since she's staying at the castle, but it's a little early for any formal introductions. Mother had invited Lady Claudette out of politeness, I imagine. After Ormond's display at the gala last night, I'm sure she regrets it, but she can't exactly un-invite her, can she? So my best guess is that she's instead inviting the member of the court she thinks most likely to have success in distracting Lady Claudette from Ormond. I'd bet my favorite mare Lady Claudette will be seated next to you, and as far away from Ormond as possible."

"I see," said Henrik, after a long moment of silence.

He could think of no other way to respond to this forthright description of his value to the group. It was confronting to realize that his tendency to flirt was considered such a certainty, the queen was apparently willing to overcome her disapproval of him to make use of it. He had never taken the banter of his peers much to heart, but to hear his reputation laid out so blandly, and by Lavinia herself, was unexpectedly painful. And her comment about his attraction to Lady Claudette was a humiliating reminder of his foolish misjudgment of the visiting Thoranian. The fact that Lavinia had clearly noticed his earlier reaction made it all the more bitter.

"Well," he tried again, when Lavinia showed no sign of breaking the uncomfortable silence. "If the queen is under the impression that there's any reason why I would be of particular interest to Lady Claudette, or her to me, I'm afraid Her Majesty is mistaken. But of course I will be honored to attend."

Lavinia gave him a measuring look before responding, and he couldn't read her expression. "Well then," she said briskly. "I suppose we'll see you in the small dining hall at noon."

Without another word, she turned away, heading out of the

training yard. Henrik sighed as he watched her walk away, her steps a little too springy for elegance. He wasn't at all sure how to feel about the interaction.

For the moment, though, he was distracted from his mixed reflections on the invitation by the frequent interruptions to the princess's progress through the yard. He ran a hand through his hair, frowning at the return of all the tumult of the night before.

He had expected to be uncomfortable around Lavinia after realizing the depth of his feelings for her, and had intended to avoid close interactions as much as possible.

He rolled his eyes. She had sabotaged that plan pretty quickly. And in fact, he hadn't found it as difficult to talk with her as he had expected. It was just impossible to be formal and uncomfortable around Lavinia for any length of time. The laughter constantly trapped inside her was always too close to bubbling over to allow him to remain serious. And her light manners, while not regal enough to satisfy her parents, had always put Henrik at ease. There was a new consciousness now, a heightened awareness of every look, every gesture. But unrequited love or not, in essence Lavinia was still the same irrepressible, likable scamp Henrik had been treating almost like family most of his life.

But she wasn't his family, as he was more acutely aware than ever before. And what he hadn't quite counted on, was how tense he would feel even watching her from a distance. Seeing the attention she attracted from every man in the training yard woke an entirely unbrotherly possessive instinct that—however unjustified he knew it to be—made it hard to avoid glaring down every admirer whose gaze lingered too long on her retreating form.

He barely held in a groan. It was bad enough that she had destroyed his temporary peace by seeking him out in the training yard. Even worse, he now had to endure a royal luncheon where, if he wanted to gain the queen's approval, he would have to give all his attention to a woman he cared nothing about. A course of action that, while it might be no more than everyone would expect, would be sure to earn the disapproval of the only woman he did care about.

CHAPTER ELEVEN

Henrik hesitated at the doorway of the royal family's private dining hall, steeling himself before entering. What he wouldn't give to have been called away on an urgent patrol. But the commander had been maddeningly ready to release him in light of the personal invitation from the royal family.

The moment he stepped into the room, his own discomforts were swallowed up by the general atmosphere of tension. He had never joined the royal family for such an intimate meal before, but he had been around them enough to know that the current mood was not normal.

The king and queen greeted him politely, Queen Marguerite giving him a break from the unnervingly observant scrutiny he had come to expect from her. She was evidently too distracted—her eyes were on her oldest son, and Ormond's unusually stony expression seemed to support Lavinia's prediction from the night before, that he had been on the receiving end of the first true scold of his life.

Lady Claudette wasn't there yet, but Lady Brielle was, and it was no surprise to see her seated next to the crown prince.

Ormond was speaking with her politely, his body language rather than his words showing that he was not entirely comfortable. Lavinia was seated on his other side, taking no part in the conversation. She looked up quickly at Henrik's entrance, flashing him a smile that he couldn't quite master himself enough to return.

He might have been pleasantly surprised that morning at how easy it was to speak with her one on one. But the very idea of trying to hide his attraction from the watchful gaze of her entire family in this intimate setting was terrifying.

Kincaid was there as well, of course, and he got up from his seat to greet Henrik with his usual friendly good humor.

"Jocelyn not coming?" Henrik asked quietly, taking the opportunity to talk with his friend while he could. He knew that Queen Marguerite was very precise about placing guests in alternating gender, so there was no hope of sitting beside Kincaid for the meal.

"I'm afraid not," Kincaid said, his expression slightly troubled. "She's still too ill."

Henrik frowned at the concern in the prince's eyes. "You look worried. Isn't this normal?"

Kincaid shrugged. "I don't know. The physician doesn't seem concerned, but I'm sure it wasn't nearly this bad last time."

"No Norik either?" Henrik looked around for the other member of the family, and wasn't sure whether to be disappointed or relieved at the boy's absence. Norik might have provided everyone with just the distraction Henrik needed to avoid any unfavorable notice during this luncheon. But then again, there was always the chance that he would say something embarrassingly accurate and revealing.

"No, he's eating in the nursery," said Kincaid absently. "This luncheon is one of Mother's proper events, not a place for children."

"Unlike the gala last night," Henrik retorted, unable to help his grin.

Kincaid glared at him, making a shushing gesture with his hands. "Keep your voice down," he muttered. "So far she's been too distracted by Ormond's behavior to remember that I brought a two-year-old into her ballroom, and I'd like to keep it that way."

Henrik glanced at the crown prince as Kincaid spoke. Ormond was still speaking with Lady Brielle, but his attention was divided as he watched the door. Henrik shook his head. He was fairly certain he knew whose arrival the crown prince was waiting for, and it baffled him how hard the usually unemotional prince seemed to have fallen for the Thoranian visitor.

Henrik had just taken his seat—as far away from the crown prince as the table allowed—when Lady Claudette finally arrived. She was accompanied by a thin, weedy man Henrik hadn't seen before, and was full of apologies for her tardiness.

The queen received the Thoranian's polite words with a thin-lipped smile that told everyone who knew her what her true feelings were, but that seemed to have no effect on Lady Claudette.

Not that the Thoranian noblewoman was paying much attention to her hostess. She had her eyes cast down demurely, but she kept sneaking glances under her lashes at Ormond. He had abruptly cut off his conversation with Lady Brielle, and was standing, smiling in welcome at the newcomer.

Compelled by politeness, Henrik also stood as a servant showed Lady Claudette to her seat which, as Lavinia had predicted, was beside his. Henrik greeted the visitor courteously, his words more stilted than usual from the awareness that both Queen Marguerite and her daughter were watching him closely as he did so. Her answering greeting was almost curt, and even though he was relieved that she seemed to have abandoned the coy flirtation she had previously employed toward him, he couldn't help the slight curl of his lips at her changed behavior. Clearly her eyes were now set on a bigger prize, and she had no attention to waste on a mere knight.

Well, that suited him just fine. He no longer had any wish to give his attention to her either. He took the opportunity while her eyes were diverted to study her face, looking in vain for any hint of the beauty that had once captivated him. But he could find nothing to admire. He was interested to see, up close, that she had a long thin scar along the line of her jaw. It wasn't especially noticeable, and it wasn't the reason he no longer found her attractive. It was just one of the many things he had apparently been unable to see before his eyes were opened to what she was truly like.

Lady Claudette didn't seem to notice Henrik's change in behavior since their last meeting. Henrik didn't mind her distraction, although he wished she would at least take her seat, so that he could politely do the same. But she still stood uncertainly behind her chair, exchanging a glance with the wiry man who had entered with her, and whom she had introduced as her servant.

This must be the servant who had stayed behind at the port to care for her guard, Feivel, when he was sick. Henrik studied the man curiously, noting the way his eyes passed along the table, taking in every detail of the assembled group. His demeanor was different from the other servants who stood behind their master's or mistress's chairs along the table, somehow, although Henrik couldn't put his finger on why.

When he returned his attention to Lady Claudette, she was looking toward Ormond and Lady Brielle, her discontent embarrassingly clear on her face. Henrik wanted to shake his head. Surely she must realize how rude it was to openly show dissatisfaction with her allotted seat. He followed her gaze, and saw that Ormond had just become aware of her placement as well, a frown creasing his usually calm face. Henrik's discomfort grew as he saw that the prince was also making little attempt to hide his displeasure at the seating.

In addition to Kincaid and a handful of other courtiers, the king and queen themselves separated the pair from Prince Ormond and Lady Brielle. It seemed Queen Marguerite wanted to take no chances.

But her oldest son clearly had other ideas. Lady Claudette had just taken her seat at long last when Ormond's confident voice carried across the room.

"Surely there's been some mistake, Mother. Our foreign guest will think she's not welcome, seated at the end of the table like that."

Henrik almost choked on the wine he had just sipped, putting his goblet down hastily as he stared at the prince, who had stood up. A hush had fallen over the small lunch party, and everyone was watching Ormond with varying levels of surprise. Henrik had never been close to Ormond like he was to Kincaid, but he knew the older man well enough to know how out of character his declaration was. Usually Ormond was as averse to making a scene as his mother.

Speaking of the queen, her normal calm looked stretched to Henrik's eye. "I'm sure everyone is quite comfortable where they are, Ormond," she said. Her tone became a little stilted as she glanced at Lady Claudette. "And I'm sure you're too generous to take offense over such a matter, Lady Claudette."

"Of course, Your Majesty," said the Thoranian, casting her eyes down with an unconvincing show of modesty. "I wouldn't wish to be any trouble."

"Nonsense," said Ormond firmly, still standing. "It's no trouble at all." His gaze fell on Lady Brielle beside him, her eyes lowered like Lady Claudette's, but with a very real flush spread across her face. Ormond looked away from her quickly, his gaze landing instead on his sister, on his other side.

"Lavinia, you won't mind changing places, will you? It won't trouble you to be seated near the end."

Lavinia raised one expressive eyebrow at her brother. She clearly disapproved, although Henrik suspected that was more to do with her opinion of Lady Claudette than any sense of scandal over Ormond's uncharacteristic outburst. Lavinia glanced toward her parents, but although they both looked extremely tense, neither of them actually prohibited the change. How could they, without making the event into even more of a scene? Lavinia shrugged one shoulder, getting up without protest.

Henrik glanced at Lady Claudette as she also rose. Again he couldn't keep his lips from curling slightly. She might be trying to look gracious, but there was no denying the hint of smugness on her face. What had he ever seen to admire in her?

He couldn't help shooting a look at the queen as well. Her face was almost expressionless, but her eyes darted between the two women changing places, and Henrik couldn't tell which she was more displeased about. It hadn't escaped his notice that in seating Henrik and Lady Claudette where she had, the queen had achieved a dual purpose in not only separating the visitor from the crown prince, but separating Henrik from Lavinia. Was he being paranoid to suspect the queen of such a motive?

"Well," Lavinia muttered, as she took her new seat beside Henrik. "This luncheon just got a bit more interesting."

"You could say that," Henrik agreed dryly, trying to keep his expression neutral as he took another sip from his goblet. "I can't help but feel like I should leave, since my function here is no longer relevant."

Lavinia chuckled, shooting a glance at her parents. "If you

upset Mother's table arrangements further, I think she might cry."

"That's hard to imagine," said Henrik.

But following Lavinia's gaze, he had to agree that both King Malcolm and Queen Marguerite looked as close to distressed as he had ever seen them. The king stood, welcoming everyone briefly, and giving a special mention to Lady Brielle. Of course nothing was said beyond the fact that she was staying in Bryford as a guest of the royal family. But Lady Claudette still looked slightly petulant at the attention being given to her rival. Unlike at the gala the night before, the king made no reference to the foreigner's presence.

Lady Brielle received the king's welcome with the quiet grace Henrik had observed in her the previous evening, but it was obvious that she was uncomfortable. It would be astonishing if she wasn't, with the way Ormond was focusing all his conversation on the woman on his other side.

"Have you ever seen Prince Ormond behave this way?" Henrik muttered to Lavinia.

Lavinia frowned. "No, I haven't," she said. "None of us have. To tell you the truth, I've never seen Mother and Father so worried." She lowered her voice. "Everything was more or less settled with Lord Thornton, and now Ormond is threatening it all." She glanced toward Lady Brielle, her expression growing more troubled. "The worst of it all is that I don't think Lady Brielle is even offended." She shook her head. "I would be, if I were her. But it seems to me she's more hurt than anything. Which means she actually likes him."

The princess's expression grew dark. "I don't care about Ormond making a fool of himself. It will do him good to look ridiculous for once in his life. But Lady Brielle doesn't deserve to be treated this way."

Lavinia's attention was claimed by the courtier on her other side before Henrik could respond, and he turned his attention to his soup. The luncheon dragged on, and Henrik found himself thinking longingly of the patrol he could have been leading at that moment.

The servants were clearing the plates between courses when a general lull in the conversation caused King Malcolm's voice to carry down the length of the table.

"I understand that your father has reached an agreement with the farmers who sought an audience with me, Lady Brielle."

"That's right, Your Majesty." Lady Brielle's voice was quieter than the king's, but by now everyone's attention was captured.

"It seems that Lord Thornton has handled the matter with great wisdom," said King Malcolm graciously.

Lady Brielle inclined her head in acknowledgment. "My father would be honored to hear you say so, Your Majesty. He has certainly tried to be fair with his tenants, and for myself, I have learned a great deal from observing his approach. I know he is most grateful for the support Your Majesty has offered. The farmers will benefit from your generosity when the harvest comes in."

"Are these the farmers who've been causing a ruckus in the city?" Lady Claudette interjected unexpectedly, her voice carrying just as much as Lady Brielle's, but not nearly as melodically.

"That's right," Ormond confirmed, when no one else answered. "They're expecting a poor harvest in the south east, and many of the farmers are concerned."

Lady Claudette raised an eyebrow. "I would think it would be everyone else who would feel concerned, with the way they've been carrying on." She glanced back at her servant. "I even heard a rumor that they might be behind the bandit attacks."

Henrik frowned, shifting in his seat. The same thought had occurred to him, but somehow it sounded less plausible and more suspicious coming from Lady Claudette.

"Is that so?" Ormond asked, clearly surprised. He looked toward King Malcolm. "Have you heard these rumors, Father?"

The king was frowning at Lady Claudette, but his expression was more thoughtful than angry. "No, I haven't. And I don't know of any basis for such a suspicion. It sounds like idle gossip to me."

Ormond bristled slightly. "I was under the impression that we hadn't identified the bandits yet. Surely any suggestion as to their motives is worth considering."

"The matter can be further considered, of course," said the king in a quelling tone. "But we must always be cautious not to start unfounded rumors."

"My apologies, Your Majesty," said Lady Claudette, dipping her head in a gesture that was somehow much less graceful than Lady Brielle's had been. "Perhaps I am unduly eager to learn the identity of these attackers, being one of their victims."

"Of course you are," said Ormond firmly, a frown marring his handsome features. "Anyone would be in your position." He looked back toward his father. "It really is unacceptable that these bandits have been allowed to go so long without consequence. I think we should follow up this lead without delay."

Lavinia shifted beside Henrik and, glancing at her, he saw that her eyes were narrowed. They were fixed not on her brother, but on the woman beside him. Lady Claudette was dabbing her mouth daintily with a napkin, looking altogether too placid considering the growing awkwardness she was creating among the group.

"Well, I suppose the crown can hardly give out gold to the farmers one day, and then punish them the next," she said, her tinkling laugh sounding artificial to Henrik. "But no doubt there is wisdom in generosity."

"Only to a certain point," said Ormond, frowning thoughtfully as he turned back to his father. "Perhaps it is hasty to give financial support to the farmers while there is still some suspicion that they might be the troublemakers."

"Forgive me, Your Highness," cut in Lady Brielle unexpectedly. "But *is* there any reason to suspect the farmers are the ones making trouble? Surely it would be most unjust to go back on the promised aid based merely on a rumor."

She drew a breath, looking uncomfortable but determined as she continued. "I am confident my father will not wish to revoke his offers of assistance to the farmers. Not without very substantial reason to do so."

"And he is quite right," said King Malcolm firmly, in a voice that seemed designed to close the topic. "A man's word is his character."

CHAPTER TWELVE

An awkward silence descended on the group, and Henrik lowered his attention to his food. But not before seeing the way Lady Claudette narrowed her eyes as she examined her rival.

"Well, that was...telling," muttered Lavinia beside him. She was frowning at Lady Claudette. "Why is it so important to our visitor to put the blame on the farmers? What's in it for her?"

Henrik followed Lavinia's gaze, surprised by the level of suspicion in the princess's voice. His opinion of the Thoranian noblewoman had certainly undergone a rapid decline, but it seemed a bit of a stretch to assume there was a plot behind her unflattering behavior.

"Does she need to gain something from it?" he asked, speaking quietly as well. "Some people just want to be right, for no better reason than that."

Lavinia rolled her eyes. "Of course you would defend her. Why does every man in the court seem to have lost his head over this girl?"

"I'm not defending her," protested Henrik, trying to keep his voice lowered in spite of his irritation. "I said she probably just wants to be right. That's not exactly a compliment, is it?" He frowned. "And I for one haven't lost my head over her," he added firmly. "Far from it."

Lavinia raised an eyebrow. "I know you were quite taken with her when she first arrived, Henrik. I'm not blind. So are you being dishonest, or just fickle?"

"Neither," Henrik insisted, frustrated all over again at how he had let himself be deceived in Lady Claudette. "I don't admire her, honestly. Am I not allowed to change my mind?"

"Fickle, then," said Lavinia, with a hint of humor that did little to soften Henrik's frustration. He looked back toward the subject of their conversation.

Lady Claudette had stopped glaring at Lady Brielle. Her eyes were lowered to her plate, although since she wasn't eating much, the posture seemed to serve no other purpose than to allow her to regularly look up under her lashes at Prince Ormond. General chatter had resumed along the table, making it impossible to follow their conversation from such a distance. But every now and then phrases like, "wouldn't wish to impose," and, "Your Highness is too kind," and, "couldn't possibly," wafted down the table toward Henrik and Lavinia.

Henrik barely held in a snort. The very tenacity with which the young woman was monopolizing the crown prince's attention was a clear contradiction of the demure manner she seemed to put on every time Prince Ormond was in the room. Henrik could only suppose that Lady Claudette considered the docility she was attempting to portray to be what Ormond found attractive.

And she seemed to be right, judging by the prince's response. But with Lady Brielle right there, her unassuming presence giving such a compelling example of the real thing, the falseness of Lady Claudette's assumed modesty was all the more obvious. Henrik gritted his teeth. And this was the kind of woman Lavinia thought he admired?

He didn't derive much enjoyment from the luncheon. He was more ill-at-ease than he had ever been before with the royal family. He was sure Queen Marguerite was watching him, and even Kincaid shot him the occasional look of confusion, as if trying to make sense of the change in his usually carefree friend's demeanor.

"You're a poor companion," Lavinia said cheerfully as the sweets were served, startling Henrik out of his reverie. "Was it terribly inconvenient for you to get out of your duties to join us?"

"Of course not," said Henrik quickly, glad she had finally thawed out from her earlier annoyance with him. "It was no trouble. I'm sorry I'm not very good company. I was lost in my thoughts."

Lavinia raised an eyebrow skeptically, but didn't comment on the polite and insubstantial answer. "You seemed to be in fine form this morning," she said, her voice still cheerful. "You looked very happy to be back with your knights. I think the royal guard will always be your first love, won't it?"

Henrik's eyes darted quickly to the king and queen, and he was relieved that they didn't seem to be listening. He had a feeling that if Lavinia's mother found out where the princess had been that morning, the fact that Henrik had not invited her, or even wanted her at the training yard, would do little to soften the queen's inevitable irritation toward him.

He turned his attention back to Lavinia, and her question. "I suppose you could say that," he said, considering the matter. "I do love the role, and I hope to rise in the king's elite."

"Well, being Kincaid's oldest friend can't hurt," said Lavinia brightly. "He'll be in charge of the king's guard one day, won't he?"

"Yes," said Henrik slowly. "But I hope to achieve a senior position long before then."

"Why?" Lavinia asked, cocking her head to the side curiously. "Are you so impatient to advance? You usually give the impression of having all the time in the world." She gave him a sage look as she bit into a pastry. "That's why all the ladies are so taken with you."

"What?" Henrik asked, distracted. "What do you mean?"

"Well," Lavinia explained, selecting another pastry with much more enthusiasm than any of the other ladies present were allowing themselves to show, "all the more important nobles, and all the oldest sons and such, are too busy and too important to spend their time charming the ladies. But general opinion is that you can be counted on to waste hours flirting if the girl is pretty enough."

"Thank you," said Henrik dryly. "Good to know my time is considered so valuable."

"At least," Lavinia continued, as if he hadn't spoken, "you used to be counted on. Word is that since you got home, you've been too much like the other nobles, aloof and distracted." She gave him a sideways look. "The rumor is that you left your heart behind you in Kyona."

Henrik made a scoffing noise in the back of his throat. "If only," he muttered.

"What does that mean?" asked Lavinia, furrowing her brow.

"Nothing," said Henrik hastily, wishing he hadn't said the words aloud. "You can assure the gossipers that every part of me returned safely from Kyona," he added firmly.

"Oh, they don't gossip to me," said Lavinia, a bit wistfully. "They're all as intimidated by the princess thing as you seem to be lately."

"I'm not—" Henrik started, but she cut him off.

"I have to get all my information through my maids. But

they're very effective at ferreting things out. My father should really consider enlisting them in his intelligence network."

Henrik chuckled, glad to have the conversation off him. "You should suggest it to him."

Lavinia grinned, her dimple appearing as she glanced toward her father. He was speaking with the courtier who had been seated next to Lavinia, and who seemed to be taking his leave. The group was starting to break up.

"Maybe I will," Lavinia said. "I'm sure he wouldn't think it was the most outrageous idea I've ever had."

"Which isn't saying much, is it?" Henrik teased.

Lavinia turned back toward him, her expression searching. "Is that why you're more distracted these days?" she asked abruptly, as though wanting to make the most of the last few moments of their unexpected time together. "Because you're impatient to advance, and you're focused on your role?"

"No," said Henrik slowly. "It's not that." He saw that his companion was waiting expectantly, and he shrugged, deciding to answer the only part of the question he could safely discuss with her. "I'm not impatient. I just meant I want to reach a senior position before Kincaid takes charge precisely because he's my oldest friend."

Lavinia frowned, looking confused, so Henrik pushed on.

"I know it's not considered important, the way my father's title is, but this role is my life, and my future. Whatever position I end up with, I want to get there on my own merit. Not because Kincaid gave it to me."

Lavinia didn't answer, looking at him with an unusually thoughtful expression.

Henrik returned his gaze to his empty plate, not sure how to respond to her scrutiny. It seemed that every time he spoke to her, she was less the irresponsible child and more the intelligent young woman. It was impossible not to wonder what, if any, changes she saw in him. Did she think him as frivolous and insincere as half the court clearly did? It was a strange feeling to be worried about whether the outrageous young Princess Lavinia thought him too immature.

"You could have been more polite to Lady Claudette, Father."

Ormond's reproachful voice cut across Henrik's thoughts, and he looked up, blinking in confusion at the sight of Ormond facing down his father with uncharacteristic irritation clear on his face.

"I do not intend to answer to you for my comments, Ormond." King Malcolm's face seemed carved from stone. "And if we are to speak of politeness, you would do well to consider your own conduct."

Henrik glanced around, realizing with a shot of discomfort that all the other guests had departed. He hadn't noticed how many had left, but only he and the royal family remained at the table. And apparently Ormond was agitated enough to speak freely in front of Henrik, the way his brother and sister usually did.

"All that talk about character," the crown prince was saying, ignoring his father's rebuke. "It was as though you were implying she was somehow wrong even to suggest reconsidering our approach to the farmers. We should consider her ideas. After all, doesn't she have some right to an opinion, as a victim of these attacks herself?"

"Ormond," said the queen quellingly. "We can discuss this matter later."

"Why can't we discuss it now?" Ormond insisted.

"She's talking about Henrik," Lavinia explained helpfully, making him wish he could sink through the floor.

Ormond glanced at Henrik impatiently, apparently noticing

his presence for the first time. "I'm sure Lord Henrik will excuse me speaking freely."

"I'll take my leave, Your Majesties, Your Highnesses," said Henrik, rising hastily to his feet and bowing to the sovereigns. "My commander will be expecting me. Thank you for your gracious invitation."

The king and queen inclined their heads in acknowledgment, their lips tight, and Henrik began to navigate around the long table.

"Oh, it's not that Henrik would mind," Lavinia told Ormond cheerfully, as Henrik began to cross the floor. "It's that Mother thinks it's indiscreet to discuss family disagreements in front of him."

"It's a little much for you to accuse me of indiscretion," said Ormond bitingly, and Henrik glanced back in spite of himself, curious and stunned in equal measure at the prince's uncharacteristic outburst. "I think you lost that right when you kissed your dancing master at only sixteen. And you've just gotten more outrageous since then."

"Ormond," said Queen Marguerite sharply, just as Kincaid also jumped in to his sister's defense.

"There's no need to rip up at Lavvy just because you're the one behaving childishly for once."

Henrik had reached the door at last, and he shut it on his friend's familiar voice with a sigh of relief. And he had thought the luncheon was uncomfortable! The scene he had just escaped was a hundred times more awkward than anything he'd witnessed among the royal family before. They were used to Lavinia's antics, and even to Kincaid's less responsible jaunts when he'd been younger. But it seemed no one knew quite how to handle a defiant Ormond.

He winced as he remembered the look on Lavinia's face when

Ormond had accused her of indiscretion. Henrik had never heard the crown prince speak to his sister like that, although he suspected it wasn't uncommon in private. He remembered quite clearly the incident a few years before, when her dancing master had been dismissed. He also remembered the rumors that had swirled at the time. The whole topic was utterly uncomfortable, and for once Henrik was in full agreement with the queen. Such matters shouldn't have been raised with him still in the room.

He started walking quickly, eager to put some distance between himself and the royal family. But he had only made it a few feet down the corridor when he was surprised by the sound of the door opening behind him. Turning, he was even more taken aback to see Lavinia striding purposefully out of the room, fire in her eyes.

"Henrik!" she called, disregarding the scrutiny of the guards stationed outside the dining hall. "Wait for me." He hesitated, and she caught up to him quickly. "I've left them to their squabble," she said curtly, tossing her curls in her habitual way. "It's nothing to do with me, after all."

She started walking down the corridor, her steps quick and agitated. Henrik followed uneasily, not sure where she was going, but getting the clear impression that she expected him to go with her. He glanced back toward the dining hall as they rounded a corner, but no one else had yet emerged.

He followed Lavinia silently down a few corridors, not paying much attention to where they were going. Neither was she apparently, because she drew up short halfway down a quiet hall, coming out of her internal fog and looking about her vaguely.

"Oh," she said. "We're going the wrong way for the training yard, aren't we?"

"You were going back to the training yard?" Henrik asked blankly.

Lavinia gave an unconvincing laugh. "No, of course not. I assumed you were, and I was going to walk with you, just until you got there."

"Oh," said Henrik cautiously. "Actually, I need to go back to my home first." He gestured to his formal attire. "I can't really train in this, can I?"

"Of course," said Lavinia stupidly, still seeming uncharacteristically vague as her gaze passed over his form, following his gesture. "I suppose you can't." She met his eyes, an unsettlingly vulnerable look in hers. "It's not true, you know."

"What's not true?" Henrik asked, confused.

Lavinia flushed. "I didn't kiss my dancing master."

CHAPTER THIRTEEN

Henrik was silent for a moment, totally unsure how to answer. "You don't have to explain anything to me, Lavinia," he said at last, his voice low.

"But I want to," Lavinia said, also speaking quietly.

Henrik glanced around. Lavinia had no maid or other companion with her, a departure from custom for which the hard-to-handle princess was well known.

In fact, no one else was in sight at all, and Henrik pulled Lavinia gently into an alcove, next to a window overlooking an internal courtyard with a small garden.

"Ormond was out of line," he said firmly. "He's the one who's been making a fool of himself the last couple of days, and he's a lot older than sixteen."

Lavinia sighed, turning her gaze out the window. "I'm older than sixteen now, too," she said. "I know everyone thinks I enjoy creating scandal, but I don't like having my past mistakes thrown around any more than the next person. It's true I flirted with the dancing master, and it was my fault he got dismissed. I still feel bad about that. But he didn't kiss me."

She met Henrik's eyes with evident effort, a twisted smile on her lips. Lips he was finding it very hard not to look at, his heart beating uncomfortably quickly at the turn the conversation was taking.

"Lavinia," he said, his throat suddenly dry. "I—you don't—" He trailed off, apparently having lost all power of speech. Her face was still flushed, and her expression more raw than he'd ever seen it. But somehow she was more beautiful than ever.

"The honest truth," Lavinia went on, clearly determined to get it out, "is that no one's ever kissed me. People like to flirt, and flatter me, but it's only because I'm a princess. And it's probably for that same reason that no one's ever been quite bold enough to actually—"

Henrik didn't know what madness seized him. All he knew was that one moment Lavinia was talking, and the next she was in his arms, her words silenced by his lips on hers. He hadn't intended to do it, but she'd sounded so lonely—which was all wrong for someone so impossibly warm and inviting—that he lost his head.

Everything about her was so utterly lovable that it was keeping him up at night. How could he simply stand there while she said outrageous things, like that people only admired her for her status?

Her startled gasp lasted a fraction of a second, then she responded with all the fiery enthusiasm that characterized her. Her hands traveled over his shoulders to link behind his neck, and she stood up on her toes to better return the kiss. She fit as perfectly in his arms and her lips were as soft and responsive as he'd imagined. The sensation was intoxicating—dangerously so.

But it was only a few heart-stopping moments of folly before sanity returned, and Henrik remembered that she was out of his reach, and that he was playing with fire even to admire her, let alone to give in to his feelings.

And that they were standing in a corridor.

He pulled away, his head reeling and his breath coming in gasps.

"I'm sorry," he managed. "That was—" He ran a hand through his dark, tousled hair, glancing guiltily around to make sure they were still alone. "I'm sorry," he repeated.

Lavinia looked a little dazed herself, but she gave him a grin that was so familiar, and so endearing, it was all he could do not to take her in his arms again.

"I hope you're apologizing for not doing that earlier."

"Lavinia," he said, with an exhale that was half laughter and half groan. "I shouldn't have...I didn't mean to..."

Lavinia's smile slid away, and Henrik's heart wrenched at the mixture of fear and frustration in her eyes. "Didn't mean to what? What are you saying?"

"Lavinia, I can't," Henrik gestured between them, "we can't..."

"Can't what?" Lavinia pressed when he trailed off. He didn't answer, and her eyes narrowed. "You can't, or you 'didn't mean to'? What, is it such second nature to you that you kiss a girl anytime you find yourself alone with one?"

"What?" protested Henrik, beginning to feel frustrated himself. "Of course not. How can you think that?" He turned, taking two agitated strides away from her before facing her again. It was all the distance their alcove allowed. "I know you think I'm frivolous, but surely you know this isn't a joke to me. Why do you think I've always been so careful? Lavinia," he took a small step toward her, "if you only knew the conflict inside me. If you only knew how hard I've been trying to—"

He cut himself off, running a hand through his hair again. Lavinia was watching him, still with that wary, slightly suspicious expression that was so out of place on her normally laughing face. He wasn't sure exactly what she expected from him, but however hopeless the cause might be, he couldn't bear for her to think he was toying with her. Telling her how he felt would make things even harder, but it was better than giving her reason to hate him.

"I want you to be mine more than anything, Lavinia," he said, his voice slightly choked. "But I can't have you, and there's no sense in torturing myself."

Lavinia's face softened slightly, and she moved toward him, closing the distance between them. Henrik stepped back, but the embrasure was too small, and her proximity wasn't helping him to clear his head.

"It didn't feel like torture to me," said Lavinia, an alarmingly attractive twinkle in her eyes. When he didn't answer, she fell silent, searching his face seriously. "I'm not saying we wouldn't have to fight for it a little. But I've never been afraid of a fight. And I thought you said you weren't intimidated by my title, Henrik."

"It's not that I'm intimidated," said Henrik shortly. "I'm just not a fool."

"And I am?"

Lavinia's raised eyebrow seemed more skeptical than angry, and Henrik wasn't sure whether to be annoyed or remorseful at the realization that she clearly still doubted him.

"I didn't mean that," said Henrik, exasperated. "Fight for it 'a little'? Come on, Lavinia, surely you realize that—"

"Henrik?"

They both jumped at the voice, alarmingly near at hand. Forgetting that he was already at the wall, Henrik tried to step further away from Lavinia as Kincaid appeared at the opening to the alcove.

"Kincaid," he said quickly, stumbling slightly as his back connected with the stone. He tried not to look guilty. "Were you looking for me?"

"Yes, I wanted to ask—Lavvy, what are you doing here?"

Kincaid seemed to suddenly notice his sister, and his brow furrowed in confusion.

"Trying to get away from Ormond," said Lavinia matter-of-factly, showing no trace of the embarrassment Henrik was feeling.

Kincaid grimaced. "I don't blame you there." He gave her an unusually searching look. "I don't know what's gotten into him, but I'm sorry he took it out on you."

Lavinia shrugged one shoulder. "It's not your fault. And although he was very rude about it, I guess he had a point." She gave Henrik a hard look. "No one can really expect to outrun their reputation, can they?"

Henrik returned her gaze ruefully, frustrated that she was taking a swing at him when she knew he wasn't free to defend himself. Yes, she was definitely doubting his sincerity. He wanted to be angry, but in spite of the sparks shooting from her eyes, he could see the hurt lingering behind them. And it made him feel more wretched than ever.

"I guess not," said Kincaid absently, scratching the back of his neck. "No offense, Lavvy, but I need to speak with Henrik."

Lavinia just shrugged again. "I'm sure it's no concern of mine," she said, flicking her hair back before starting down the corridor, without so much as another glance at Henrik.

"A word, Henrik?" said Kincaid, before she was even out of earshot. He glanced around, jerking his head toward a nearby door. "In there?"

Henrik followed his friend into what seemed to be an unused guest room, his heart racing almost as quickly as it had in the moment before he kissed Lavinia. He'd forgotten to add best friend's little sister to the list of reasons for him not to do what he'd just done.

"What are you doing out here, by the way?" Kincaid asked, as Henrik closed the door behind him. "The guard said you'd gone this way, but I couldn't for the life of me guess where you were headed. I thought you were going back to the training yard."

"Oh, I uh…I…" Henrik trailed off, his mind blank of any acceptable explanation for why he and Lavinia had been alone in a secluded corridor of the castle.

"Never mind," said Kincaid, his voice unusually serious. "Henrik, I need to speak with you."

Henrik swallowed, wishing he could locate the courage that came without difficulty in a life-threatening fight.

"Kincaid, let me explain."

"There's something not right about Lady Claudette," Kincaid barreled on, before cutting himself off in confusion. "Explain? Explain what?"

"Uh, nothing," said Henrik, thrown. "I was just—did you say Lady Claudette?"

"Yes, I did," said Kincaid grimly, clearly oblivious to his friend's turmoil of mind. Henrik must not look as disheveled as he felt. "I didn't want to say it in front of Lavvy, because she'd probably run off and do something rash, like accuse her in front of everyone. But there's something I don't trust about her. I can't put my finger on it."

"Well, her behavior at the luncheon today certainly didn't paint her in a very pretty light," said Henrik cautiously.

Kincaid snorted. "That's an understatement. But it's not her behavior that has me so suspicious. It's Ormond's. I've never seen him lose his head like he has over this girl. I mean, she's basically a stranger!" Kincaid lowered his voice, even though they were alone in the room. "And to be honest, she's not even very pretty. I'll admit that when she first arrived, I thought she was quite attractive. But seeing her up close at the luncheon today…" He shrugged. "I can't quite figure out what has Ormond so devoted to her." He frowned. "Honestly, it makes me angry."

"I agree," said Henrik, "about all of it."

Well, all of it except the anger, he added silently.

He thought it was as strange as Kincaid did, but he was finding it hard to care very much at that moment about anything to do with either Ormond or Lady Claudette. His thoughts were following Lavinia, wondering what she was doing and thinking after what had passed between them.

But Kincaid's comment about changing his mind on Lady Claudette's appearance caught his interest. It was peculiar that they had both had that same experience.

"What exactly is it you want me to do?" he asked, forcing his attention back to their conversation.

"I want you to see if you can find out whether she's up to something," said Kincaid. "I can't go anywhere without being conspicuous, and I don't want to ask a guard to do it—who knows what Ormond would do if word got out I was having her followed?"

"You want me to follow her?" Henrik asked, his heart sinking. Lady Claudette was the last woman he wanted to be following around at that moment.

"That's right. I want to know more about her and what she's really doing here. It's strange that I didn't even question it at the time, but the more I think about it, the stranger her story sounds. Why didn't she just wait, and come with the rest of Cody's delegation? She arrives here, with nothing but a letter of introduction from Cody's father-in-law, a couple of servants, and a guard."

"Feivel," said Henrik thoughtfully.

"What?"

"The guard's name is Feivel," Henrik explained. "I sparred with him just this morning, in the training yard. There's something...off about him."

"There's something off about the whole thing," said Kincaid darkly.

Henrik nodded slowly. When Kincaid said it all so plainly, Lady Claudette's story did seem very odd.

"All right," he said decisively. "I'll see what I can find out."

"Thanks, Henrik," said Kincaid, sounding relieved. "I knew I could count on you."

Henrik squirmed slightly, trying not to look guilty as he imagined what Kincaid would think of his recent actions.

He didn't linger with Kincaid, turning his steps toward home at last, and changing quickly into something he could train in. When he had said it to the king and queen, it had only been an excuse to get away from the awkward family scene after the luncheon, but by now his commander probably really was expecting him.

Henrik strode back to the training yard with fresh purpose. He had told Kincaid he would help, but he didn't actually intend to trail Lady Claudette around. He had a much better idea. He just needed to figure out where to find Feivel.

CHAPTER FOURTEEN

Henrik arched his back, trying to relieve the ache that had been spreading up it for the last hour. He let out a quiet breath of frustration, trying to remember why he had been fool enough to turn down a rematch with the polearms for this.

Following Feivel had seemed like a fantastic idea in theory. But in practice, it had meant hours of fruitless inactivity. And the last thing Henrik needed was endless space to think. A vigorous training session would have been the ideal way to distract his mind from what had happened with Lavinia. Instead, he was sitting motionless in a corner of the royal stables, concealed behind a bale of hay as he watched the entrance to the soldiers' barracks where Feivel was sleeping.

It was a situation that meant, firstly, that he had become far more familiar with manure than he had ever wished to be. And secondly, that he had hours in which to relive how incredible it had felt to kiss Lavinia, and how much more gut wrenching it made the knowledge that he had no hope of actually winning her.

Not to mention all the time he had spent flicking between irritation and regret at her parting words. He couldn't help but be irked that after he had been vulnerable enough to admit the depth of his feelings, she had walked away suspecting him of toying with her after all. But however much he was annoyed at Lavinia over her reaction, he was more annoyed with himself. Because he knew that there was a reason she doubted his sincerity. He had been far too liberal with his attentions, entertaining himself with flippant flirtations with just about every other girl in the court.

He could hardly blame Lavinia for not realizing that she was the one girl he had never spoken to insincerely. How could she know how careful he had been around her? How intentional his failure to flatter her had been? She probably thought he had refrained from complimenting her, or seeking her out, because he still thought of her as the annoying younger sister of his childhood friend.

Thoughts of Kincaid did nothing to lift Henrik's mood. He couldn't quite decide whether his friend would be more likely to be furious with Henrik if he knew the true nature of his thoughts about the prince's beloved little sister, or to be thrilled at the prospect of a closer relationship between them. A relationship that only Kincaid would be oblivious enough to think possible.

The sound of raucous laughter drew Henrik's attention, and he gratefully abandoned his circular thoughts. Darkness had well and truly fallen, but the courtyard which the soldiers' barracks came off was well lit by lanterns. He peered through the stable's open doorway, trying to make out the source of the noise. Even as he looked, the sound cut off again.

Henrik stood up, edging forward on stiff legs until he was right in the doorway. It seemed someone had opened the door to the barracks, allowing the sound of the soldiers' merriment to temporarily spill out of the building. The door was closed again now, but the figure could still be seen striding quickly across the empty courtyard.

Henrik felt a surge of satisfaction as he looked the figure over. Strong and muscled, with a short, confident gait. It was Feivel, he was almost certain. So the hours of waiting and watching hadn't been utterly pointless after all.

He slipped out of the stable, running a hand over the hilt of his weapon as he stole across the courtyard. He didn't intend to take any chances.

The man made his way through the city with a familiarity which suggested he had taken this route before. Henrik followed at a discreet distance, trying to look nonchalant for the sake of the various night time wanderers he passed. It was getting late, but the night wasn't so far advanced that the streets were deserted.

At one point the man paused under a torch, glancing around him before turning down a side street. Henrik fell back a step, trying to look inconspicuous. His unknowing guide didn't see him, but the quick glimpse of his profile was enough to confirm Henrik's guess. It was Feivel.

The Thoranian made his way to a large public garden that ran alongside one of the castle's outer walls. Henrik knew the place vaguely—in good weather, parties were sometimes held among the decorative plants. It could be accessed from the castle by a series of gates, all of which were presumably locked for the night, but as a public garden, it could also be reached from the city.

Feivel strolled in as if he owned it, wending his way between trees. Henrik had some difficulty following him without being seen, and he was forced to fall further behind than he would have liked. No one else seemed to be using the garden—it was almost midnight, after all—and Henrik's curiosity was piqued. Feivel's choice of location for a late night stroll surely meant that he was trying to hide something. And Henrik had every intention of finding out what it was.

After a few minutes, he lost the guard in the winding pathways, but he continued to creep forward, focusing on not making himself visible. If there was no one else in the garden, it would surely be possible to find Feivel again, once he had reached wherever he intended to go.

Sure enough, a short time after he had stopped hearing the sound of footfalls, Henrik caught a quiet voice issuing from behind a large shrub.

"Feivel, there you are. You're late."

Henrik raised an eyebrow at the distinctly feminine voice. He may not have wanted to follow Lady Claudette, but it seemed that following Feivel had achieved the same result. He crawled as silently as he could into the shelter of another, larger, shrub nearby.

Feivel grunted in response to the reproach. "Rowdy night in the barracks. Had to wait until no one was paying attention."

Lady Claudette gave a very unladylike snort. "You mean you stopped for a game of chance. Don't you realize how risky it is for me to hang around here waiting for you?"

"Relax Claudette," said Feivel. "You know I won't let anyone hurt you."

There was a pause, during which Henrik's eyebrow went back up at the guard's casual manner of addressing his mistress. When Lady Claudette spoke again, her voice was softer.

"I know."

"I don't like all this subterfuge," Feivel grunted, and it took Henrik a moment to identify the emotion behind the words. It was the frustration of a man wanting what he couldn't have, an uncomfortably familiar feeling to the knight. "I don't like watching that idiotic prince fawn over you."

Henrik fought the urge to shift his position, reminding himself to be still and silent. A curl of distaste was spreading through him. He wasn't sure what he'd expected, but it hadn't been this. If the nature of Lady Claudette's relationship with her guard was romantic, eavesdropping on them suddenly became much less daring and much more sordid.

"I know," Lady Claudette said again, her voice caressing. Somehow the sound wasn't pleasant—perhaps because Henrik's eyes were filled with the vision of her simpering over Prince Ormond earlier that day. "But you know it's just a means to an end. It will all be worth it when I'm queen."

Both Henrik's eyebrows shot up this time. It wasn't as though the Thoranian woman's ambitions were a surprise. But somehow hearing her say it so brazenly was still shocking.

"That won't be for a long time," said Feivel dryly.

"Nonsense." Lady Claudette sounded annoyed. "The crown prince is clay in my hands. I've used everything we learned, and it's worked just as I hoped. I wouldn't be surprised if he proposes tomorrow."

"I'm not doubting your work," said Feivel, his voice so low that Henrik had to lean forward to hear. "But even if you're right, even if he marries you before the delegation comes, I think you overestimate how much power a crown princess has. It will be a long time before you're queen, like I said."

"Well, neither of us can see the future, Feivel," said Lady Claudette briskly. "So let's focus on what we can control, and let what follows take care of itself."

Henrik frowned. The words were spoken lightly enough, but there was still something ominous about Lady Claudette's comment.

Feivel gave another grunt. "You always have such confidence in your luck."

"It's not luck," said Lady Claudette firmly. "It's the ability to adapt. There's always a solution. You all said we shouldn't come when we were delayed so long in Thorania. But I was right, wasn't I? We have enough time to do what needs doing. We just need to turn what we find to our advantage. Like the princess being incapacitated. You call that good luck, I call it a resource."

A shot of fear raced through Henrik, and it was all he could do not to burst out of the bush. Incapacitated? What did that mean? Had something happened to Lavinia in the hours since he'd seen her?

"No, I don't call it good luck," Feivel said shortly. "She shouldn't be here at all. I call it *bad* luck that her condition caused her to return early from her trip."

Henrik started breathing again. Of course, he should have realized they were talking about Jocelyn. There might always be only one princess in his mind, but since her marriage, Jocelyn was Valoria's princess as much as Lavinia was. He frowned. But why was it bad luck that she had returned early from Kyona?

"It was unfortunate," Lady Claudette conceded. "But like any obstacle, it can be overcome. As I said, I've been able to use it in full force the last couple of days." The frown was evident in her voice. "Although not without risks, I admit. It's possible I've pushed it too far. I thought that husband of hers was as oblivious as the rest of them, but this afternoon he started to behave suspiciously."

So she knew Kincaid was onto her, did she? Henrik wasn't sure whether to be satisfied or alarmed. Just how far was this woman willing to go in order to become queen of Valoria? And how had she made such a powerful impact on the usually steady Ormond?

"But I had to act quickly," Lady Claudette was continuing.

"The window is smaller than we realized, with the king and queen almost ready to announce the prince's betrothal to that irritating local girl." She made a noise of disgust. "Her and her weak-minded views on handing out gold every time a farmer has a bad harvest. The royal coffers would be empty in no time with her as queen. Honestly, the royals are bigger fools than I expected."

Henrik felt his lip curl. Even without whatever underhanded plot was clearly going on, having this woman on one of Valoria's thrones would be an utter disaster.

"They need you to bring them into line," said Feivel, with a touch of humor. "I think once you've joined their number, we can find some better uses for Valoria's riches."

Lady Claudette chuckled. "I should think so." Her tone turned businesslike. "We have some work to do before then, however. Like I said, the younger prince is suspicious of me, and I think the hotheaded little princess might be, too. And the queen is ready to throw me off a cliff for getting in the way of her plans for her precious son. Prince Ormond is fully under control now, I have no concerns about him. But there may be trouble from elsewhere. Are the others ready, and close by?"

"They are," Feivel confirmed, as Henrik's heart beat uncomfortably in his throat. Who were these others, and what exactly were they ready for?

"Good," said Lady Claudette briskly. "Then I should return to my rooms before it gets any later. Ginny is supposedly keeping the gate secure for me, but you know what a fool that girl is. Can you take this message to the rest of them?"

Feivel grunted his assent. "I'll take it tomorrow. You be careful in there with all these North Landers."

Lady Claudette laughed. "Relax, my suspicious one. It's not all bad. The women of Valoria might hate me, and the royals might be starting to question me, but the men are all *very* taken with me. It would be quite entertaining if I had time to get distracted by such things."

"But you don't," Feivel reminded her. "You said it yourself, the window is small. Do whatever you need to do to get that prince to propose to you tomorrow."

"I will," cooed Lady Claudette reassuringly. "You'll be calling me 'Your Highness' before you know it."

Feivel made an impatient noise in the back of his throat. "Well, until then, be careful, *My Lady*."

The words were followed by the firm tread of footsteps going back the way Henrik and Feivel had come, and a moment later, another lilting step could be heard, heading toward the castle.

The conspirators were gone, leaving Henrik crouching, frozen, in the bush. He made himself count to a hundred before emerging, even though his blood was pumping and his every muscle was longing for action.

He walked slowly from the garden, telling himself over and over to be smart. As satisfying as it might be to run after Feivel and fight it out with him then and there, it would achieve very little. He needed to tell Kincaid what he'd heard, and most likely the two of them needed more information before they took anything to the king and queen.

Henrik drummed his fingers on the hilt of his sword as he walked, frustrated at how many questions still weren't answered. He didn't have the luxury of time, not if Lady Claudette was planning to secure a betrothal the next day. It seemed absurd to think that she could achieve that, but remembering the astonishing behavior he'd so far witnessed from Ormond, Henrik didn't feel safe to bet against it.

However, there was nothing to be done. If Feivel wasn't taking his message to his accomplices—whoever they were—

until the next day, it seemed likely he was going back to the barracks now, to sleep. There was no point continuing to watch him through the night. And Henrik couldn't go barging into Kincaid's rooms at midnight, not now his friend was married.

As much as it chafed, he would have to wait until the morning.

CHAPTER FIFTEEN

Henrik was up before the sun, full of nervous energy. Even though he wasn't due for active duty for some hours, he donned the livery of the king's guard, thinking he might want to remind his listeners of his official position.

He didn't put on chain mail, but he armed himself, slipping on the lighter weight metal arm guards that provided some defense in the absence of a shield. He strapped his sword on last, reassured by the comforting familiarity of the weapon. He had no idea what the day would hold, but he had no intention of being caught unaware.

He hurried toward the castle just as dawn broke, intent on finding Kincaid. He knew the prince was unlikely to have emerged from his rooms yet, but his errand had waited long enough. He was hoping to speak with Kincaid and return to the soldiers' barracks before Feivel left. With any luck, he might be able to follow the guard and find out the location and identity of the group Lady Claudette had spoken about the night before.

His steps slowed as he entered the royal wing of the castle. He might be used to running free here, but not usually so early in the morning. He noticed one of the guards watching him as his eyes passed from the door to Kincaid's suite, to the suite the princess occupied further down the hall. Reaching a quick decision, he remained at the end of the wing, turning to the closest guard.

"I need to speak with Prince Kincaid," he said, as confidently as he could.

The guard regarded him expressionlessly. "The sun is barely up, My Lord. Their Highnesses haven't yet emerged."

"I know, but it's urgent," said Henrik. "I'm reporting to him at his request." He kept his face impassive. It was sort of true. Kincaid may not have said anything about predawn reports, but he had asked Henrik to find out what he could about the visiting Thoranians.

The guard frowned for a moment, then gave in with a sigh. "All right, then." He strode to the prince's door, giving it three short raps. "Your Highness?" He waited a moment, then knocked again.

After a delay, the door opened, and a bleary-eyed Kincaid appeared in the opening. "Did you knock?"

"Yes, Your Highness," said the guard, standing at attention. "Lord Henrik is here to speak with you."

Kincaid's posture straightened at once, his eyes flying to his friend some distance down the hall. "Henrik! You have something to tell me?"

Henrik gave a curt nod, his eyes sending a silent message that Kincaid clearly understood. The prince's sleepiness fell away, and he spoke briskly as he glanced back into the suite behind him.

"Not here. The nurse has taken Norik to the nursery so Jocelyn can sleep, and I don't want to wake her. Give me a minute, and I'll join you."

He disappeared back inside the room, closing the door

behind him. Henrik waited impatiently, still hanging back at the end of the corridor, as the minutes went by. A number of servants gave him curious looks as they passed. He tried not to fidget as he kept his eyes determinedly from looking in the direction of Lavinia's rooms. He reminded himself that no one else knew of what had passed between him and the princess. No one would think it unusual for him to hang around the royals' wing, as he had so often done. So why did it feel like every pair of eyes was on him?

The prince finally emerged, dressed and looking much more alert. "Come on," he said, joining Henrik at the end of the corridor. He glanced around in confusion. "Why are you all the way back here?"

"Didn't want to intrude," said Henrik shortly.

"If you say so." Kincaid stifled a yawn, clearly not caring enough to question his friend's behavior at that moment. "Let's find somewhere to talk."

The prince led the way through the castle, nodding vaguely to the various people they passed. They were all servants and guards of course—certainly none of the courtiers were abroad so early. One of the servants who bustled past caught Henrik's eye, and he felt a stirring of unease as he recognized the wiry man who had attended Lady Claudette at the luncheon the day before.

The Thoranian's demeanor set him apart as much as his coloring. The rest of the servants barely raised their eyes, dipping into respectful bows or curtsies when they saw the prince and his companion. But this man, although he bowed stiffly, kept his eyes on the duo, seeming to take in every detail with a scrutiny Henrik had rarely observed in servants.

Henrik watched the man surreptitiously, making sure he had passed out of sight before they turned the corner. Kincaid didn't seem to have noticed the encounter, but soon after he chose an anteroom, apparently at random. Having checked that it was empty, he waved Henrik inside.

"Did you follow her?" he asked, as soon as the door was closed. "Did you find something out?"

Henrik moved away from the door, lowering his voice just in case the servant had doubled back. "I didn't follow her," he said. "But I may as well have. I followed Feivel, her guard. He's staying in the soldiers' barracks, but late last night he met Lady Claudette in the public gardens." His voice was grim. "It was quite an illuminating conversation."

As best he could remember, he recounted what he had overheard to his friend. Kincaid's expression grew stormier by the second, and he was pacing back and forth by the time Henrik finished.

"I knew she was scheming something. I mean, it's obvious she wants Ormond's crown, but the fact that all her people are apparently in on it..." He gritted his teeth. "They think they can take our family for fools, do they? And all the time she's most likely involved with her guard, anyway." He made a noise of disgust. "Doesn't anyone have any sense of boundaries anymore?"

Henrik fidgeted self-consciously, but Kincaid wasn't paying him any attention. The prince's scowl was fading, his expression becoming more thoughtful.

"But how is she doing it? How is she making Ormond lose his head like this?" He met Henrik's eyes, his own troubled. "I would suspect some kind of magic, like what that Thoranian advisor Rasad was playing with when he tried to turn his kingdom into an empire. But all of Rasad's experiments were destroyed by the dragons. Apparently they burned his home to the ground, and destroyed all the artifacts he was carrying as well."

Henrik nodded, his own expression thoughtful. He hadn't

been part of the delegation that went to Thorania a few years before, but he had heard all about the events that had transpired there. He would like to think that his own failure to recognize Lady Claudette for what she was earlier could be attributed to some kind of enchantment. But if that was the case, why was he no longer under it?

Kincaid made a frustrated noise. "I wish I could speak to Lucy. She knows more about everything that happened in Thorania than I do. She might be able to tell me if there's any way this could be connected to Rasad's magic. But she's far away in Kyona."

"Like you and Jocelyn were supposed to be," said Henrik slowly. He'd forgotten to mention that part of the conversation, and he quickly repeated the strange comments the Thoranian pair had made about Kincaid's wife.

The prince's scowl returned, a hint of alarm behind his anger. "I don't like that at all," he said, glancing toward the door. "I think I will wake her. I want to talk all this over with her."

More like you want to check she's all right, thought Henrik, smiling to himself in spite of the situation. But he didn't protest. He had been alarmed enough himself when he thought the conspirators were talking about Lavinia, and he had far less right to feel protective of her than Kincaid had with Jocelyn.

"I'm going to see if I can find Feivel," he said, cutting in on Kincaid's evident distraction. "I'm hoping I can follow him when he goes to meet with whoever they were talking about."

"Yes, good idea," said Kincaid briskly. "Although I think what you've already heard is enough to justify me speaking to my father." He frowned. "But I'll have to be careful how I do it. Ormond was even worse after the luncheon yesterday. Honestly, Lady Claudette's not completely crazy to think he might be on the point of proposing to her." He met his friend's eye. "It would be best for you to tell my father what you heard firsthand, but I think following this Feivel is more important. You can confirm it all to my father when you get back, and hopefully have something more to add."

Henrik nodded, already turning toward the door.

"And Henrik," Kincaid added, causing Henrik to look back at him. "Be careful. I don't want word of any of this to get out, but you should take a couple of other knights with you, if there's someone you can trust. We don't know what we're dealing with yet." He grimaced. "Just don't give them the impression that this is an official royal command. I have no idea how my father is going to react to any of this."

Henrik nodded again. He hurried out into the corridor, his mind already reviewing the knights most likely to be discreet enough for such a mission. Kincaid was hard on his heels, following him from the room and disappearing back toward the royal wing without further conversation.

Henrik turned in the opposite direction, heading for the front entrance of the castle. He was only halfway there when he heard his name, and turned impatiently.

"Lord Henrik!"

His frustration turned to alarm when he saw who was hailing him. Lady Claudette was hurrying toward him, looking less polished than she had the last time he had seen her, as though she had gotten ready in a hurry.

"Lady Claudette," Henrik said cautiously, trying to read her expression. "You're up early."

"So are you," she said with a smile that bordered on flirtatious.

Henrik couldn't bring himself to return it. He supposed he should be trying to avoid suspicion. But the memory of her smug tone when she told Feivel that all the men of Valoria were in love with her was too fresh. It was all he could do to keep his lip from curling instead.

Her smile dimmed slightly. "I'm not one for lying in bed all morning," she said, shrugging one shoulder. "Especially on such a glorious day as this." She gestured toward a nearby window. "Won't you take a walk with me, make the most of this beautiful morning? There's a lovely public garden nearby."

Henrik narrowed his eyes at her mention of the garden, then tried to smooth out his expression. Was she testing him?

"Actually," he said, with his best attempt at politeness, "I can't linger. I'm on my way to the training yard."

"Oh?" Lady Claudette smoothed her skirts with both hands, the movement a little too studied. "Official royal business, I assume? You being part of the king's guard and all."

"No," said Henrik carefully, remembering Kincaid's warning. "Just morning training, you know."

"Well, then," said Lady Claudette winningly, "surely you can afford a few minutes to enjoy a sunny morning first?"

Henrik hesitated. He was increasingly becoming convinced that her servant had reported to her about his early morning rendezvous with the prince, and that she had sought him out to try to learn what, if anything, he knew. He glanced in the direction of the castle entrance, wondering if he would be wisest to just extricate himself.

But he shook the thought off quickly. He would have to be careful, but if he made good use of this opportunity, perhaps *he* could be the one to find out what *she* was hiding.

"Of course I can," he said, offering her his arm with his most gallant manner. "You're right—my training can wait a few minutes."

Lady Claudette smiled, the expression a trifle smug, and it was all Henrik could do to keep his arm steady as she put her hand on it. His skin seemed to crawl beneath her touch. He led the way through the corridors, reaching the castle's entrance to the public gardens within minutes.

"Oh," said Lady Claudette, looking up at him from under her lashes. "So you know this garden, too, do you?"

"Of course," said Henrik steadily. "The public gardens are well known. They're a popular meeting place among the court."

"Are they?" Lady Claudette asked, looking hastily away from his scrutiny.

Was it his imagination that she looked a little unsettled by this information? He smiled grimly as he stood back, politely waiting for her to go through the gate first.

"So what brings you to the castle at this hour?" Lady Claudette asked, once they were strolling down one of the tree lined pathways. "From what I've seen, most of the court, and the royals, don't start their day so early."

"Oh, nothing of importance," Henrik lied cheerfully. "I'm not quite like the rest of the court, you know. Being a knight, I'm used to an early start. Our commander likes us up with the sun."

"I can see you're not like the rest of the court," said Lady Claudette, stopping unexpectedly.

Henrik did the same, and realized that while he had been intent on their conversation, the Thoranian woman had navigated them into a secluded corner. No doubt she'd already become familiar with several such hideaways in the gardens, from her midnight rendezvous with Feivel.

Distracted, it took Henrik a moment to realize that Lady Claudette was looking up at him expectantly. He returned her gaze, his own expression blank as he tried to remember what she'd been saying.

"In fact," she tried again, her manner undeniably coquettish, "you're not at all like the rest of the men I've met in Valoria." Her hands were folded demurely in her skirts, and she tilted her face up invitingly as she spoke. "Quite apart from being by far the most handsome man I've met in Bryford," her artificial giggle grated on Henrik's ears, "I suspect that your desire for action is the least of your...admirable qualities."

Henrik jumped slightly when the Thoranian woman laid a hand on his chest. He stepped back, fighting to keep his disgust hidden. He wanted to find out what she was up to, but there was only so far he was willing to go in that pursuit.

"You flatter me," he said, his voice flat. "I'm really nothing out of the ordinary."

Lady Claudette's smile faltered, but she showed none of the embarrassment Henrik would expect after a rejection. She looked frustrated, certainly, but if anything, Henrik would describe her expression as confused. He narrowed his eyes slightly.

"So modest," Lady Claudette said, with another tinkling laugh. "But that's not what I hear. I hear you're a deadly fighter, for one thing." She batted her eyelashes. "And the ladies certainly love you."

"You heard I'm a good fighter, did you?" Henrik asked, raising an eyebrow. "From who? Your guard?"

Lady Claudette took a small step back, her expression suddenly veiled.

"My guard?"

"I sparred with him yesterday," Henrik explained, his voice casual but his eyes keen. "He's quite formidable himself."

"Oh, sparring," laughed Lady Claudette, still holding herself a little stiffly. "Why do men love to fight so much?"

"Maybe because we don't have the weapons you have at our disposal," said Henrik, watching her closely.

"The weapons I have?" Lady Claudette repeated, looking unnerved.

"You know, feminine wiles," Henrik said casually.

Lady Claudette gave an unconvincing laugh, one Henrik was sure had an edge of relief. Interesting.

"Now you're the one flattering me," said Lady Claudette. "I'm sure I don't have any 'wiles' beyond what the next woman has." She took another step back, and Henrik moved forward slightly.

"Really?" he asked pleasantly. "I can't agree. Prince Ormond certainly seems to have been very much impacted by your company." He leaned forward slightly. "If you don't claim any particular charms, what type of weapon is at work there?"

Henrik knew he ran a risk in showing his suspicion so clearly. But Lady Claudette's expression had become hard, and he was starting to hope that she was goaded enough to slip up and reveal something.

She opened her mouth to speak, but before she had said a word her eyes slid over his shoulder, latching on something behind him. Henrik frowned, wondering if she was trying to distract him. He started to turn his head, to see what she was looking at, so he had no warning before she suddenly launched herself toward him.

He reached instinctively toward the hilt of his sword, but it seemed Lady Claudette had an altogether different type of attack in mind. Before Henrik knew what was happening, she was pressed against his chest, and her lips were on his.

Startled, he stumbled back, his exclamation stifled by the contact. His eyes flew in shock to Lady Claudette's face, but she wasn't looking at him. She was again looking past him, her hand to her throat in apparent dismay, and her lips parted in an unconvincing gasp of surprise.

Henrik whipped his head around at last, and his heart seemed to drop into his stomach at the sight of Lavinia, standing rooted to the spot a few yards away.

CHAPTER SIXTEEN

A dozen emotions seemed to flit across the princess's face before her eyes slid to Henrik's, and an expressionless mask descended on her countenance.

"Well," she said, one eyebrow slightly raised. "It seems I'm interrupting." Without waiting for a response, she turned on her heel and disappeared around the corner of a hedge.

"Lavinia, wait!" Henrik called. He took a step toward her, then turned, his furious gaze falling on Lady Claudette.

She met his gaze steadily, her expression smug. "Oops."

"Oops?" he repeated, his anger growing. His lips were still prickling unpleasantly from the unwelcome contact. Lavinia's appearance had brought their own kiss the day before forcibly to mind, and the comparison filled Henrik with repulsion as he looked at the scheming, manipulative woman before him. "What's wrong with you? Why did you do that?"

Her smirk dropped away, replaced by a look of cold calculation. "Call it a friendly warning," she said, her change in demeanor so complete as to be shocking. "Stay out of my way."

And with that, she brushed past him, striding off in the opposite direction from Lavinia. Henrik stared after her for a moment, then decided that whatever she was up to would have to wait. He turned, sprinting in the direction Lavinia had taken.

The princess was walking quickly, but he had no trouble catching up with her before she left the garden.

"Lavinia!" he called, as soon as she was in sight.

A slight falter in her gait was the only sign that she heard him. She kept walking away from him, her posture stiff and her head held high.

"Lavinia," Henrik said again, catching up to her and grabbing her arm. "Wait. That wasn't what you think."

Lavinia turned, her eyebrows raised as her gaze traveled slowly from his hand on her arm to his face.

He released her quickly, thinking ruefully that she had the haughty princess role perfected. There was certainly no sign of a dimple now. Just a blazing fire in her eyes to match that in her unrestrained hair. Like Lady Claudette, she appeared to have readied herself in a hurry. But while it made the Thoranian woman look sloppy, Lavinia looked natural and fresh, more appealing than ever.

In spite of the deathly glare.

"It seems I was right to be suspicious of Lady Claudette's intentions toward my brother," Lavinia said once he'd let go. "But while I had a lot of guesses as to what I might find if I followed her, I must confess I didn't expect that. I suppose I should have."

"Lavinia, listen," said Henrik desperately. "I didn't—"

"I think you mean Your Highness," interrupted Lavinia. Henrik winced at her freezing tone. "And there's no need to explain anything to me, *Lord* Henrik. It's not as though I'm surprised. Your reputation is well known."

"Lavinia, will you just listen?" Henrik cut in, torn between frustration and fear. If he couldn't make her believe him...

"I'd rather not," she said shortly. "I think I've heard enough of your eloquent speeches in the last day or two." She gave him a disdainful look. "Your performance yesterday was especially skillful. What was it? Something about 'the conflict inside you'? Well, I'm so pleased to see that you've resolved that conflict so quickly. Now you don't need to—what was the phrase?—*torture* yourself anymore."

"I meant what I said to you yesterday!" Henrik insisted. "I'm not interested in Lady Claudette!"

Lavinia's eyebrow went up again. "Aren't you? That doesn't really put your conduct just now in a better light, you realize."

"What conduct?" said Henrik, frustrated. "I didn't do anything—she threw herself at me."

Lavinia made a scoffing noise. "So she lured you into a secluded corner of the garden to accost you, did she? That would be more convincing if she wasn't so obviously chasing Ormond and his crown." Lavinia cast a scornful eye over Henrik's form. "With such a prize within her grasp, it's hard to believe she'd risk losing everything for a dalliance with you."

Henrik felt a flush rising up his neck, as much at the disdain on Lavinia's face as at the reminder of how far below the royals his position really was.

"I know you're in the habit of thinking no woman can resist you, but believe me, that's far from true."

"That's not fair," Henrik protested, but he had no chance to explain himself further.

With her parting shot, Lavinia had again swept away from him. She made straight for the gate leading from the public gardens into the castle, the guard at the entrance nodding respectfully to her. Henrik knew there was no use in following her. She would make sure he had no chance to speak to her in private.

He ran his hands through his hair, stunned and horrified at the turn things had taken. Lady Claudette was more cunning than he'd realized. It had been clear from her parting warning that she had a pretty good idea of how heavy a blow she'd just landed him. She must be more observant than he'd given her credit for. The thought was chilling in more ways than one—how many others could see what he'd been trying to hide?

But he pushed the thought aside, focusing instead on his anger at Lady Claudette and her schemes. It was much more invigorating than the quagmire of humiliation and hopelessness that sucked him in when he thought of what Lavinia had just seen, and how completely it had confirmed her suspicions about him.

So the Thoranian woman thought she had him cornered, did she? She thought she could threaten him into giving up on finding out what exactly she was up to? She had underestimated him. It was gut wrenching to remember the look on Lavinia's face when she'd seen Lady Claudette kissing him, certainly. But it wasn't like he'd ever had any real hope of the princess, so he hadn't lost anything that was ever his to begin with.

He directed his steps out of the garden with determination. He would follow Feivel as planned. And once he knew the extent of whatever the visitors were up to, he'd take that information to the king, and bring the vile schemer down. Regardless of what it might cost him.

He reached the training yard quickly, his steps still agitated but his purpose clear. A couple of his peers called greetings to him, but he ignored them. He scoured the area for his commander, but he wasn't in sight. An older knight caught his attention, one he had often been on patrol with. Henrik strode toward him. Not only was the man trustworthy, he could be relied on to be at the training yard before dawn every day.

"Morning," Henrik greeted him.

The older knight looked up from the sword he was polishing, nodding in acknowledgment before returning his attention to his work.

"Do you know where the commander is?"

"Talking with the night patrol, I think," the knight responded in his deep, steady voice.

Henrik grunted, frustrated. Then he drew closer, lowering his voice. "Has that Thoranian guard, Feivel, been here this morning?"

The knight looked up, his attention caught. "Not that I've seen. And I've been here since first light."

Henrik nodded, frowning. He hoped his unplanned interlude with Lady Claudette hadn't made him miss his opportunity to follow the guard. He scowled at the memory of the disastrous morning, until a chuckle brought him out of his abstraction.

"Want a rematch, hey? I heard about your interrupted fight."

"What?" Henrik asked blankly. "Oh, that." He made an impatient gesture. "No, I don't care about who's a better fighter." Well, not much. "This is something else." He glanced around to make sure no one else was in earshot. "You on active duty this morning?"

The knight shook his head, raising an eyebrow at Henrik's conspiratorial tone.

"I heard the guard say he was meeting someone today," Henrik explained. "And I want to know who it is."

"Do you?" grunted the older man. "Sounds like your own affair."

"Actually," said Henrik, "it's a little more than that. The prince asked me to find out who he's meeting, if I can."

The knight frowned at him. "This is starting to sound dangerous."

Henrik shrugged. "Could be. Not sure yet."

"All right," said his companion, with a sigh. "I'd better come and make sure you don't get hurt."

"Thanks," Henrik chuckled, taking no offense at the slight on his abilities. He knew he was young for his position, and it never bothered him when the more experienced knights treated him in a fatherly way. It was so much like the long-suffering treatment he got from his family, it made him feel quite at home.

In no time at all, the two knights were making their way to the soldiers' barracks where Feivel was staying. As he had on his previous visit, Henrik slipped into the royal stables nearby rather than approaching the barracks directly. His companion followed him.

"Morning, Lord Henrik," said an under-groom cheerfully. "Need your horse saddled up?"

"That depends," said Henrik, smiling in greeting. The groom was a friendly boy, who often lingered to chat when Henrik visited his horse. "Has that Thoranian guard been through here yet this morning?"

"Yep," said the boy brightly. "Rode out about twenty minutes ago. He's got an excellent seat, you know. They say the Thoranians don't even use saddles half the time."

"Blast," muttered Henrik, not paying attention to most of the groom's speech. He exchanged a look with the other knight. "Do you know where he went?"

"North, I think," said the boy vaguely. "Don't know any more than that."

"Twenty minutes isn't long," said Henrik decisively. "We'll ride out now, and try our luck."

"As you like, My Lord," said the groom cheerfully. "Won't take a minute."

It was a little longer than that, but the boy was efficient, and soon Henrik and his companion were riding through the city, toward the north gate. The guards on duty at the gate confirmed that Feivel had ridden through it some fifteen minutes before, so at least they knew they were going in the right direction. But beyond that, there wasn't much to work with.

They rode for some time along the main north road, pushing their mounts as fast as practical on such a well-trafficked route. But after about ten minutes, Henrik was forced to conclude that their chances of catching up to Feivel weren't good.

He pulled up his horse, and his companion did the same.

"Where to now, lad?" the older man asked. "Am I right in thinking we have nothing at all to go on? Or do you know something I don't?"

Henrik frowned, turning the question over in his mind. He did know significantly more than the other knight did about Feivel. Surely there was some clue he could make use of.

"We could head back for the city," he said slowly. "Wait for him to return, and intercept him then. But that won't tell us anything about where he's been or who he's been meeting with."

"It won't," agreed his companion. "But I can't say I have any other ideas. Do you? It's clear we're not going to catch him. Maybe if he was riding very slowly, but that doesn't seem likely. The boy at the stables said he had an excellent seat."

"He did, didn't he?" said Henrik thoughtfully, the comment tickling something in his memory. "Apparently most Thoranians are very good riders." He glanced back toward the city, then out again, toward the north east. "I do have one idea. Something's been bothering me since the bandit attack my patrol intercepted out this way." He gave a decisive nod. "I can locate the place again. We might find nothing, but then we won't find much sitting by the city gate."

"Lead on, then," said the older knight compliantly. "This is your venture, I'm with you."

Henrik nodded his thanks, then spurred his horse into motion again, heading further up the northern road. After several minutes of hard riding, he took a turn off toward the north east, making for the copse of trees where he and his patrol had come upon the attempted robbery. They reached it in less than half an hour, and Henrik slowed his horse as soon as they entered the trees.

He was approaching it from the opposite direction now, so it was difficult to be sure of the right place to leave the road. But he chose a spot according to his best recollection, and the two men led their horses through the trees, picking their way slowly up the wooded slope. When the trees began to thin, Henrik saw the boulder-covered ground he remembered, descending down toward the grassland below.

"What exactly are we looking for?" the other knight asked quietly, his brow furrowed.

"I'm not exactly sure," Henrik admitted. "Any sign of people, I suppose. It struck me when I saw the attack here that the bandits must be good horsemen to navigate this terrain as quickly as they did. I'd forgotten at the time that Thoranians are supposed to be so good with horses."

The knight raised an eyebrow. "You think the bandits are Thoranians? I thought that noblewoman only had a couple of servants with her, not a whole group."

Henrik shrugged, wondering how much to disclose to the older man. "I'm not sure what I think. But the guard definitely said he was meeting a group today. And whether they're Thoranians, or Valorians, or from somewhere else altogether, I don't think their intentions are friendly."

The knight gave him a shrewd look. "I think there's a deal to this that you're not telling me, lad."

Henrik just shrugged again, remembering Kincaid's comment that he didn't want word of the situation getting out before he could report it to his father. The older man regarded him silently for a moment, before evidently deciding to let it go.

The two of them split up, guiding their horses at a walk as they explored between boulders in opposite directions. Henrik soon slipped from his mount, leading the horse by its halter as he picked his way across the uneven ground, looking for any sign of recent passage. His training included the basics of tracking, and after several minutes, he thought he saw certain telltale indents in the grass. He paused, bending low to examine them more closely. He followed the direction of the tracks, a rush of excitement shooting through him as the marks began to resemble a trail.

He was just picking up his pace when he caught the sound of voices, not far ahead. The accent marked the speakers as Thoranian, even before Henrik was close enough to hear their words. His excitement mounted.

Looking around, he saw an enormous boulder not far ahead, and he led his mount silently toward it. The rock was large enough to conceal both horse and rider, and Henrik positioned himself behind it, running his hand down his horse's nose in a soothing gesture. Hopefully the creature would remain quiet enough to avoid detection.

"All right, then," came a voice that Henrik recognized as Feivel's. "I'd better return to Bryford. But don't forget, I want everyone ready to ride out at any time. I think we can afford to stay quiet for now, but it's possible we might need another incident. It just depends how today unfolds."

"Understood," said a curt voice Henrik didn't think he'd heard before. "We're more than ready for action. Just give us a better job to do next time. The men don't like being told not to get their hands dirty."

"Well, tell them to keep their eyes on the goal," responded Feivel sharply. "The bandit attacks aren't for fun. Do the men need to be reminded how great a risk we run every time? If one of them was unmasked..."

"Relax," said the other man dismissively. "No one's been unmasked."

"Yet," Feivel retorted, his voice grim. "I still don't like it. If the staged attack on Claudette and Ginny hadn't raised so much suspicion, we would never have staged the other attacks, you know that. We just had to make it seem like it wasn't an isolated incident. Claudette is trying to convince everyone that the farmers are behind it, but who knows if that story will stick? It's imperative that no one finds out her role in it all, so no foolish risks!"

"Who said anything about foolish?" said the other man, sounding sulky. "You like to think you're the boss, but some of us have our own reasons for being here."

"You're losing focus," said Feivel sharply. "This is about securing a permanent future. It isn't about revenge."

The other man snorted. "We haven't lost focus, don't worry. Don't think any of us will forget how much gold we've been promised. But not everyone cares about that. You can tell *Her Ladyship* that revenge is the only thing that brought some of the men here. We're not all going to get a crown out of this."

"Don't lose your head," snapped Feivel. "And don't pretend you're the only one who lost everything. I had it worse than you, and I'm not going to get some grand position like Claudette. But I still know how to be patient."

"Personal guard to the crown princess is a pretty good position if you ask me," grumbled the other man. "None of the rest of us are getting that."

"You'll get enough," Feivel said dismissively. "Once she's a royal, she can start maneuvering positions for everyone. Trust me, I've seen what it's like in the castle. There's plenty of gold in Valoria, and plenty of power to go around. The prince is completely in Claudette's control. And the king is used to trusting his son's judgment. The prince's word goes. As long as he's a puppet on her string, she'll lead the court any way she wants. If we keep her path clear, we'll get what's due to us."

Henrik narrowed his eyes. This was certainly enough to prove their villainous intentions. He just wished he knew how many were in this group of conspirators. He still had very little idea what he was dealing with.

"We'd better," the other man was muttering.

Feivel didn't respond, and after a moment Henrik heard the sound of footsteps. It seemed the two men were parting ways. He debated for a moment about what to do next, but he decided there was little need to follow Feivel now. He had said he was going back to Bryford, and Henrik knew where to find him there. If he followed the other man, he might be able to find out the location and number of Lady Claudette's group of supporters. He glanced around, wishing the other knight was within sight, but he could see no sign of the man.

Just as he was edging around the boulder, trying to catch a glimpse of where the unfamiliar man had gone, his horse apparently reached the limit of its patience.

The creature stamped a hoof, letting out a whinny that, while quiet, carried clearly through the still air.

CHAPTER SEVENTEEN

"Who's there?"

Henrik stifled an oath at the sound of Feivel's voice. He remained silent, thinking through his options. A heavy footstep sounded, and he placed a hand on the hilt of his weapon. There was no hope of escaping undetected, not with his horse in tow. He could mount up and ride away before the guard reached him, of course, but he didn't consider that option for more than a second. He had never been one to run from a fight.

Feivel rounded the edge of the boulder a moment later, and his expression instantly went from suspicious to furious.

"You!" He growled deep in his throat. "Followed me, did you? You're a thorn in my side."

"Well, I can't let you have it all your own way," said Henrik calmly.

The Thoranian was reaching for his weapon, and Henrik released his horse, letting out a long high whistle as he drew his own sword. Hopefully the older knight would hear the signal and respond. There was no sign of Feivel's companion—it seemed he had already passed out of hearing range.

"It's time I taught you your place, little knight," said Feivel mockingly. "You got lucky the last time we fought."

"Some call it luck when their opponent runs out on the fight," said Henrik provocatively, as he dropped into a fighting crouch. "I just find it unsatisfying."

The Thoranian guard growled again, clearly infuriated by the suggestion that he had fled their previous encounter. He lunged aggressively, and Henrik stepped nimbly to the side, parrying the attack.

"So you like the look of Valoria, do you?" he asked lightly, as Feivel drew back, his eyes roaming over Henrik, looking for an opening. "Looking to—what was it? *Secure a permanent future*?"

Feivel's eyes narrowed at this evidence that Henrik had truly overheard his conversation. Henrik whipped his sword up in front of him, reading his opponent's intent in his eyes.

Feivel's second attack was less fierce. The movement was controlled, more precise, and Henrik could tell that he was serious now. Henrik had learned too much—the Thoranian meant to eliminate him.

Henrik gripped his sword with grim determination as he deflected the other weapon. That wasn't going to work out quite as the guard hoped.

His horse had shied away, so Henrik didn't have to worry about being trampled. But space was limited between the huge rocks, and Feivel was trying to push him back against the nearest boulder.

Henrik allowed the guard to press him, moving steadily backward until he felt the rock behind him. Then he dropped to one knee in a lightning movement, thrusting upward and forcing his opponent's sword wide as he swung himself around and out of the tight space. He sprang to his feet with a grunt of effort, his sword still engaged with Feivel's.

The Thoranian's expression was stormier than ever as

Henrik threw off his sword at last. The older man was clearly frustrated at Henrik's skill. His distraction was a weakness that Henrik had every intention of exploiting.

"Hoped for an easy kill, did you?" he panted, stepping back in the hope of drawing the Thoranian onto better ground.

The other man grunted, murder in his eyes as he advanced. "I've faced worse than you, believe me."

His sword flashed out, but Henrik's was quicker, and in the clash of steel there was no time for further baiting. He would have to let his weapon talk for him. Feivel threw all his superior strength into his advance, and Henrik had to fight hard to hold him off. He ducked and weaved, his blade dancing back and forth with deadly precision. He was quick, often flashing under Feivel's guard. But he wasn't quick enough to end it, the Thoranian always managing to recover in time to avoid a fatal blow.

For a few minutes they fought in grim silence, except for the clang of their blades, and the thud of their feet on the uneven turf. Henrik's breath was loud in his ears, but he was alert and determined, full of energy and confident in his skill. As in their last fight, he could tell that he was better trained than his opponent, as well as fitter. If it came to it, he was sure he could outlast Feivel, as long as he made no foolish mistakes.

The knowledge that this was no sparring match—that a foolish mistake would cost him his life not his pride—only sharpened his focus. He was at a disadvantage in that he was determined to bring Feivel before the king alive, whereas the Thoranian clearly wanted to finish him. But he didn't allow himself to be distracted by the thought.

Feivel, on the other hand, had shown himself to be vulnerable to distraction. A tool to make use of.

"Do you really think," Henrik panted, raining a series of tight blows on Feivel's upraised sword, "the prince will tolerate," he ducked, dodging a thrust from the other man's weapon, "a wife who's dallying," he leaped back out of reach, "with her guard?"

Feivel grunted, his eyes narrowed as he advanced. Henrik's sword flashed up, deflecting a blow that was less precise than before.

"Can you tolerate it?" he huffed, pressing his advantage. "Watching her simper over him?"

Feivel's growl came from deep in his throat, and the rage in his eyes gave Henrik a second's warning before the guard charged at him.

He brought his sword around with both hands, deflecting the wild attack with ease. An enraged enemy was much easier both to predict and to defeat than a calm, determined one.

Henrik side-stepped the charge, bringing his foot out to connect with the back of Feivel's knee as the guard passed him. The Thoranian man stumbled, and Henrik followed up his attack, using his blade to disarm his opponent in a practiced motion. The other man's sword went spinning out of his hand, hitting a boulder with a clang. Henrik surged forward, pressing his blade to Feivel's throat.

"Surrender," he said curtly, his breath coming in short gasps from the exertion of the fight.

The Thoranian was also panting, but the hatred in his eyes was as fierce as ever as he stared Henrik down. He said nothing, but he made no move to continue the fight. Henrik had succeeded in grazing Feivel's arm, and the Thoranian clutched at the shallow wound, from which blood was slowly seeping.

Following the motion with his eyes, Henrik saw that although Feivel was once again dressed in a full-sleeved tunic, the gesture had caused one sleeve to ride a few inches up his arm. Henrik's eyes widened at the sight of the mangled flesh revealed between the guard's wrist and elbow. The wounds weren't the result of the fight—they looked like burns, healed but leaving a permanent mark.

Not that Henrik was interested in their origin, particularly. It was their familiarity that caught his interest. He'd seen that type of wound, recently.

"It *was* you," he breathed.

He was still staring at the ruined skin of his opponent's arm, thinking he had Feivel covered. But his distraction cost him, and the sudden movement from the guard was too quick. In a flash, Feivel produced a dagger from his boot, lunging toward his captor.

Taken by surprise, Henrik blocked the attack clumsily. With his longer blade, he managed to deflect the knife, but Feivel was ready to take advantage of his distraction.

Before Henrik grasped the guard's intent, Feivel had launched himself forward, barreling into the Valorian knight before Henrik could bring his sword in front of him again. Feivel was no longer armed, but he grasped Henrik's sword arm, forcing it outward with every bit of his strength.

The leaner, younger knight struggled grimly as Feivel attempted to disarm him. He knew his life hung in the balance. No matter how strong Feivel might be, Henrik simply had to resist.

"Henrik? Where are you, lad?" The other knight's voice came drifting from somewhere behind them.

At the sound, Feivel seemed to reach a decision, suddenly abandoning the attempt to wrest Henrik's sword from him. Henrik raised his arm, but he wasn't quick enough to deflect the next attack. Bringing his fist around with alarming speed, Feivel landed a hefty blow to Henrik's temple.

For a moment Henrik's vision spun wildly, the older knight's voice ringing in his ears with a strange metallic whistle.

Then everything went black.

. . .

"ALL RIGHT, LAD, EASY NOW."

Henrik cracked his eyes open, wondering why the light was so blinding, and why his head was pounding so furiously. The voice speaking to him was vaguely familiar, but he couldn't place it for a moment.

"That's it," said the voice again, in the tone someone might use when soothing an overexcited child. "You'll do."

Henrik became aware that he was lying on grass, and he pushed himself into a sitting position, groaning as he did so. The rest of him seemed to be fine, but his head was still throbbing painfully.

The face of an older knight from the king's guard came slowly into focus, and Henrik frowned, still confused. He knew the man, but not especially well. Why were they here together, wherever here was?

He glanced around, trying to collect his wits. His gaze fell on his familiar sword, discarded on the grass nearby, and memory came surging back.

"Feivel!" he said sharply, struggling to his feet. He looked around wildly, but there was no sign of the Thoranian guard. Just the other knight, and their two horses, grazing peacefully nearby.

The knight stood slowly, examining Henrik with a critical eye. "Careful, now. Don't rush it. You've taken quite a blow."

"It was Feivel," said Henrik, furious with himself at the memory of how he had become distracted at the crucial point of their fight.

"Aye, I figured as much," said the knight calmly, walking toward his horse. "But he wasn't anywhere to be seen by the time I arrived. Can't have been far ahead of me, I reckon. I can only assume he heard me coming and ran for it, otherwise I guess he'd have finished you off." The man retrieved Henrik's horse, leading it back over to where the younger knight was still standing. "I thought about going after him, see if I could spot him. But you were in a bad way, and I thought I'd better stay nearby, make sure no one came and did you in while you were unconscious."

"Thank you," said Henrik, taking his horse's reins and trying not to scowl at how they had been bested by the Thoranian. "I'm grateful."

"Well, I came along to keep you alive, didn't I?" said the knight, as placid as ever. "Thought I'd better do my part." He had returned to his own horse, and he stroked its nose, preparing to mount. "I didn't find anything, but it seems you had more success."

"If you could call it that," agreed Henrik ruefully, swinging into his saddle with a wince.

"What did you discover? Was he meeting with someone?"

"He was," said Henrik grimly. "I think the meeting had already happened. By the time I arrived, he was just speaking with one man, saying goodbye."

"And?" the knight pressed.

"They're up to something, all right," Henrik said, as the two men urged their horses into a trot. Even that pace was excruciating for Henrik's throbbing head, but he pushed his horse faster. He was eager to return to Bryford. "Lady Claudette is at the heart of it. I didn't hear the details, but there seems to be a whole group of them. They're determined to see her married to Prince Ormond, and everyone intends to benefit from it."

The other knight grunted. "Not altogether surprising, is it? Of course her friends would hope to benefit from it if she made such a match."

Henrik shook his head, frustrated. "It's more than that, I'm sure of it. There's something sinister going on. They're behind the bandit attacks, for a start." He narrowed his eyes. "That's why the attacks were so clumsy. They had no idea which roads were most likely to be used by wealthy travelers, and at what time. They don't know the area at all."

The knight raised an eyebrow, but didn't comment. It wasn't clear whether he was convinced. Henrik hesitated for a moment, wondering whether to tell the older man his discovery about Feivel. He decided he had better wait until he could discuss the matter with Kincaid first.

"Why would her 'friends' be hiding out here instead of openly staying in Bryford, for one thing?" he said instead.

"That is strange," the other knight agreed. "Most suspicious."

But his tone was still placid, and it was clear he didn't view the situation quite as grimly as Henrik did. Probably because he didn't just get clobbered on the head, Henrik thought ruefully.

They had reached the trees by this time, and conversation ceased as they picked their way through the foliage. When they reached the open road, they spurred their horses into a canter, and there was no more opportunity for discussion.

In spite of how small a head start Feivel must have, Henrik had little expectation of overtaking him. They knew the guard to be an excellent rider now, and with the pounding of Henrik's head, he couldn't sustain the pace he had set when they rode out from Bryford.

Henrik had no idea what the Thoranian would do now that he knew someone was onto him, and he was eager to speak to Kincaid, so they could come up with a plan for talking to the king. But first he had to reach Bryford, and the trip back to the capital felt tortuously slow.

At last they rode through the city's northern gates. Henrik paused to speak to the guard on duty, who confirmed that Feivel had returned almost half an hour before. Henrik scowled. That was far too long for the Thoranian to have the lead on him.

He made straight for the castle, his companion following

without comment. Henrik relinquished his horse to a groom in the courtyard, taking the steps toward the castle two at a time.

But he never made it to his destination. He had almost reached the doors when he was intercepted by two members of the royal guard.

"Lord Henrik, you're to come with us," one of them said gruffly, sounding like he didn't relish his task.

"What?" Henrik said sharply, glancing at the older knight behind him, whose eyebrow was slightly raised. "Why?"

"Your presence is required," said the other royal guard curtly. "At a royal audience."

CHAPTER EIGHTEEN

Henrik opened his mouth to protest, but quickly closed it again. There were plenty of people milling around the castle's entranceway, and the group was starting to attract attention. There was nothing to be gained by arguing with the guards. He would have to save it for someone who could actually do something about it.

He submitted with a tight nod, and to his relief the guards didn't seize him, allowing him to walk between them unhindered as they made their way toward the royal audience hall. The other knight trailed behind, saying nothing.

As they walked, Henrik's initial shock fell away, replaced by growing irritation. He had a bad feeling that Feivel had made the most of his head start. Well, the Thoranian had obviously underestimated the standing Henrik had as a member of the king's elite. The knight had nothing to fear from stating his case before King Malcolm. And once the king knew the details of Feivel's conversation with his co-conspirator—not to mention his liaison with Lady Claudette the night before—they would see who would find himself being seized by guards.

But when the guards led him through the doors into the

broad audience hall, Henrik's stomach dropped unpleasantly. There was no sign of King Malcolm. The throne at the end of the hall was empty. Instead, standing in front of it on the raised dais, was Prince Ormond. And—Henrik could hardly believe her brazenness—Lady Claudette stood beside him.

"Lord Henrik," said Prince Ormond without preamble. "I have just heard a report about you that is deeply concerning."

"Then you must have been misinformed," said Henrik through gritted teeth, his gaze hardening as it rested on Lady Claudette. She wore the falsely demure expression again, the one that didn't quite succeed in covering her smugness.

"I would watch my words, if I were you," said Prince Ormond in a hard voice. "I won't tolerate any...insinuations."

Henrik drew a deep breath, trying to keep his temper in check. He could see he would have to tread carefully. He still had no idea how Lady Claudette was doing it, but it was clear that it was no exaggeration that she had the crown prince under her control. He felt a flicker of sympathy for the normally steadfast prince, but it was quickly drowned out by Ormond's next words.

"What do you have to say for yourself, in regards to your behavior toward Lady Claudette?"

"What behavior?" Henrik asked blankly. His thoughts had been full of the fight with Feivel, and the prince's words caught him by surprise.

"She reports that you accosted her in the public gardens this morning," said Ormond, his face set in grim lines. "And it has further been reported that when her personal guard sought you out to challenge you on your conduct, you attacked him."

"What!?" Henrik's blood thundered in his ears at the accusation. He wasn't sure what enraged him more—Ormond's sanctimonious disapproval, or Lady Claudette's barely concealed smirk. "That's utter nonsense!"

Ormond's lips tightened into a thin line, and Henrik shook out his shoulders, trying to master his anger. It was on the tip of his tongue to say that it was Lady Claudette who had accosted him, but he stopped himself in time. If he had been speaking to King Malcolm, as he had expected, he wouldn't have hesitated to tell the truth of that encounter. But it was clear that making such an accusation to Ormond would not have a happy outcome.

"There's been some mistake," he said instead, as evenly as he could. "Lady Claudette's guard didn't seek me out, I sought him out. And he was the one who attacked me. If you ask the guards at the north gate, they can confirm that he left the city before I did."

Ormond raised an eyebrow. "You say you followed him? So you admit that you've been harassing Lady Claudette and her retinue?"

"Of course not, Your Highness," said Henrik quickly. "I haven't been harassing anyone. I followed him because I have reason to think that he's plotting against the crown. He and his conspirators are the ones who've been carrying out the bandit attacks!"

"How dare you?" gasped Lady Claudette. If the situation hadn't been so grave, Henrik would have rolled his eyes at her dramatic tone. "Can't you accept rejection with honor, My Lord? Must you look to cause trouble for me and my servants out of spite?"

"Your conduct reflects poorly on yourself and your position," agreed Ormond sternly, before Henrik could retort. Which was probably for the best, given what he wanted to say to Lady Claudette.

"Your Highness, no part of these accusations is true," he spat furiously, keeping his eyes away from the Thoranian woman with an effort. "I spoke with Lady Claudette in the gardens this morning, but I certainly didn't accost her. And I followed her guard out of the city to see who he was meeting. I overheard him speaking with another Thoranian man, and when he discovered my presence, he attacked me, with the intent to kill me."

"Nonsense," said Lady Claudette dismissively. "My guard went for a ride this morning, but he wasn't meeting with anyone. And this talk of him posing as a bandit, and trying to kill a knight of Valoria, is absurd. What would he have to gain from such outrageous behavior?"

"The question, My Lady," said Henrik through gritted teeth, "is rather what *you* would have to gain."

But apparently even that was pushing it too far.

"Enough," said Ormond angrily. "You will speak respectfully to your future queen."

Henrik froze, too stunned to respond. It was worse than he'd thought. After everything, was he already too late?

Prince Ormond exchanged a sickeningly love-struck look with Lady Claudette before his gaze returned to Henrik, his expression growing hard. His eyes passed to the knight still standing behind Henrik.

"Why are you here?" he asked, his brow furrowed.

The knight cleared his throat, also looking a little stunned by Prince Ormond's declaration. "I accompanied Lord Henrik out of the city this morning, Your Highness," he said. "As he has indicated, we left Bryford in pursuit of the Thoranian guard called Feivel, on the understanding that he intended to meet with someone clandestinely."

Lady Claudette clucked her tongue. "Where did you get this information from?"

"Well," the knight hesitated, throwing Henrik an apologetic look, "from Lord Henrik, My Lady. He informed me that the prince had asked him to find out who this Feivel was meeting."

"I did no such thing," said Ormond hotly.

"I assumed, Your Highness," said the knight carefully, "that Lord Henrik was referring to Prince Kincaid."

"Ah," said Ormond, looking grimly back at Henrik. "Of course he was. Again, you bring yourself no honor by trading on your friendship with my brother to try to make your personal mission of revenge appear legitimate."

Henrik opened his mouth, a furious protest on his lips, but Ormond pushed on, his attention back on the other knight.

"And did you witness any clandestine meeting taking place?"

"Yes," interjected Henrik angrily. "I did. Feivel met with—"

"I wasn't speaking to you," Ormond cut him off. His gaze shifted to the older knight. "I was asking you."

"Well," the knight hesitated, glancing at Henrik, "I didn't witness it myself, Your Highness. Lord Henrik and I split up, and I wasn't with him when he overheard the conversation. But for what it's worth, I don't doubt his account at all. When I found him, he had certainly taken a blow to the head."

"He probably fell off his horse," said Lady Claudette dismissively.

The knight cleared his throat. "I don't think so, My Lady."

"I wasn't asking for your speculation," said Ormond shortly. "Just what you actually witnessed."

"Prince Ormond," said Henrik, trying to keep his voice even, "you know me. You know that I would have no reason to lie to you about such a matter. I'm telling you, there's a plot to—"

"Yes, I do know you," interrupted Ormond, pinning Henrik with his most disapproving frown. "And I know that you've always been irresponsible, and far more interested in adventure than reality." He glanced at Lady Claudette, his frown deepening. "And I know that the pursuit of a beautiful woman might justify in your mind behavior that I would consider entirely unacceptable."

Henrik ground his teeth. The sanctimonious prince didn't

know him at all if he really thought that. But it was about what he imagined Ormond's true opinion of him might be.

He didn't know whether to shout in frustration or to laugh derisively at Ormond's description of Lady Claudette as a beautiful woman. The prince was blinded, all right. And the more extreme his behavior became, the less Henrik could believe that it was prompted by a natural attraction. Whatever weapon Lady Claudette was employing, it was powerful. And Feivel and the others were clearly in on it. But what could Henrik do? If Ormond was under an enchantment of some kind, he wasn't going to be convinced by anything Henrik might say.

"Your Highness, I'm sorry to hear that you think my behavior was inappropriate," he said at last. "There's been a misunderstanding. My intention has only been to serve the crown, and to fulfill my duty as a member of the king's guard to protect our kingdom."

"Empty words," said Ormond dismissively. "I'm disappointed that you're not taking more responsibility. I had hoped you might be brought to see that you'd been in the wrong, and to apologize for your conduct toward Lady Claudette this morning. But if you persist in trying to disguise your own behavior with these outrageous accusations against her and her party, you will have to face the consequences."

"Consequences?" Henrik asked blankly.

"Surely you don't think I will simply let it go that you accosted the woman who will soon be my wife?" said Ormond sternly.

Henrik raised an eyebrow, his gaze transferring to Lady Claudette. He was past the point of being outraged by the accusation that he had forced his attention on her. "The woman who'll soon be your wife?" he repeated grimly. "How soon?"

Prince Ormond ignored him. "You will spend some time in the dungeon, to reflect on your choices."

"Surely he should be stripped of his position," interjected Lady Claudette, her eyes lingering triumphantly on Henrik. "Having failed so significantly in his *duty*, as he put it."

Henrik barely bit back a growl in time. The malicious little schemer.

"Sadly, that is not in my power," said Ormond tightly. "He is a member of the king's guard, and only my father can strip him of his position."

"But you're the crown prince," Lady Claudette pouted. "Surely you can exercise the same authority as the king, if he's not present to do it himself."

"I'm afraid it doesn't work that way," said Ormond patiently.

"Hm." Lady Claudette looked petulant, her displeasure at Ormond's lack of authority clear.

"I will speak to my father about it," said Ormond quickly.

If the situation hadn't been so serious, Henrik would have rolled his eyes. It was embarrassing to watch his future king making such a fool of himself over this childish pretender.

"Your Highness, there's been a misunderstanding," he tried again. "Let me speak to Prince Kincaid, and I'm sure he can—"

"I don't think so," said Ormond flatly. "Your friendship with my brother won't get you out of trouble this time."

"I should think not," said Lady Claudette, a sneer on her face. "Presumably that's how he got his position in the first place."

Henrik balled his hands into fists, controlling his anger with an effort.

"Most likely," agreed Prince Ormond dismissively. He nodded at the guards who were flanking the doorway. "Take him down to the dungeons."

"Wait!" said Henrik quickly, as the guards moved forward. "If you won't let me speak to Prince Kincaid, then I insist on speaking to the king."

"Certainly not," frowned Ormond.

"It's my right as a member of the king's elite," Henrik insisted. "To state my case before him in response to this accusation. You have no right to throw me in the dungeons without his approval."

Lady Claudette stepped forward slightly, raising an eyebrow. "You're going to let *him* tell you what authority you have? Is that the kind of leader you'll be?"

"Of course not," said Ormond quickly, glaring at Henrik. "Stop being so foolish. A few hours in the dungeons won't kill you. You're just making it worse for yourself."

Henrik's eyes were on Lady Claudette, and his unease grew at the unveiled smugness on her face. A few hours wouldn't do him any harm, it was true. But what might she be planning to achieve during that time? He had to speak to Kincaid.

But the guards, who were now standing ready on either side of him, stepped close at a nod from Prince Ormond. They were royal guards, not knights of the king's guard like Henrik was, but they were both known to him. And he could tell from their demeanor that they were uneasy with their prince's instructions. But of course neither of them was in a position to disobey.

They each placed a hand lightly under his elbow, and he submitted to their guidance without protest. His thoughts were racing, trying to figure out what he should do next, so he barely even glanced at the prince as he began to walk from the room.

But he did notice the displeasure on Lady Claudette's face. She was clearly not impressed with the lenient treatment her enemy was receiving, and the calculating look in her eyes filled Henrik with foreboding. He had underestimated her when he had thought she was only after the luxury of a royal position. This was someone who wanted power, and she wouldn't be satisfied with anything less than total control.

He remembered Feivel telling her that she had overestimated how much power the wife of the crown prince would hold. He had to agree with the guard, and he couldn't help but be apprehensive of what she might be willing to do to increase that power. It was clear from this encounter alone that she was dissatisfied both with Ormond's authority, and with his willingness to exercise it.

He and his escorts had only made it halfway out of the audience hall when all of these concerns were driven momentarily from Henrik's mind as the door to the corridor burst open.

CHAPTER NINETEEN

Henrik's heart leaped for a moment, hoping that Kincaid had come to intervene, or even King Malcolm. But he had no such luck.

He groaned quietly at the sight of Princess Lavinia, her astonished gaze passing from him to her brother up on the dais. She was the last person he wanted to witness this humiliating spectacle. Her opinion of him had already taken enough of a dive that day, and it wasn't as though she could help him, even if she'd been inclined to do so. There was no way Ormond would listen to her. He thought her as irresponsible as he thought Henrik.

Which was ironic, Henrik reflected, since she seemed to have been the first to recognize that something wasn't right about Lady Claudette. Well, the first except for Norik, perhaps. But the toddler always seemed to see things adults didn't.

"What in the kingdom is happening here?" Lavinia demanded blankly, her eyes on Henrik but her words addressed to her brother. "Ormond, what are you doing?"

"It's no concern of yours, Lavinia," said the crown prince dismissively.

"Are you..." Lavinia's gaze passed between the guards on either side of Henrik, her astonishment evident. "Are you having Henrik thrown into the dungeons?"

Henrik winced. It was somehow even more humiliating when he heard it said aloud. But he would expect nothing less than plain speaking from Lavinia.

"I am, and you can be sure I have good reason," said Ormond, his tone clearly designed to discourage further questions. "As I said, it's no concern of yours."

"Maybe not," Lavinia retorted, clearly far from discouraged. "But does Father know you're using his audience hall to pronounce judgment in his absence, and throwing one of his own knights into the dungeon?"

Ormond shifted uncomfortably, his frown deepening. "Stay out of this, Lavinia," he said, his tone defensive. "It's not a matter that's appropriate for you to get involved in."

Lavinia snorted. "Appropriate? I'm not a child, Ormond. What's he been accused of?"

Lady Claudette gave a tinkling laugh that made Henrik want to cover his ears. "My word, princesses are given a great deal of license in Valoria. I'm sure the royal family of my own kingdom would be astonished. Of course, King Abner's children are older now, with children of their own. It's hardly surprising if they're a little more...steady."

Lavinia narrowed her eyes at the Thoranian woman, but Ormond's frown was still directed toward his sister.

"On the contrary, age has nothing to do with it. We have high expectations of our princesses in Valoria as well. Unfortunately, my sister frequently needs reminding of that fact."

Lavinia tossed her head in a familiarly defiant gesture, her eyes narrower than ever.

"Do you think you could take me to the dungeons now?" Henrik muttered to one of the guards.

The man's lip twitched ever so slightly. Presumably he was as eager as Henrik was to avoid witnessing one of the sibling squabbles which had recently become more public among Valoria's royal family. Honestly, the dungeons seemed like an appealing alternative.

But for once, Princess Lavinia showed more restraint than her brother. She didn't speak immediately, taking a deep breath before repeating her question.

"What's he been accused of, Ormond?"

"If you must know," said the prince, his scowl growing heavy, "he accosted Lady Claudette in the public gardens this morning. And once she made it clear she wasn't interested in his attentions, he sought to make trouble for her and her servants, making all kinds of accusations against them."

Henrik wanted to sink through the floor, but he couldn't help himself from watching Lavinia for her reaction to the accusation. The princess's face had drained of color at the mention of the early morning meeting in the garden, and she was determinedly avoiding looking at him. But to her credit, despite her evident discomfort, her voice was steady.

"He accosted her, you say?" One eyebrow was meaningfully raised. "Forced his attention on her? It certainly didn't look that way to me."

"Didn't look that way to—Lavinia!"

Henrik was still facing the door, but he could hear the growing outrage in Ormond's voice.

"Are you telling me you actually witnessed the incident? Have you no shame?"

"I'm not sure why *I* should be embarrassed about your *betrothed*," the scorn in Lavinia's voice made Henrik wince again, "kissing another man in the gardens."

"How dare you?" Ormond said, sounding angrier than Henrik had ever heard him.

"The dungeons, I'm begging you," Henrik muttered to the guards, and with an uncertain glance back, they started to hustle him out of the room. To the clear relief of all three men, neither of the royals protested their exit.

"Henrik."

Henrik paused in the corridor, turning at the voice. He had momentarily forgotten about his fellow knight. The older man glanced at the guards, then spoke quickly, his voice low.

"I don't know what's going on here, but something is clearly amiss." He looked back toward the audience hall. "What do you want me to do for you, lad?"

"Find Prince Kincaid," said Henrik quickly. "Tell him what's happened. Tell him I need to speak with him urgently."

The knight nodded curtly, turning on his heel without another word. Henrik watched him go gratefully. Maybe they could still stop whatever disaster was looming.

The remaining three men made their way quickly to the dungeons. Henrik was grateful to the guards that, beyond removing his weapon, they didn't actually lay hands on him. But it was still mortifying how many people watched them march him to the dungeons, from wide-mouthed servants to scandal-loving courtiers. He would never live this down.

Although he'd been to the dungeons a number of times, he'd never actually been inside a cell before. It was cleaner than he expected, but there was still an unpleasantly lingering smell. The guards locked him in with expressions that were almost apologetic, then hurried out of the dungeon. Henrik sighed as he leaned against the bars, resigning himself to a long wait.

He was therefore pleasantly surprised after only about half an hour, when he heard a hurried step on the stairs leading down from the rest of the castle. Within moments, a familiar face appeared, and Henrik straightened, gripping the bars with both hands.

"Kincaid!"

"Henrik." His friend hurried the last few steps, gripping his arm through the bars. "This is a nightmare, I'm so sorry. I got you into this mess when I asked you to follow that Thoranian guard."

"Never mind me," said Henrik impatiently. "You got my message?"

Kincaid nodded. "Yes, your friend sought me out. Tell me everything."

"We were too late to actually follow Feivel out of the city," Henrik started, without preamble. "But I had a hunch that he might be headed for the spot where that last bandit attack happened. We went that way, and my hunch turned out to be right. I overheard him saying goodbye to whoever's in charge of the group that's hiding out there."

He did his best to recount the conversation, emphasizing the comments about revenge, and the intention that Lady Claudette would find powerful positions for the rest of the group once she was part of the royal family.

"Revenge for what?" asked Kincaid, nonplussed.

Henrik shrugged. "They didn't say. But that guard, Feivel, said something about having lost everything. I get the sense that not all of them—whoever they are—care about influence, or even gold. I think some of them just want blood. The other man said that the group didn't like being told not to get their hands dirty."

"And they really said they were the ones carrying out the bandit attacks?" Kincaid asked, frowning.

"Yes," Henrik confirmed grimly. "It's all been Lady Claudette, since the moment she arrived. And I have proof."

He told his friend quickly about the scars he'd seen on Feivel, and how he'd seen those same types of wounds the day they'd arrived home.

"He's the man I fought when I intercepted the attack on Lady Claudette, I know he is." He frowned. "Not that it was actually an attack, of course." He made an angry noise as something occurred to him. "That's why she fell out of the carriage at that inconvenient moment. It wasn't an accident at all—she knew exactly what she was doing. She had to stop me from unmasking him, and showing that he was one of her Thoranian companions."

He struck a hand against the bars uselessly. "If only I had! Her little game would have been over before it began."

"Well, unfortunately it's far from over," said Kincaid darkly. "Have you heard that Ormond is now declaring publicly that he intends to marry her?"

Henrik's scowl deepened. "He said something along those lines, yes."

Kincaid shook his head. "It makes no sense. Her behavior has only gotten more outrageous, but half the court are celebrating the betrothal as if it's excellent news. Some of Father's advisors are singing her praises, and even Father himself doesn't seem to realize what she really is." His expression grew dark. "I don't understand how they can all be so blind. Every time I see her with Ormond, it makes me angry. Angrier than I've felt in a long time."

Henrik raised an eyebrow. His normally easygoing friend certainly did look angry. He seemed to be taking the whole thing very personally. But Henrik didn't comment on that.

"There must be some enchantment at work," he said instead, frowning as he remembered his veiled discussion with Lady Claudette about a weapon of some sort. "It wouldn't be the first time someone brought magic here from the South Lands, intending to make mischief, would it?"

Kincaid grimaced at the reminder of Scanlon, the Balenan who had used dragon magic to insinuate himself in the Valorian court several years earlier. It was probably a particularly unpleasant memory for him, given that Scanlon had abducted Jocelyn while Kincaid was away from Bryford, almost certainly intending to kill her. Fortunately she'd been a lot more capable than Scanlon had bargained for.

"It wouldn't," the prince acknowledged. "But if it's magic, why are you and I not affected? I never fell under Scanlon's influence, but that was only because I had almost no exposure to him." He made a face. "I've had enough contact with Lady Claudette to last me a lifetime."

Henrik shuddered, the memory of her unwelcome kiss that morning rising forcibly to his mind. "So have I."

He remembered thinking that she looked confused as well as frustrated when she failed to captivate him with her flirting. Was that just because of his reputation? Or was it further proof of some kind of enchantment? One that for some reason he was immune to?

"I must confess, I didn't say anything about the suspicion of an enchantment to my parents," said Kincaid. "They still get very uncomfortable any time they're reminded of how completely they were taken in by Scanlon. It wasn't the proudest moment in our family's history. I think they'd be resistant to the suggestion that it's happening again. I was hoping you'd have more proof after following Feivel, and we could use it to convince them."

"I'm sorry I didn't actually see stronger evidence of the group," Henrik said heavily. "It seems that all I achieved was to give him and Lady Claudette a new sense of urgency." He paused. "And to make them both determined to get rid of me, in their different ways," he added grimly.

Kincaid shook his head. "It's not your fault. I'm just glad you took someone with you, or it sounds like you might not have made it back."

Henrik said nothing. The memory of Feivel besting him still rankled, in spite of the much larger issues at stake.

Kincaid sighed. "I did tell Father what you told me this morning. He agreed it didn't reflect well on her that she was discussing such things with her guard at midnight. But it wasn't enough to convince him of a plot. And there was no time to argue with him about it. I wasn't able to speak to him privately until hours after we spoke, and I'd barely finished repeating it all to him when we heard about Ormond's betrothal." The prince scowled. "We were both a little distracted after that."

"She certainly didn't waste any time," said Henrik, scowling himself.

"And she doesn't intend to waste any more," Kincaid agreed. "Ormond's pushing for an immediate wedding, but I guess we know who's really behind that." He rolled his eyes. "Ormond's never been in a hurry to do anything in his life. That's how we're all in this mess in the first place. He should be married by now, and then we wouldn't all be vulnerable."

"Or Lady Claudette would have just eliminated any obstacles in her path," said Henrik grimly. "I'm telling you, she's determined. More than I realized at first." He shook his head as he remembered not only her veiled comments to Feivel, but her manipulation of Henrik's apparently not-so-secret heartache, and her brazen accusation against him a short time before. "I don't think there's much she wouldn't do to get what she wants."

He frowned thoughtfully. "I'm not surprised she wants to secure Ormond straight away. Her guard said something about her needing to be married before the delegation arrives. I'm guessing there are some things that will come to light when Cody and the others get here."

Kincaid didn't seem to be paying much attention to his friend's musings, lost in thoughts of his own, but he looked up at Henrik's last comment. "That's still weeks away, though. I don't think we can hold off that long." His tone turned brisk. "The question is whether your word is enough to convince Father that Lady Claudette is behind the bandit attacks. Surely that would give him enough justification to delay the wedding while the matter can be properly investigated." He made a frustrated noise. "If only I could speak to him immediately."

"Why can't you?" asked Henrik, alarmed. "You should have seen Lady Claudette in the audience hall earlier. She was ready for war. I got the sense that there's no time to lose."

Kincaid shook his head. "I know there isn't, but Father isn't in Bryford right now. He may not seem to realize how awful Lady Claudette is, but he's certainly not blind to the ramifications of Ormond's infatuation. He rode out to meet with Lord Thornton as soon as Ormond made his announcement. I mean, my parents had basically finalized the betrothal between Ormond and Lady Brielle, and now they have to try to clean up Ormond's mess."

Henrik groaned. It wasn't a good time for King Malcolm to be absent from the city. But at least that explained why he hadn't been there to see Ormond using the royal audience hall to pass judgment, as if he was already king.

"He'll be back in a couple of hours, at most," Kincaid said. "And if I hurry, I can be back by then too."

"Back?" Henrik asked sharply. "Back from where?"

"I'm going after this group of renegades," said Kincaid grimly. "The knight who went with you this morning said he could find the place. I'm going to take a few squadrons, have them search the area thoroughly. If they haven't found anything by the time I need to return, I'll leave them to continue without me."

"I don't know, Kincaid," said Henrik slowly. "I don't like the idea of you putting yourself in danger. I'm telling you, we shouldn't underestimate how far these people are willing to go."

"I won't be in danger," said Kincaid dismissively. "Like I said, I'm taking three squadrons. And I won't even be doing the actual searching myself. But if we can find a group of armed Thoranians hiding out in the place where Lady Claudette's guard attacked you, it might be all we need to stop any wedding from taking place."

The prince glanced around, not waiting for a reply. "But what am I doing? You're still in the dungeon. Hi there!" He raised his voice. "Guard!"

After a moment, a guard came into view, making his way down the steps. "Your Highness?" the man asked cautiously.

"Let Lord Henrik out," said Kincaid imperiously. "This whole situation is ridiculous."

The guard swallowed, looking uncomfortable. "He's in there by order of the crown prince, Your Highness."

"Yes, I know that, thank you," said Kincaid impatiently. "But it's a mistake. I'll deal with Ormond."

"It's just..." The guard hesitated, his eyes passing nervously between the prince and the prisoner. "Prince Ormond gave very specific instructions about Lord Henrik's imprisonment. That is, instructions about any...intervention."

"What are you talking about?" Kincaid asked, looking perplexed, but Henrik was pretty sure he understood.

"Let me guess," he grunted, remembering Ormond's scathing comments in the audience hall. "He told the guards not to let my royal friend release me."

The guard acknowledged it with an uncomfortable one-shouldered shrug.

"He said what?" blustered Kincaid. "That puffed up—"

"Don't worry about it, Kincaid," Henrik said, cutting his friend off before he could say something about his brother that he might regret. Henrik knew from personal experience how quickly gossip could spread through the ranks of the guards. "It won't kill me to be in here for a little while. You can't afford to waste time on this."

Kincaid frowned, obviously not liking it, but looking as though he really was eager to be off.

"I'll be fine," Henrik said encouragingly, trying not to let it show on his face how unexcited he felt about the prospect of a prolonged stay in the dungeon.

"The whole thing is ridiculous," Kincaid muttered again.

He had turned to follow the guard, who had already hurried back up the stairs, but he hesitated.

"Oh," he said, glancing back at Henrik. "I forgot to ask. I assumed *she* wanted you thrown in here because you know too much, but Ormond was spouting some story about you insulting her. He talked on and on about how he wasn't going to tolerate it, but I couldn't get a straight story out of him. What was he talking about?"

Henrik rolled his shoulders uncomfortably. "She appeared this morning, after we spoke. I think her servant saw us, and reported it to her. She was trying to find out what I know." He scowled. "I stupidly thought I could be the one to find out what she was up to, and I let her lead me into the gardens. She sort of...threw herself at me." There was a moment of silence, and Henrik sighed at Kincaid's look of confusion. "She kissed me," he clarified. "Needless to say, it wasn't welcome."

Kincaid's bewilderment grew. "Why would she do that?"

Henrik shrugged, more uncomfortable than ever. Was it his imagination, or was it hotter in the dungeon than an underground room should be?

"I don't know," he hedged. "Maybe she foresaw the need to have something to accuse me of."

"Still seems odd," said Kincaid, frowning. "I mean, she's obviously telling a lot of lies. She could've just made something up without actually having to do it. With the state he's in, Ormond would swallow anything she told him."

"Probably," Henrik agreed evasively. "But I thought you were in a hurry."

"Oh, you're right," said Kincaid quickly, instantly distracted from the question. He cast his friend one more rueful glance. "I'm sorry to leave you in here. When my father gets back, we'll sort out this whole mess."

Henrik waved him off. Being stuck in the dungeons was slightly less frustrating if it got him out of explaining to Kincaid exactly why Lady Claudette had considered it an effective attack to kiss him at that particular moment.

There was no longer any reason to wait hopefully at the bars. He settled himself in the corner of the cell, suspecting that Kincaid had been optimistic in estimating that the king would return in only two hours. Lord Thornton's lands were some distance from the capital. And who knew how long it would take for Henrik to be released after that? With everything going on, he didn't expect his situation to be the king's top priority.

He sighed as he leaned against the wall, trying to get comfortable on the straw scattered across the stone floor. Valoria's royals weren't generally given to throwing people in the dungeons, and he had no company down there. Even the guard remained out of sight at the top of the stairs.

It was hard to judge time in a windowless dungeon, but Henrik was certain, when he heard the guard hailing someone, that it hadn't yet been two hours. Maybe half that time. Certainly not long enough for Kincaid and his squadrons to reach the copse of trees and return to Bryford.

"Your Highness. Surely you don't wish to enter the dungeons?"

Henrik tilted his head to the side, frowning in confusion at the guard's salutation. Perhaps Jocelyn had emerged in order to try to get him released. His mood lifted instantly at the thought. It would be like the kind-hearted princess, and the guard might find it hard to say no to her.

"Obviously I wish to enter the dungeons, or I wouldn't be here."

Henrik's hopeful mood disappeared instantly at the familiar —and clearly unimpressed—voice. It was a princess, all right, but not one who was currently inclined to be kind to him.

CHAPTER TWENTY

Apparently the guard made no attempt to actually prevent the princess's passage, because a moment later Lavinia's slim form appeared at the top of the steps. Henrik scrambled to his feet, trying to muster whatever shreds of dignity he had left to him.

Lavinia paused when she caught sight of him, her expression difficult to read as she hovered at the bottom of the stairs. Henrik watched her warily. When she showed no sign of breaking the silence, he cleared his throat.

"Princess Lavinia. What uh…what brings you here?"

"You, obviously," she said, her voice a little softer than he'd expected. She glanced around. "There isn't really any other competition, is there?"

Henrik gestured to the empty dungeon, a rueful smile on his face. "No, down here I seem to be the king."

Lavinia regarded him in silence for a moment, and when she spoke, her tone was brisk.

"I came because I want to talk to you about that scene in the audience hall."

Henrik grimaced at the reminder that she had seen the humiliating display.

"I want you to explain what Ormond said, about why you've been put in here."

Henrik scowled. "What is there to explain? It's all lies, but if you wouldn't believe me when I told you this morning, I don't know why you would now." He paused, shifting his feet uncomfortably. "Thank you, by the way. For speaking up for me. I know you don't believe me when I say I'm not interested in Lady Claudette, but I'm glad you still know me well enough to know I wouldn't force my attention on a woman who—"

"I don't want to talk about that," Lavinia cut him off ruthlessly. The softness was gone from her expression. "I want to talk about the other part. Ormond said that you'd been making accusations against her, and her servants. I want to know what you're accusing them of."

"Oh." Henrik blinked, trying to adjust his mind to the conversation's abrupt change in direction. "They're plotting. Against the crown."

Lavinia inclined her head expectantly. "Can you be a little more specific?"

Henrik let out a sigh of frustration, running a hand through his hair. "Not as specific as I'd like to be. I know she's plotting to marry Ormond, and get a crown."

"Yes, I think we'd all figured that out," said Lavinia dryly. "I assume there's more to your accusations than that, or she wouldn't have had you thrown in the dungeons."

"So you know she's behind it?" Henrik said eagerly, gripping the bars as he leaned toward her. "Then you must know that there's nothing romantic between us. It was all a scheme on her part, to try to discredit me, so that I—"

"I know my brother," Lavinia said, cutting him off again. "And I know this isn't him. As much as I want to throttle him half the time, he's not this unreasonable, this closed to all criticism. I can see that he's her puppet. What I don't know is how."

"I don't know that either," said Henrik, frowning. "Although Kincaid and I suspect there's some enchantment at work."

Lavinia's expression mirrored his. "The same thing has occurred to me," she said. "But I can't find any proof of it." She looked at him thoughtfully. "Is that what you accused her of? No wonder Ormond looked ready to murder you."

"No, of course not," said Henrik quickly. "I'm not a fool, and I could see there was no point trying to make him see reason where Lady Claudette is concerned. But I tried to tell him that her guard met with a group of others this morning, and that they're the ones who've been carrying out these bandit attacks. And that when I overheard them, he attacked me."

"Attacked you?" Lavinia repeated, startled. Her eyes roamed over his form, as if she expected a nasty injury to suddenly appear. "Were you hurt?"

Henrik shrugged an impatient shoulder. "It was my fault for being careless. I had him disarmed, but I let myself get distracted, so he knocked me out."

Lavinia's eyes were wide, and in spite of his impatience, Henrik couldn't help but be warmed by the concern in her eyes.

"Never mind that," he said. "Do you know what's happening up there?" He jerked a head toward the ceiling of the dungeon. "Did you speak to Kincaid before he left?"

"Kincaid?" Lavinia said, looking confused. "No. Is that why I couldn't find him? Where did he go?"

"He took a few squadrons to try to find the group of Thoranians who've been hiding outside the city. At the moment the only proof we have that they're behind the bandit attacks is my word." He glanced ruefully around his accommodations. "And my word isn't worth a great deal right now. Kincaid was hoping to be back by the time your father reached Bryford."

"Well, I wouldn't be surprised," said Lavinia, her brow creased. "I can't imagine that Father will be able to straighten this mess out in a hurry."

"Yes, I heard about the betrothal," said Henrik grimly. "I'm guessing Lord Thornton isn't too happy about his daughter being jilted."

Lavinia shook her head. "I didn't mean the betrothal, although there's also that. I was talking about Ormond's little scene with the farmers."

"What do you mean?" Henrik asked quickly. "You mean his comments at that luncheon?"

"You haven't heard?" Lavinia raised an eyebrow. "It's much worse than that. Ormond—or I guess we should say his puppet master—called a meeting with the key farmers from Lord Thornton's lands this morning. Neither of my parents knew about it. He accused the farmers of wreaking havoc in the city, and said that the offer of aid was being withdrawn."

Henrik felt his own eyes going wide. Kincaid had failed to mention that aspect of Ormond's behavior, apparently too distracted by his anger at Lady Claudette. "He told them he suspected them of being behind the attacks?"

Lavinia shook her head. "He didn't go quite that far. He just said that the crown was looking into certain accusations about their conduct." She made a noise of disgust. "According to one of my maids, the gossip among the servants is that Her High and Mightiness wasn't satisfied even with that. She was in a bit of a huff that he didn't do more."

"Just like with my 'punishment' earlier," muttered Henrik grimly. It wasn't a good sign as to what it would be like if Lady Claudette were to achieve a position of greater power.

"Anyway," Lavinia continued, "when my father found out, he overruled Ormond at once. That's the other reason he went out himself to Lord Thornton's lands. To reassure the farmers that the offer of assistance hasn't actually been revoked."

"Did he contradict Ormond publicly?" Henrik asked, an ominous feeling growing inside him.

Lavinia nodded, her expression uncharacteristically grave. "I think it hurt him more than Ormond to do it. Ormond's always been so steady, so reliable. But I guess he couldn't just let it go. Lady Claudette was furious. To be honest, I think he was trying to prove something to her more than to Ormond. To show her that she's not going to get her way just because she has Ormond wrapped around her finger."

"That's what I'm afraid of," said Henrik, running a hand through his hair.

"What do you mean?" Lavinia frowned, watching Henrik as he stepped back from the bars, striding up the confined space and back.

"I mean he's demonstrated to her that as long as he's around, she won't have the power she wants, even married to Ormond."

Lavinia shrugged. "Why is that a bad thing? Maybe if she realizes it's not worth her while, she'll back off."

"I don't think so," said Henrik grimly. He remembered Lady Claudette's casual comment to Feivel in the gardens, that neither of them knew how soon she might be queen. It had unnerved him at the time, for reasons he couldn't put his finger on. But after watching her with Ormond today, he thought he under-stood her better.

He had admired her for her determination once. The admi-ration had been artificial, but the determination had been real. He had told Kincaid that he didn't think there was much she wouldn't do to achieve her ends, and he had meant it.

"You say King Malcolm rode out to Lord Thornton's lands himself?" Henrik asked suddenly.

"Yes," said Lavinia, still frowning. "He left hours ago, though. He might be on his way back by now."

"And everyone knows that he went?"

"I think so. You know how quickly news spreads in the castle, and it was a bit of a scene earlier." Lavinia raised her eyebrow. "What are you getting at?"

"But he took guards with him, didn't he?" Henrik asked, his anxiety growing. The bars of his cell were starting to chafe. He longed to be out, to have his sword in his hand. "He didn't travel alone?"

"Of course he didn't travel alone," said Lavinia, starting to sound unnerved. "He would have taken some of his personal guards with him. But I can't imagine he was expecting trouble. I mean, surely the bandits wouldn't be bold enough to attack the king! And even if they were, there have only ever been what, four or five of them? Father's guards could take care of them in a heartbeat."

"But they're not really bandits, remember?" Henrik argued. "The attacks were all staged! It's Lady Claudette behind it. And we don't know how many men she really has with her."

A chill passed over him as he remembered the conversation between Feivel and the other man, just that morning. The guard had said that everyone was to be ready for action at a moment's notice. He had also said that the king was used to trusting Ormond's judgment. Feivel—and presumably his mistress—had seemed to believe that the prince's power was enough to get Lady Claudette whatever she wanted, as long as she controlled him. And now King Malcolm had proved that belief wrong.

What was the phrase Feivel had used? *If we keep her path clear, we'll get what's due to us.* Just how far would these men go to clear Lady Claudette's path to power?

Remembering how Feivel's companion had said the men were spoiling for revenge, and wanted the chance to get their hands dirty, Henrik had a horrifying suspicion that he had his answer.

"Lavinia," said Henrik suddenly, meeting her eyes. "I have a very bad feeling about this. I need to get out of here." He took a breath. "I know this is going to sound outrageous."

Lavinia gave a dry chuckle. "I don't have any problem with outrageous."

In spite of everything, Henrik almost smiled at the truth of that statement. Some of the sparkle was back in Lavinia's eyes. But the situation was too serious for distraction.

"I think Lady Claudette is going to try to have your father killed. Another bandit attack maybe, or an unlucky accident."

All hint of humor was gone from the princess's face. "She can't, surely. She's here at the castle, with Ormond. She never leaves his side now."

Henrik gripped the bars, shaking his head in frustration. "I don't mean she'll do it personally. She'll have her henchmen make the attempt. And if they've harnessed some kind of magic, they might even be able to succeed."

Lavinia didn't answer immediately, her face unusually pale.

"Do you really think his life is in danger?" she asked at last. "This isn't some kind of prejudice, or revenge, because of whatever's been going on between you and Lady Claudette?"

"Of course not!" said Henrik, frustrated. "Do you think I would make light of something like this? We're talking about regicide! He might be your father, but he's also my king!" He beat a fist against the embroidered emblem on his livery. "I took an oath when I joined the king's guard, to protect the crown, with my life if necessary."

He paced away again, running a hand through his hair as he let out a frustrated noise. "For the first time since I took that oath, I genuinely believe the king's life is in danger. And I can't do anything about it locked in this dungeon!" He drew a long breath, his voice turning to a mutter. "The worst of it is, it's my own fault I'm in here. I only have myself to blame that apparently it's not difficult to believe I would go to any lengths to throw myself at the latest girl to dance across the court."

He stopped pacing, returning his gaze to Lavinia with an effort. The princess was watching him thoughtfully, having listened in silence to his tirade.

"Lavinia," he said quietly. "I know you don't want to hear it. But I still need to say it. There's nothing between me and Lady Claudette. There never was. I've known for some time that she was up to something, and that's why I was with her this morning. I was trying to find out what, but she bested me." He gritted his teeth at the memory. "I made it too obvious that I suspected her, and that's why she did what she did. To try to silence me."

Lavinia let him speak without interruption, but she was frowning by the end of his account.

"That doesn't make sense to me. I still can't see why she would kiss you. How would that silence you?"

Henrik rolled his shoulders, torn between relief that the princess was finally hearing him out, and discomfort at being forced to make himself vulnerable yet again.

"She only did it because you were there," he said shortly. "She's more cunning than you realize. I don't think she misses much, and she knew it would hurt me more than any other type of attack."

For a moment his words hung between them, the silence stretching out uncomfortably. Henrik forced himself to look Lavinia in the eye, but he couldn't read her expression.

"Well," she said at last. "You're right that this isn't a matter to take lightly. If you really think my father is in danger, this is no time to argue about motivations." She frowned. "The trouble is, with Ormond useless and Kincaid not here, we don't have a lot of options. Let's be honest—no one's going to take me seriously if I try to mobilize a squadron to go after Father."

"And as we've already established, my word isn't currently much good either," said Henrik heavily, casting another glance around his cell.

"Well, we'll just have to do it ourselves," said Lavinia briskly.

Henrik looked at her blankly. "Do what?"

"Go after Father and, I don't know, save the day."

"But..." Henrik fought a mad desire to laugh as Lavinia raised her eyebrows expectantly. "But you can't really fight, and I'm, you know...stuck in here."

"Unhelpful on both counts, I agree," said Lavinia, still speaking in that decisive tone. "I'm still furious that Mother and Father wouldn't let me be trained in swordsmanship, even after learning that Jocelyn had been taught to fight from a young age." The princess rolled her eyes. "Some nonsense about her being more responsible with a weapon than I would be."

Henrik's lip twitched slightly. He couldn't deny that he could see the sovereigns' point. But in all honesty, he found the thought of Lavinia armed and capable quite enchanting. There was no doubt she had the determination necessary to pursue extended training.

"But as for you," the princess was pushing on, "it's not an insurmountable barrier. Surely we can get you out of there."

Henrik sighed, flicking the fingers of one hand against the bars in irritation. "Kincaid already tried. Apparently your dear oldest brother was very insistent that I be left in here, and the guard wouldn't budge."

"Ah, but that was Kincaid," said Lavinia, her dimple appearing. "He doesn't have the...talents I have."

Henrik frowned. "What's that supposed to mean?" he asked ominously.

Lavinia laughed, a roguish sparkle in her eyes. "I saw the guard on duty. I don't think I'll have any trouble."

"Lavinia," started Henrik warningly, but she was already on her way to the stairs, tossing her hair mischievously. The minutes she was gone somehow felt longer than the hours that had come before them, Henrik pacing his cell fretfully.

But eventually she reappeared, looking triumphant. Henrik raised an eyebrow, and she grinned, lifting a ring of keys with a satisfying jangle.

"How did you—?" Henrik protested, but she just shrugged, a smile lingering on her lips. Her eyes were sparkling more than ever, and Henrik could only shake his head. She was dangerously attractive when she was in this humor, there was no denying it.

Although perhaps that was because she was his liberator. As the door of the cell finally swung open, it was all Henrik could do not to sweep her into his arms with a cry of grateful delight. But he wasn't at all sure how that would be received, so instead he swung his arms awkwardly, stretching as though he'd been locked in a box rather than a cell.

"Thank you," he said, trying not to stare at the princess.

She suddenly felt tantalizingly close, with no bars to separate them. The only things separating them now, he thought ruefully, were her status and her parents' opinion of him. And his uncertainty about her true feelings toward him, of course. Not to mention her anger and suspicion over the whole incident with Lady Claudette.

So still a bit to contend with.

"Shall we?" she asked, tilting her head toward the stairs.

Henrik nodded mutely, falling a step behind her as they made for the exit. Was he supposed to be sneaking past the guard, or had the man willingly given Lavinia the keys?

But Lavinia's step was too confident for deception. Besides, Henrik reflected, that wasn't really her style.

He tried to mimic her certainty, although he avoided looking the guard in the eye as he collected his sword from where it had been placed, pending his release. He couldn't help overhearing Lavinia's parting words, however.

"Thank you," the princess was saying brightly, "for being so brave."

Henrik barely refrained from rolling his eyes as he followed Lavinia out of the dungeon. A glance back showed that the guard looked a little awestruck, and Henrik felt a stirring of sympathy for the young man. He would probably get in trouble for this, but the stakes were too high to worry about such things.

They picked up their pace as soon as they emerged into a corridor on the ground floor of the castle. Lavinia looked over at Henrik, grinning as she caught his expression.

"What?"

"Do I even want to know?" he asked dryly.

She chuckled, tossing her hair over her shoulder. "Probably not."

Henrik shook his head, not sure whether to be amused or irritated. "You're outrageous, Princess."

"You're one to talk," scoffed Lavinia, and Henrik let the matter drop.

After all, he reminded himself grimly as they hurried toward the royal stables, there were more important matters to worry about.

CHAPTER TWENTY-ONE

Henrik glanced back toward Bryford, trying to calculate their chances of intercepting the king before he left Lord Thornton's lands.

Not good, was his guess. The afternoon was wearing on, and it was all too likely that King Malcolm and his guards had begun their journey to the capital long before Henrik and Lavinia even set out. If Henrik's fear was justified, and Lady Claudette's henchmen intended to attack the group while they were on the road, relatively vulnerable, then it was impossible to guarantee the groups would cross paths before that happened.

Henrik couldn't help fretting, worried that they'd taken too long to leave Bryford. But while Lavinia had done whatever she'd done in order to appear at their meeting place outside the city with no chaperone, he'd thought it worthwhile to make some inquiries of his own. He'd needed to be careful, of course, since he wasn't certain who knew that he was supposed to be locked in the dungeon. He wasn't entirely sure what would happen if someone alerted Lady Claudette to his escape, but he didn't want to find out.

Fortunately, however flighty the court might think him,

Henrik had the respect of the guards, and many of the servants. He also knew where to go to discreetly find the type of information he wanted. That was how he'd learned that Feivel had left the capital, again heading north, almost as soon as Henrik and the other knight had entered it that morning. A discovery that, while it justified the delay, sharpened Henrik's alarm considerably.

If Feivel had gone straight back to his men with instructions to lay a trap for the king, the Thoranian renegades were probably gone from their hideout before Kincaid ever reached them. The prince and his squadrons would be searching fruitlessly, while an unknown number of attackers were on their way to ambush the king.

Henrik pulled his gaze away from the city behind him, his eyes falling on Lavinia. She was riding beside him, her expression intent as she urged her horse forward. He hadn't been riding with her since she was much younger, and he had to admire her horsemanship. No one would guess that she was riding a random mare the friendly young groom had saddled up for Henrik in the royal stables, rather than her own familiar mount. Her hair streamed behind her, the unrestrained tresses glinting red and gold in the afternoon sunlight, seeming, as always, like the embodiment of her irrepressible spirit.

"What?" she asked, suddenly glancing over and catching him looking. "Are you worried that we made the wrong decision not to try to gather a squadron? I'm telling you, you would have just ended up back in the dungeons." She grimaced. "And I would probably have been locked in my rooms."

Henrik shook his head, reflecting ruefully that it was all too likely. "No, I wasn't thinking that. The slim chance of anyone believing us wasn't worth the time it would take to argue about it." He hesitated. "Although I do wonder if we should have reported our suspicions to the queen."

"Trust me," said Lavinia dryly. "Mother is the last person we should have gone to if we didn't want to be held up for hours. I don't think she would have taken our suspicions very seriously, somehow. Apparently she wasn't too impressed about Kincaid racing off to follow up the rumor of a group hiding out to the north east. But she didn't actually try to stop him—believe me when I tell you that she wouldn't have shown the same forbearance with me."

Henrik nodded, not doubting the princess's assessment for a moment. "Or with me, I imagine," he said. "Honestly, I think I was lucky to make it out of Bryford without being apprehended by one of Ormond's people. If I'm any judge, the guard on duty had a pretty good idea that I wasn't supposed to be leaving. I'm just fortunate I know him well, and he was willing to turn a blind eye."

Lavinia nodded. "So what is it, then?" she pressed, after a moment. "You were giving me the strangest look." Her forehead suddenly creased in a frown. "I hope you weren't going to say something enraging, like that I should have stayed behind, or—"

"I wasn't," Henrik cut her off, laughing in spite of himself at her scowl. "When have I ever tried to restrain you?"

"Never, I suppose," said Lavinia fairly, tilting her head to the side as she considered the point.

"I wouldn't be so foolish," said Henrik, smiling slightly.

I was only staring at you because everything about you is glorious, he added silently. But he knew how unlikely Lavinia was to believe that extravagant compliments coming from him were sincere, so he kept it to himself.

"I was wondering how in the kingdom you're riding out of the city without an escort," he said instead.

Lavinia flashed him a grin. "What do you mean? Aren't you my escort?"

"Somehow I don't think my presence would make it better in anyone's mind," he said dryly.

Lavinia chuckled. "Probably not."

"I meant—"

"I know what you meant," she interjected with a smile. "I have my ways. I'm generally acknowledged in my family to be by far the most skilled at giving my minders the slip. Not that most of them see it as a quality, but I think Joss and Kincaid are sometimes a little envious of what I get away with."

Henrik shook his head. "Your guards can't be very good at their role. How haven't they learned your tricks by now? I mean, you could be anywhere at this moment, and they would have no way of knowing if you were in danger, let alone protecting you."

Lavinia narrowed her eyes, although there was still a twinkle lurking there. "You're starting to sound strangely like my mother."

Henrik frowned, thinking that he'd never been more in sympathy with Valoria's austere queen. He'd never thought twice about Lavinia's antics before, but somehow her ability to shrug off her protectors was suddenly more alarming than entertaining.

"Well," he said gruffly, "I still say your guards don't deserve their position. If I had the job of protecting you, I wouldn't be so useless."

"Wouldn't you?" said Lavinia, with a hint of humor.

Henrik didn't answer immediately, returning his eyes to the road as unease curled in his stomach. He was well aware that there was an edge of guilt to his disapproval of her guards' failure.

"I know you'll be angry with me for saying it," he said at last. "But if I thought I could get away with it, I would have tried to leave you behind."

He glanced over, and saw her eyes narrowing.

"Don't eat me," he said quickly. "It's not that I think you're helpless, or that I don't want you here." He sighed. "I hope I'm wrong about my fears, but if I'm not, I'm leading you into danger, and that scares me more than all the rest."

Lavinia was silent for a moment, as Henrik wrestled with his thoughts.

"But the truth is," he said gruffly. "I need you." He looked at her again, and saw that she was raising an eyebrow. "I mean," he hastened to add, "even if we reach the group in time, I don't have any proof. Your father's guards probably won't listen to me, and your father has no reason to take me seriously. But I doubt any of them will ignore you."

"Good to know I have some purpose," said Lavinia curtly, sounding less than impressed. "I am curious to know how you think you could have stopped me coming, if you'd decided I wasn't useful after all."

"I doubt I could have stopped you," Henrik said, smiling slightly in an attempt to soften his admission that he wished he'd been able to leave her behind. "To be fair, it's a bit of a stretch to say that I'm leading you anywhere. Without your help, I'd still be pacing the dungeon. So I guess it's really the other way around."

"Should I be apologizing for leading you into danger, then?" Lavinia asked, a hint of her usual good humor returning. But a moment later her face was serious again. "You're not wrong that actually leaving the city is being a little more outrageous than normal."

She shrugged a shoulder. "There'll be a tremendous fuss made when I get back." She paused. "That is, if this turns out to be a false alarm." She was silent for a moment, her eyes on the road ahead of them. "And yet, I wouldn't mind that." She looked over at Henrik, her dimple gone and her expression troubled.

"You really think these renegades are going to ambush Father, don't you?"

Henrik nodded, all other concerns disappearing at this reminder of what they were doing. "I really do."

Lavinia gave a single decisive nod, her characteristic determination clear in her eyes. Without another word, she spurred her horse forward, and Henrik matched her pace. Soon they were riding too fast for speech to be practical, and the capital rapidly fell away behind them.

They covered the ground quickly, and Henrik was encouraged by the fairly regular appearance of other travelers on the road. Surely if a disaster was waiting for them up ahead, people wouldn't be traveling to and fro as normal. But after almost half an hour of hard riding, Henrik's muscles tensed at the sight of a pair of horsemen approaching. Their familiar livery identified them even from a distance as members of King Malcolm's personal guard.

"Lavinia," he said sharply, reining his horse in to a trot.

The princess followed his gaze, and he heard her draw a sharp breath as she also slowed.

"Where's Father?"

Henrik shook his head, his expression grim. The king's absence was conspicuous. They both pulled their mounts into the middle of the road, making it impossible for the guards to bypass them.

"Hi there," Henrik called, as soon as the men were close enough. "Where's His Majesty?"

The guards pulled up, looking confused. Henrik recognized one of them, a middle aged man who'd been a member of the king's personal guard for years. But the man didn't respond to him, his eyes skating over the knight to land with evident surprise on Henrik's companion.

"Your Highness?" The man's raised eyebrow said it all. "Is all well?"

"I hope so," said Lavinia tersely. "Where's my father?"

The man glanced between them again, looking bewildered but—to Henrik's relief—not alarmed. Surely nothing dire could have befallen the king if his guards were this relaxed.

"His Majesty is further back up the road," he said. "With the rest of his guards."

"Why have you separated?" Lavinia asked, her voice infused with unexpected authority.

"His horse threw a shoe, Your Highness," the guard responded. "Since we're so close to the capital, he instructed us to ride ahead and return with another mount rather than risk causing injury to the beast."

Henrik and Lavinia exchanged a look, the princess's eyes mirroring the alarm Henrik felt. How often did the king's horse throw a shoe? Henrik wished he could believe it was a coincidence, but he couldn't shake the thought that the Thoranians were known for their skill with horses. It was all much too convenient. He looked between the two guards. Normal protocol would be for the sovereign to travel with six guards. That left only four protecting King Malcolm. It wasn't enough.

"So the king is just waiting around on the highway?" he demanded.

The older guard bristled at his accusatory tone. But after a glance at the princess, he evidently accepted that he had to answer. Henrik had been right—her presence was clearly the only reason they were getting any information from the guards at all.

"Of course not," he said gruffly. "There was a small side road near where we stopped. King Malcolm and the other guards were going to stop a little way up the lane, off the main thoroughfare."

Henrik didn't need to look at Lavinia this time—the hiss of her breath between her teeth told him that she had reached the same realization as him. It sounded like the perfect set up for an ambush.

"How long ago did you part ways?" he asked urgently.

The guards exchanged a glance, clearly unsettled by his change in tone. The second guard, who had so far been silent, spoke up.

"Not long. Not much more than five minutes, I'd say."

Henrik's heart beat uncomfortably in his throat. Maybe it wasn't too late. "Never mind getting the king a new mount," he said quickly. "We have reason to believe His Majesty's life is in danger. We need to go to his aid at once."

"But—" The guards exchanged another look, but Henrik wasn't paying attention to them.

"On second thought," he said, frowning, "one of you should continue to Bryford with all possible speed. Bring back a squadron."

"Bring back a squadron?" repeated the first guard. "On whose authority are we supposed to do that? Yours?"

"Never mind the posturing," cut in Lavinia sharply. "Just do as Lord Henrik says." Her gaze passed to the second guard. He was younger, and looked stronger, and Henrik could only assume she had decided he was most likely to be useful in a fight. "And you can show us where my father is."

"Yes, Your Highness," said the guard, again proving Lavinia's usefulness to the mission. He glanced briefly at his superior before wheeling his horse around. "Follow me."

The older guard still looked less than impressed—after all, princess or not, Lavinia actually had no more authority than Henrik to give orders to a member of King Malcolm's personal guard. But he made no effort to stop them.

Henrik assumed the man would continue on to Bryford, but

he didn't wait to make sure. Reaching the king was more pressing. If they could beat the renegades there, they would remove the element of surprise, and the numbers might not be so crucial. But were they too late to beat them there? How precisely could Feivel and his men plan this type of sabotage? Henrik wished he knew more about horses.

They pushed their horses as quickly as the public road allowed, and it was less than five minutes before the guard, riding just ahead of them, pointed silently to a laneway coming off the side of the main thoroughfare.

Henrik strained his ears for any sounds of conflict as they started down the laneway, but he couldn't hear anything out of the ordinary. After a few more minutes, a small group of men came into sight, dismounted and lingering in the shade of a large apple tree. Henrik's heart leaped at the sight of his king, clearly unharmed. He checked his pace slightly, for the first time realizing the potential for humiliation if all his fears proved groundless. But if there was any chance the king was in danger, it was a risk worth taking.

"Your Majesty," he said, spurring his horse forward again as he drew close to the group.

King Malcolm looked up, his gaze passing from the guard in front to the knight behind him, a look of blank surprise on his face.

"Lord Henrik? What are you—" The king's words cut off as his eyes flicked to the third rider, and a look of long-suffering came over his face. "Lavinia," he said, his voice a little sharper. "What's going on?"

"Father," Lavinia started, her voice holding the same relief Henrik was feeling. "We thought that—"

Before she could finish, the distant sound of thundering hoofs reached Henrik's ears. He surged forward, acting on instinct without even turning toward the sound.

"Your Majesty, mount your horse!" he cried. "You're in danger!"

He swung his own horse around, hoping the king was taking him seriously, but not able to afford the time to convince him. King Malcolm was far too vulnerable on the ground, and Henrik needed to cover him for long enough to allow him to remount.

He heard sounds of astonishment—and amusement if he wasn't mistaken—from a couple of the king's personal guards, but he kept his eyes ahead. The hoof beats were growing louder, their source hidden behind a bend in the lane.

"Lavinia," he said tensely, suddenly remembering the princess's presence with a spike of alarm. "Get behind me, with your father."

"Henrik—"

"Please." His eyes flicked from the road, latching on to hers as he cut off her protest. For a moment he forced himself to disregard everything else, trying to put the full weight and sincerity of his emotion into his gaze. "If not for yourself, do it for me. Please."

For a moment Lavinia was frozen, several emotions following one another across her face as her eyes searched Henrik's. But the earnestness of his tone seemed to penetrate through her natural stubbornness. With a curt nod, she sprang into action, pushing her horse toward her father.

Henrik turned away, his relief and gratitude quickly swallowed in the grim determination that always gripped him at the prospect of a fight. He drew his sword purposefully. He knew that as soon as the attackers rounded that corner, there would be no room for other considerations. All the more reason to be glad one of the royals at least had taken his warning seriously. He would have to trust Lavinia to convince her father of the urgency of the situation.

His focus was on the approaching riders, still not visible, but

Henrik was still aware of his more immediate surroundings. He knew that only a couple of the guards had gathered around their king, the others muttering among themselves at the audacity of the young knight in instructing his sovereign.

But there was no time to convince them. The next instant, the approaching group finally came into view. Henrik gripped his sword grimly. As he had expected, their faces were swathed in fabric. His eyes passed over the would-be bandits quickly, ignoring the shocked cries of the guards. His heart lifted as he counted only half a dozen of them. Fewer than he had feared.

"The bandits?" The voice of one of the guards reached him through the scuffle of movement that signaled that they were finally forming up. "They would dare to attack the king?"

"They're not bandits," Henrik said curtly, without looking back. "It's a front—they're here to kill the king."

CHAPTER TWENTY-TWO

There was no chance to assess the impact of his words. The group was almost upon them now, and Henrik pushed his horse forward, determined to put some distance between the king and the inevitable fight.

He knew a brief moment of regret that he didn't have his lance with him. Nevertheless, he wouldn't relinquish the benefit of being mounted if he could possibly avoid it. At least none of the approaching riders seemed to be carrying the longer weapons either. Pushing such thoughts aside, he swung his sword meaningfully, letting out a cry of challenge as he charged the man leading the group of renegades.

The supposed bandit faltered, his surprise at the preemptive attack evident even with his face covered. The moment of hesitation was all Henrik needed. Wielding his sword skillfully, he pushed past the man's hasty defense, running his weapon through the man's shoulder and twisting it mercilessly.

It was an attack that Henrik knew wouldn't be fatal, but would remove the man from the fight. He would settle for any outcome that saw the king and the princess emerge unharmed, but hopefully, if at least one of the Thoranians survived, they could get some answers as well.

He yanked his sword free, turning his attention to the next rider without pausing to watch as the first man toppled from his horse with an anguished cry. The next man was ready for him, steel clashing on steel as he raised his sword to deflect Henrik's attack.

Henrik heard battle cries arising—somewhat belatedly—from King Malcolm's guards behind him, and he pulled back from his fight. With him there to replace the missing guard, they should be able to form a loose ring around the royals, as they had all been trained to do.

He fell back, glancing behind him to make sure he was moving in the correct formation. His eyes caught on Lavinia, sitting atop her horse beside her father, who was thankfully now mounted as well. A shot of equal parts fear and pride surged through him at the sight of her calm, still figure, clutching a dagger she had produced from who knew where.

He ripped his gaze away, pushing all distractions aside as he raised his sword with renewed vigor. As he watched, another attacker fell to the guard who had ridden back with Henrik and Lavinia. The group was clearly faltering, and Henrik's heart leaped hopefully. Perhaps being ready to fight back was all it would take.

But even as the optimistic thought flashed across his mind, his sharp ears picked out the sound of more horses approaching. Within moments, another half a dozen masked riders appeared, from the opposite direction from their fellows, to swell the numbers of the attackers. Henrik's heart plummeted at how uneven the fight was about to become. Even if the other guard returned to Bryford at full speed and managed to rally a squadron, they wouldn't arrive in time to make a difference.

He swung his sword again, his eyes on the new arrivals. It

was up to him and the others, then. There was no outside help coming. With the thought came a surge of fresh determination. He drew on that wave, all fear and calculations falling away as he let the fight take his full focus. As the first of the riders reached him, he stopped thinking even of what was at stake. There was nothing but this moment, this swing of the sword, this deflection, this foe.

He fell on his enemy with ferocity, aware of the others fighting alongside him. He drew strength from their shared purpose without allowing himself to become distracted by whether his fellows were winning or losing their own battles.

His sword flashed in front of him as he brought it down with all his force again and again. The clash of metal was deafening as his opponent held him off with increasing desperation. Whether in strength or determination, Henrik soon outmatched the other man. The renegade's defense faltered, and Henrik brought his sword down in one final attack. This man wouldn't be surviving to answer any questions.

He turned his attention away at once. His fight had taken him around the circle, and he now found himself on the battle's other flank, where the new arrivals had appeared.

He glanced behind him to reassure himself that both King Malcolm and Lavinia were still unharmed. As he looked, he saw one of the masked attackers bring down a member of the king's private guard. The man surged forward, instantly taking advantage of the gap in the circle, and Henrik realized with a rush of alarm that he recognized the figure.

Strong, thickly muscled. Blood beginning to seep through one undamaged sleeve, as if an existing injury on the man's lower arm had reopened.

Feivel.

Henrik stifled an oath as he urged his horse into motion, determined not to let the Thoranian guard reach the king. Feivel must have been in the second group, waiting to emerge if backup was required. Henrik was sure he would have recognized him if he'd been part of the initial charge. They must have hoped that half a dozen would be enough—the smaller group was more credible in the role of bandits.

Henrik's alarm grew as Feivel's horse strained and plunged. The fighting had pushed the ring around the royals tighter than he realized, and the guard had almost reached his target. Henrik was out of time to cut him off. Pulling his horse alongside Feivel's, he launched himself from his saddle with a shout, gripping the guard with both arms from behind, pulling his adversary from the saddle.

Both men tumbled to the ground, and for a moment everything was a terrifying blur of stamping hooves and shocked shouts. Shaking his head clear, Henrik leaped to his feet, seizing his sword from where it had fallen beside him.

Feivel recovered himself just as quickly, grasping his own sword in one gloved hand as he turned to face his attacker with a growl. No part of the Thoranian's face was visible, but Henrik could tell from Feivel's posture that the guard had recognized his recurring adversary immediately.

Henrik didn't wait for any pleasantries this time. He lunged forward, slashing at Feivel's chest as he threw himself between the guard and the royals. Feivel met the challenge with brutal force, the larger man's strength more evident than it had ever been before. The Thoranian didn't intend to lose this fight.

Henrik deflected Feivel's blade, his sword flashing rapidly as he employed every trick he knew to conserve his energy while still holding the stronger man off. Feivel attempted a feint, but Henrik's scrutiny was too sharp, his whole focus on the fight. He recognized the bluff easily, driving his sword toward Feivel's suddenly exposed side with lightning speed.

The older man brought his blade around rapidly, but not

quickly enough to avoid contact. Henrik's sword, driven off course, sliced shallowly into the Thoranian's side. Henrik drew back quickly, anticipating the counter-attack that inevitably followed.

He spared a brief glance around. The circle was even tighter now, the royals trapped in its middle. He could hear the nervous stamping of the king's and princess's horses right behind him. The fighting was too close to them. And everywhere he looked, the Valorian guards were fully occupied by the superior numbers, no one able to race to Henrik's aid.

All of this he ascertained in a couple of seconds, before he forced his attention back to Feivel. The older man lunged, and although Henrik held him off, he knew that he needed a new strategy. Feivel was pushing him hard, trying to drive him backward, and Henrik couldn't afford to give any more ground.

He took a risk, allowing his blade to continue its momentum as he parried the attack. He lunged past Feivel, giving the guard a clear path to the royals. As Feivel surged forward, Henrik jabbed back, slashing his opponent in the leg. Feivel stumbled, stifling a cry, and Henrik brought his forearm, steel arm guard and all, up with full force. He smashed it into the side of Feivel's head, and the Thoranian staggered sideways, allowing Henrik to once again place himself between the royal pair and their attacker.

Feivel spat on the ground, leaving a red stain in the mud. All Henrik could see of the man were his eyes, but he could still read the murder in their depths. Henrik pushed down his own emotions, anger included. He had no intention of allowing himself to be distracted this time.

He dropped into a fighting crouch, his eyes assessing his opponent for any weakness. He was still on his own, and the fight was still much too close to the king for his liking, but now Feivel had an injury to his leg and hopefully a pounding head to accompany the slash to his side and the wound to his arm from earlier in the day.

Before the two could join blades again, a shout went up from behind Feivel. Henrik's eyes flickered briefly to the source of the noise before returning to his opponent. It was one of the Valorians who had cried out. Like Henrik, he was no longer mounted, but that was all his quick glance had confirmed.

"It's true!" the man shouted. "They're not bandits. This one looks like he's from the South Lands!"

Feivel glanced behind him with a curse, and Henrik allowed himself another brief look. The Valorian guard was kneeling beside one of the fallen attackers, and he had ripped the fabric off the man's face.

"They're Lady Claudette's henchmen," called Henrik, bringing Feivel's attention instantly back to him. "She was behind all the bandit attacks."

The space was suddenly filled with exclamations, some sounding skeptical, some merely shocked. Henrik even heard the sharp intake of breath from the king behind him, and Lavinia's quiet voice, presumably assuring her father of the truth of the claim.

But he ignored all of this, his eyes on Feivel. The Thoranian man reached up to rip the covering from his own face, apparently accepting that the deception had run its course. Henrik almost took a step backward at the hatred in the other man's eyes. This fight was personal to Feivel, more than Henrik had realized.

Feivel fell on Henrik with furious force just as another shout rang out to one side of them. Henrik could barely hear the words over the clash of steel, but it seemed that Feivel had been recognized as Lady Claudette's personal guard.

If Feivel heard it, he gave no sign, except perhaps the narrowing of his eyes. Somewhere in the back of his mind,

Henrik grasped how dangerous Feivel's decision was to discard his disguise. In order to achieve the intended goal, of making everyone believe that the king had been killed by bandits, Feivel and his men would need to ensure that no one in the group was left alive. Not the king, not the princess, not any of the guards.

But Henrik didn't dwell on the thought. He couldn't afford to worry about the stakes. There was only room for this struggle, this moment. Feivel was fighting with more precision now, and Henrik realized with some chagrin that the other man had been hampered by his disguise before. The knight shouldn't expect any more easy hits.

"Did you think—" Feivel puffed, as if reading Henrik's thoughts, "—that you could best me?"

Henrik didn't reply, sweat beading on his forehead as he fought with all his strength not to let Feivel push any further forward.

"You think—you can—protect them?"

Henrik's own eyes narrowed as he saw Feivel's gaze slide past him, to the king and princess behind.

Feivel dropped back a step, his eyes roving over Henrik's form, looking for an opening.

"You think you can stop me?" he taunted, his breath coming in pants. "After what I've seen, you're child's play."

Henrik didn't respond, refusing to be baited. Feivel must think him a poor knight to believe he could so easily be distracted. But he was more than ready to make use of his opponent's desire to talk instead of fight.

Without warning, Henrik's sword flashed out, aiming for the heart this time. Feivel brought his own blade up with a grunt, intercepting the attack before Henrik could make full contact. But just like the first time they fought, his sword slashed at the other man's tunic, not deeply enough to pierce flesh, but enough to rend the fabric. And unlike the day Henrik returned to

Bryford, when he saw only a glimpse of Feivel's wounds, this time his sword sliced along the entire length of the garment.

Startled gasps sounded from the royals behind him. In spite of his determination not to be distracted, Henrik felt his own eyes widening at the mangled flesh exposed by the ruined tunic. The skin buckled and stretched, an angry red in some parts, in others crisscrossed with spiderwebs of white. Feivel's whole torso seemed to be covered in the scars, and remembering the man's tendency to wear long sleeves even in the hottest weather, Henrik could only assume his arms were in the same condition.

"What's the matter?" Feivel spat, rage just below the surface of the words. "I thought you North Landers loved your pet dragons. Don't you like seeing what dragon fire looks like?"

Henrik's eyes passed from Feivel's chest to his face, confusion creasing his brow.

"Dragon fire?"

"Thought they were all tame, did you?" Feivel scoffed. "Or was it just that you didn't care how many South Landers were burned when you and your allies called in your dragon army to set fire to our lands?"

Henrik was silent. He knew that Kincaid and Jocelyn had a closer friendship with the dragons who lived off Valoria's coast than any human had boasted in generations. And thanks to their success in reconnecting the dragon colony on Wyvern Islands with that in Kyona's mountains, it wasn't unheard of now to see the great beasts wheeling overhead, traveling across Valoria to visit their kin.

But beyond those distant glimpses, Henrik had never so much as seen a dragon, any more than he'd been to the South Lands. Whatever grudge this Thoranian was holding had nothing to do with him, but Feivel clearly didn't see it that way.

"Well, we didn't all burn," the guard added grimly. "We

survived. *I* survived. And now I'm going to make sure you lose everything, just like I did."

The guard glanced over Henrik's shoulder, menace in his eyes. Henrik raised his sword, his hand steady. He had as little intention as ever of being distracted by Feivel's words, but all at once he realized that Feivel's eyes, their expression full of malice, weren't lingering on King Malcolm, as he had assumed.

For some reason, Feivel's frustration and anger about what he had suffered had all come to rest on Henrik. He had decided to make the fight personal, and just like Lady Claudette, he had apparently identified exactly where Henrik was most vulnerable.

That was the only explanation for why his murderous gaze now rested not on the king, who was supposed to be his target, but on the young woman mounted beside him.

Henrik willed himself not to lose focus as fury rose up within him. He couldn't afford to let Feivel inside his head. What did it matter what Feivel's intentions were? Henrik's hadn't changed—his one job was to keep Feivel from reaching the royals at all.

But even as the thought went through his mind, a warning shout from Lavinia made him whip his head around. While Henrik's focus had been on Feivel, another of the Thoranian attackers had broken through the defenses. Henrik felt a flash of alarm as he saw that the new challenger was still mounted.

Before Henrik could do more than turn, the man drove his horse into the king's. King Malcolm raised a sword that Henrik hadn't even realized he was carrying, but he wasn't quick enough to stop the man from barreling straight into him. The momentum caused the plunging horses to veer wildly into Lavinia's mount, crammed too close to her father's in the confined space of their protective circle.

Henrik let out a cry of horror as all three riders crashed to the ground. He started forward, a flash of movement behind him reminding him a moment too late of his original adversary.

Feivel took full advantage of Henrik's distraction, thrusting his sword toward his retreating enemy. The knight's hasty deflection, while enough to save his life, wasn't enough to prevent Feivel's blade from slashing into Henrik's leg.

He stifled a cry, shifting his weight to his uninjured leg as he held off Feivel's continued attack. He was still half-turned, frantically trying to discover the state of King Malcolm and Lavinia while still keeping Feivel in view.

They both seemed to have made to it to their feet without being trampled by the rearing horses or felled by the blade of the attacking Thoranian. To Henrik's relief, Lavinia seemed to be entirely unharmed, at least for the moment. But King Malcolm was holding himself in a way that told Henrik he was in pain. Not surprising after being thrown from his horse.

"Henrik, look out!" Lavinia screamed, and once again Henrik realized he had taken his eyes off his own opponent for too long. He turned hastily back to Feivel, raising his sword ready to deflect.

But the Thoranian wasn't looking at him. To Henrik's rage and terror, he saw that Feivel's eyes were fixed on Lavinia, vindictive determination in their depths.

And as Henrik turned, ready to throw himself between Feivel and the princess, he saw with a thrill of horror that the second attacker, also having recovered his footing, was lunging for King Malcolm.

For the briefest of moments, time seemed to slow, Henrik's reflexes slowing with it. He couldn't intercept both Feivel's attack on Lavinia and the separate attack on the king, not on his own. And there was no one else to help. His oath to protect his king flashed through his mind, but his eyes were on Lavinia, his mind full of the awful thought of her sparkling eyes going out, her fire quenched forever.

There was no time to think. Abandoning any attempt to weigh his responsibilities against his heart, Henrik threw himself forward. The pain in his leg faded to insignificance as he hurled his body between Lavinia and her attacker.

CHAPTER TWENTY-THREE

This time there was no deflection, no struggle. Henrik fell on Feivel with single-minded ferocity.

The guard had lunged right past Henrik, clearly taking the gamble that Henrik would race to protect his king rather than take advantage of Feivel's exposed position.

It cost him his life. Feivel's sword was inches from Lavinia—who had raised her dagger in a determined but futile attempt to deflect the attack—when Henrik's blade ran him through.

He fell to the ground, unmoving. Henrik didn't need to look closely to know that it was over. His eyes scanned Lavinia's form for a frantic second, assuring himself that she was still standing. Then he turned desperately to her father, terrified of what he would see.

Against all hope, King Malcolm was upright, his sword still in his hand as he held off his attacker. The king was clearly spent. And judging by the blood running down one shoulder, in Henrik's moment of distraction he had sustained a sword injury to accompany whatever wound had been caused when he was thrown from his horse.

But he was still alive.

"To the king!" Henrik shouted, racing forward to assist.

The Thoranian attacker faltered as cries went up all around, and he turned his attention—and his blade—to Henrik.

There was no room for either anger or fear in Henrik's thoughts. His guilt and his relief he pushed aside completely. His sole focus was protecting his king, and the unknown Thoranian didn't last a minute under his unrelenting attack.

As soon as the man fell, Henrik looked up, searching the area for the next threat. But there was a lull in the fighting. The Thoranians were hesitating. The Valorians had acquitted themselves well—more than half a dozen of the attackers lay dead or injured on the ground. Most of those still standing were unmasked, like Feivel had been. Their gaze rested uneasily on their fallen leader, and Henrik realized with a surge of determination that the battle could be won right then, if the Valorians seized the opportunity.

"Their leader is dead! Advance!" he shouted.

There was a crucial moment of hesitation, before King Malcolm's voice cut through the still air.

"Do as he says!"

The Valorians advanced, some making use of the moment to remount their own or their fellows' horses. After a moment of indecision, the remaining Thoranians turned, fleeing as one. The Valorians turned to their king for instruction.

"Let them go," King Malcolm said, wincing slightly as he took a step forward. "We're still too exposed."

The most senior of the guards barked an order, and the remaining few took up defensive positions around the royals. One dismounted, beginning to check the bodies on the ground.

"Your Majesty," Henrik said sharply, starting forward with his eyes on his king's injured shoulder. "You're hurt."

Lavinia's presence burned against his awareness like an open flame, but he refused to let himself look in her direction. Trying to master his guilt, he ripped a length of fabric off his tunic, binding it around the king's wound.

"Forgive the roughness of the binding, Your Majesty," he said gruffly. "We must get you back to the castle and the royal physician urgently." He hung his head slightly, not quite able to meet his king's gaze. "And forgive me," he said, his voice a little strangled, "for failing to protect you."

"Lord Henrik," King Malcolm said, his tone difficult to read. "Look me in the eye."

Henrik looked up at once, trying to keep his face impassive. He blinked rapidly, taken aback by the softness of the king's expression. He had expected anger and reproach. But he could see nothing of the kind.

"I saw what happened," King Malcolm said, so quietly that no one else could hear.

Henrik swallowed hard, his guilt once again threatening to overwhelm him. But he held his head up, determined to accept with honor whatever consequences would come. He had abandoned his oath in the moment where it mattered most, but he was still a member of the king's guard.

"I'm a father as well as a king," said King Malcolm, again catching Henrik by surprise. "And you didn't fail me."

The king's gaze flickered to Lavinia, and Henrik finally allowed himself to follow with his own eyes. She was looking at the scene around her with admirable poise. Nothing but the paleness of her face would lead anyone to guess how close to death she had just come.

"Quite the reverse," King Malcolm added, drawing Henrik's attention back to him. The king gave a stiff smile, putting a hand gingerly to the makeshift bandage on his injured shoulder. "I wouldn't be much of a king if I couldn't defend myself for the few moments it takes for my knights to first ensure the safety of my children." He winced as he rolled the shoulder.

"I'm not as young or as quick as I once was, but I did have my sword, and unlike my daughter, I've been trained to defend myself."

His face creased in a slight frown as he again glanced at the princess. "I never took her requests to receive that type of training very seriously before, but suddenly I see her point. Perhaps we should follow the example of our Kyonan allies in this area."

"I'm sure the princess will be delighted to hear you say so, Your Majesty," said Henrik, with a wry smile. A moment later his conscience pricked him again. "Although you could just as truthfully say that she wouldn't have needed such training if I hadn't brought her into danger. But Prince Kincaid wasn't available, and I didn't think anyone would listen to me without her support."

"I'm afraid you're probably right," acknowledged King Malcolm. He sighed, his voice taking on a long-suffering tone. "And you must think I don't know my own daughter if you believe I need to be persuaded that no one can really bring her anywhere. I suspect it was quite the reverse."

Henrik grimaced. He may have admitted as much to Lavinia, but he wasn't sure he wanted to admit it to his king.

"Are you all right, Father? That looks painful."

Henrik jumped guiltily as the anxious voice of the princess herself cut in on their conversation about her.

"I will recover," said the king calmly. "Thanks to Lord Henrik's intervention." His eyes remained on his daughter. "Are you truly unharmed, Lavinia?"

She nodded, her uncharacteristically serious expression showing that she knew how nearly that hadn't been the case.

The king let out a long breath. "For that I am grateful," he said, in his usual, steady voice. His gaze lingered for a moment on the body of Feivel, not far from where they stood, then returned to pass between Lavinia and Henrik. "Now I think the two of you had best explain what happened here."

Henrik remained silent, allowing Lavinia to take the lead in the narrative as he bound his own wound as effectively as he could. He interjected when required, explaining his encounter with Feivel the night before, as well as his fight with the guard earlier that day, out toward the north east.

The king's lips pursed as he listened to their account of Prince Ormond's unsanctioned judgment in his father's royal audience hall, but he made no comment about his son.

"You really believe Lady Claudette is using some kind of dragon magic?" he asked, a frown creasing his forehead as he looked at Henrik.

"I do, Your Majesty," Henrik said seriously. "It's the only explanation that makes sense. Plus, there's obviously some connection between all this and the dragons." He briefly recounted what Feivel had said about the dragons, and the king's frown deepened.

"Valoria has never called on dragons to burn anything down," he said curtly.

Lavinia had her head cocked to one side, clearly deep in thought. "I doubt they would see it that way. I know Elddreki, Joss's dragon friend, broke her and Kincaid out of prison when they were in the Thoranian palace. Apparently there was a fair bit of damage, and even if it wasn't Valorians who asked for it, it was Valorians who benefited. Could Feivel have gotten burned then?"

"Maybe," shrugged Henrik.

"Well," King Malcolm said, his thoughts clearly going in a different direction, "whatever means have been used, we have more than enough proof of our Thoranian guest's true intentions." He sighed. "I can't deny that while it would be alarming in some ways, in others it would be a relief to discover that dragon magic had been at work in Bryford these last weeks."

"You mean," said Lavinia helpfully, "it would be a relief to know that there's some external reason for why Ormond has suddenly gone from utterly dependable to embarrassing our royal house like the spoiled brat he usually accuses me of being."

Her father sent her a quelling look, but he didn't actually correct her. Henrik hid a smile. The memory of Feivel charging toward Lavinia with sword raised and murder in his eyes was distressingly fresh. He was relieved beyond words to see Lavinia not only in one piece, but restored to her usual lively self.

She glanced up at him unexpectedly, and the urge to take her in his arms and assure himself that she was safe was suddenly overwhelming. Henrik turned away with an effort, hoping that the king wasn't watching too closely. He felt sure his emotions were written all over his face.

"Your Majesty." The guard who had dismounted earlier stepped forward. "Do you wish to wait here while we send someone back to the city for reinforcements?"

"No," said King Malcolm briskly. "I think we've already lingered too long in what is evidently an exposed location." He glanced around at the grim evidence of the recent battle. "Are they all dead?"

"No, Your Majesty," said the guard. "A couple of the Thoranians are simply unconscious."

The king nodded. "Good. Tie them up. We will hope that they remain here until reinforcements can reach them." He turned to the other guards. "We will depart for Bryford without delay. Lord Henrik will ride with my daughter and myself."

"But, Your Majesty—" the senior guard began, shooting a skeptical glance at Henrik at this allocation of the most important role to him.

"That is all," King Malcolm cut him off firmly, and the guard bowed before turning to do as instructed.

Henrik felt a bewildering mixture of pride and shame at the king's trust in him. He couldn't regret saving Lavinia's life, but he still felt as though he had failed his duty as a member of the king's elite.

"And now," said King Malcolm, his voice grim. "There's a matter requiring our urgent attention back in Bryford."

"Yes, Your Majesty," said Henrik quickly, springing into action.

He spared his fallen enemy only a brief glance as he retrieved his horse. He felt no sense of victory at the man's defeat. Feivel's scarred body was sad in death, his strength gone, and his injuries making him look small somehow.

But regardless of Feivel's fate, the plot he had taken part in wasn't over yet, Henrik reminded himself. There was still a mess to be untangled back in the city.

King Malcolm had already mounted his own—still unshod—horse, but Henrik paused before following his lead. Lavinia's borrowed mare seemed to have disappeared in the melee, and she was attempting to coax the horse of one of the fallen guards to come to her. Henrik hurried over to help, limping on his injured leg. The two of them soon had the horse under control. He turned to reclaim his own mount, but was stopped by the princess's soft voice.

"Thank you."

"Of course," Henrik nodded, but Lavinia shook her head.

"Not for the horse. For saving my life." She looked down. "You chose me." She swallowed. "You shouldn't have, but you did."

Henrik glanced behind him, making sure that the king was occupied watching the activities of the other guard. Then he turned back to Lavinia, putting a gentle hand on her chin, and lifting her head until their eyes met.

"There was no choice."

For an endless moment their gazes were locked, their communication bypassing words as they lived again the raw emotions of the past hours. Then Lavinia took a shuddering breath, and Henrik dropped his hand.

"I believe you, by the way," she said, accepting his assistance to mount the horse. "About, you know," she waved a hand in an all-encompassing gesture, "everything."

Henrik said nothing, just smiled up at her with no attempt to hide the affection in his eyes. He knew it didn't really change anything, not where the future was concerned. But his heart still felt incredibly light at the knowledge that she no longer doubted him. It would have to be enough.

The ride back to Bryford passed quickly. Henrik hadn't thought he'd made much of an impression on the guard they'd intercepted on their way out of the capital, so he was surprised when they encountered a small group of guards not long before they reached the city's gates. King Malcolm sent most of them on to deal with the mess they'd left behind them, but a few of them turned to swell the king's escort as he rode the short distance remaining to reach the safety of the castle.

The king strode into the castle with a firm step that belied his injuries, Henrik and Lavinia hurrying behind him, the knight still limping. The king's steward appeared almost immediately, his eyes starting in horror at the state of his sovereign.

But King Malcolm dismissed the man's entreaties for him to see the royal physician before doing anything else.

"I will see the physician in good time," he said impatiently. "Where is Prince Ormond?"

"I believe he's in the small dining hall, Your Majesty," said the steward nervously. "With Prince Kincaid. And Lady Claudette."

The king's face hardened at the mention of the Thoranian noblewoman. "Summon all three of them to the throne room."

"Yes, Your Majesty," said the steward, bobbing into a bow. "At once."

Henrik and Lavinia exchanged a glance as they followed the king, Lavinia matching her pace to Henrik's slower one. The knight pushed himself as quickly as he could, holding in a frustrated grunt. His injury was painful, but that wasn't what bothered him. It was the limitation of having to go slowly on his wounded leg. He didn't want to fall behind—he wasn't entirely sure whether he was supposed to be part of the coming encounter, but this time he didn't offer to discreetly remove himself from the family conflict. Whatever was about to happen, he wanted to see it for himself.

King Malcolm strode the length of the long hall, turning expectantly toward the doors with a face like flint. He didn't ascend the dais, or sit on the throne, but he didn't need to. His authority radiated off him with his every movement.

Henrik positioned himself off to the side, some distance from the king. To his surprise, Lavinia came to stand beside him rather than joining her father. In a very short time, the doors burst open, Ormond entering the room with long strides, his eyes on his father. Lady Claudette was at his side—as brazen as ever, Henrik thought darkly—and Kincaid wasn't far behind them. The younger prince looked furious. From the demeanor of the two brothers, Henrik would guess that their father's summons had caught them mid-argument.

"Father, what is the meaning of—" Ormond cut himself off mid-sentence, a sharp gasp escaping him as he took in his father's bloodied state. "What happened?"

"Father!" Kincaid cried, hurrying forward to stand beside his brother. "You're injured!"

"I am," said King Malcolm, an edge of deadly purpose beneath his habitually calm tone. He turned to Lady Claudette. "As for what happened, perhaps our guest can explain that better than I can."

Henrik saw that Lady Claudette had a wary look on her face, and her weedy manservant, who had unobtrusively followed her in, was holding himself with unnatural tension. Ormond, of course, instantly stiffened at his father's tone.

"What is that supposed to mean, Father? I've tolerated enough rudeness today toward my betrothed, and—"

"Enough," King Malcolm cut him off mercilessly. "Do not make more of a fool of yourself than necessary, Ormond." The crown prince fell silent, looking stunned at the harsh words, but the king's attention was already back on the Thoranian woman. "Lady Claudette knows what I'm speaking of, and soon you will, too."

His eyes passed to his younger son. "I heard about your errand, Kincaid. What did you find?"

Kincaid stepped forward eagerly. "We found evidence of a camp, but there was no one there. I left a squadron behind, to apprehend the renegades when they return to their base."

"They won't all be returning," said King Malcolm grimly, glancing toward Henrik and Lavinia.

Ormond followed his gaze, starting as he seemed to notice the pair for the first time. "What are you doing here?" he demanded furiously, narrowing his eyes at Henrik. "How did you get out of the dungeon?" His eyes passed to Lavinia, narrowing even further. "But I suppose I have my answer. Do you have no sense of loyalty, Lavinia?"

The princess opened her mouth to retort, but her father cut her off.

"Your accusations are misdirected, Ormond," he said sternly. "I am astonished to hear that you had one of my knights thrown in the dungeon, and we can all be very grateful that Lord Henrik wasn't detained in there for long."

The king spoke to his son, but his eyes lingered on Lady Claudette's face. She still looked cautious, but Henrik had to admit that she was maintaining her calm much better than he would have expected.

"Perhaps you can explain to me, Lady Claudette, why a group of your countrymen, led by your personal guard, attacked me on my way back to Bryford."

Kincaid drew in a sharp breath, but Ormond just looked shocked. "Father! Surely there is some mistake!"

"There have been a great many mistakes," the king agreed. "The first of which was mine in accepting this woman as a guest based on so little evidence of her connection to the approaching delegation."

"Your Majesty," said Lady Claudette smoothly. "I can assure you that there is indeed some mistake. I am horrified to learn that you have been targeted by these bandits, but I can assure you that neither I nor my guard has anything to do with it."

Henrik raised an eyebrow. Still trying to push the story of bandits? She was certainly bold. But his astonishment increased enormously as he watched a flicker cross King Malcolm's face.

"I appreciate a direct answer," the king said gruffly. "And I am hesitant to blame you for events for which you were not present." He frowned, as if trying to recapture his previous thought. "But there is still some explaining to do."

"Hesitant to blame—Father, she tried to have you killed!" Kincaid exclaimed.

Henrik stared between the king and the prince, trying to understand what was happening. He would not have thought it possible that King Malcolm could be distracted from his anger after what had just passed. Lady Claudette must be using a weapon that Henrik couldn't see—a powerful one. But any enchantment strong enough to bend the mind of the king would surely have captured Kincaid as well.

Not to mention Henrik. And yet, he was as disgusted by Lady Claudette's deceit and manipulation as ever.

"How dare you?" Ormond hissed at his brother.

Before Kincaid could respond, the door to the throne room swung open, and everyone turned to see the new arrivals. Queen Marguerite hurried into the room with something less than her usual stateliness, her eyes wide as they rested on her injured husband.

A sharp gasp drew Henrik's attention to Lady Claudette's servant, and he looked up in time to see the Thoranian woman —her own posture suddenly stiffer—throw her underling a furious glance. The man fell silent, but Henrik had already seen the trajectory of his gaze. And it wasn't the entrance of the queen that had rattled him.

Princess Jocelyn was following close behind her mother-in-law, her face pale but her expression determined. Perched on her hip, his brown eyes taking in the scene with great interest, was Norik.

"Jocelyn!" Kincaid hurried forward to meet his wife, while the queen joined her husband in front of the dais.

"You need the physician," said Queen Marguerite, with an admirable attempt at her usual calm.

"My injuries can wait," said the king curtly. "I am in no immediate danger."

Kincaid had been speaking quietly with Jocelyn, but he turned at his father's words. "Unlike Ormond," he said darkly, throwing a fulminating glance at Lady Claudette. "Who's still in great danger from that scheming, lying—"

"You will not speak of her that way," hissed Ormond, turning on his brother with balled fists. "She is the gentlest, sweetest—" his voice choked slightly in his throat, and he turned his gaze to the woman beside him. "Just because she has tolerated the insults against her today with such grace, doesn't mean I'll stand by while my own family—not now, Norik!"

"But why do you like her, Uncle Ormond?" chimed in Norik unexpectedly. The little boy had wriggled free of his mother's hold while his parents talked, toddling up to the rest of the group. He was now tugging insistently on his uncle's leggings. "She's not very nice at all. Actually, I think she's mean."

CHAPTER TWENTY-FOUR

A sudden hush fell over the group at the toddler's words. Henrik braced himself for Ormond's inevitable outrage at the insult to his beloved, or even a reproach from Queen Marguerite. But neither came.

Instead the silence lengthened as Ormond's gaze passed slowly from Norik to Lady Claudette, his eyes widening as his nephew's words washed over him. His expression of total disillusionment would have been comical if the situation wasn't so serious.

"C-Claudette?" he said, looking as confused as if the woman in front of him had suddenly transformed into someone else.

Henrik narrowed his eyes, remembering his own moment of clarity where Lady Claudette was concerned. The transformation had felt that absolute to him as well.

The Thoranian woman gave a tinkling laugh, and Henrik could tell from the slight wince on Ormond's face that the sound now grated on his ears as much as it did on Henrik's.

"Valorian children are given such license," she said.

No one responded, either to defend or chastise the young

boy. Ormond and King Malcolm were both still staring at Lady Claudette, and everyone else was staring at Ormond.

"You're using magic," said Jocelyn suddenly, her eyes narrowed as they passed to the Thoranian woman. "I can sense it." She shook her head in disgust. "It's familiar—how did I not feel it before?"

Kincaid took a step forward, his expression menacing as it rested on Lady Claudette. But her servant moved to intercept him, his own face hard. Henrik strode out from the side of the room, standing beside his friend. The servant's eyes flicked between the two men, and Henrik finally recognized the calculating scrutiny he had observed in the man before now.

"You're not a servant," he said suddenly, and the man's gaze jumped to him warily. "You're a guard." He looked past the man, his eyes settling on Lady Claudette. Her expression was mutinous. "And Feivel wasn't really a guard, was he? Not a trained one, anyway. What was he? A soldier? Or just a groom with an aptitude for fighting? He was certainly good with horses."

Henrik took a small step forward, his eyes narrowing. "So were you playing a part, too, *My Lady*? You're not a noblewoman at all, are you? You were never going to be part of Cody's delegation. You're just an opportunistic impostor."

Lady Claudette—or rather, just Claudette—wore a pronounced sneer now.

"Anyone who needs a title in order to get anything done isn't worthy of it. I would have made a better queen than the soft-minded fool you want to put on the throne."

Henrik glanced at Ormond, and saw that he looked stricken at the reminder of the absent Lady Brielle. Henrik felt a flicker of sympathy for the prince. He had done more than just make a fool of himself. Under Claudette's influence, he had possibly destroyed his best chance of securing a suitable marriage.

Henrik stepped forward again, his expression stony. "You

think someone so desperate to be queen that she was willing to kill the king in order to get there faster could ever be worthy of a crown?"

"My, my," said Claudette. She raised an eyebrow, looking pointedly at Henrik's hand, which he hadn't even realized he'd placed on the hilt of his sword. The Thoranian woman's gaze passed maliciously to Lavinia, standing just behind Henrik. "How quickly he goes from wooing a woman to wanting to wound her, wouldn't you say, Princess?"

Henrik felt his anger bubbling up, but Lavinia's expression was simply scornful. "That's enough from you, you snake," she said, stepping up to stand beside Henrik.

"More than enough," agreed King Malcolm. He nodded to the guards who had accompanied him into the room. "Seize them both."

The guards started forward, two of them grabbing the servant, or guard, or whatever he was, after a brief scuffle.

But Claudette was quicker than her companion. Like lightning, she lunged forward, seizing Norik by the arm with one hand while the other one produced a dagger seemingly out of nowhere.

The shocked cries and outraged gasps were quickly stifled, everyone in the room freezing as Claudette raised the knife. Only Norik moved, squirming and squawking as he tried to pull free of her grip.

"Norik, hold still," said Kincaid sharply, barely concealed panic in his eyes. "It will be all right."

"That's right, listen to your father," said Claudette mockingly. Norik stopped moving, his eyes as wide as a stunned rabbit's.

Claudette's gaze hardened as it fell on Jocelyn. "Trust you to come in at the last minute and ruin everything. All my hard work, years of preparation. See how you like it when you lose what's precious to you. You can tell your friend how it feels, so she knows what she did to us."

"My friend?" Jocelyn asked carefully. Her eyes were as wide as Norik's, but she was keeping her head. She had a restraining hand on Kincaid's arm, her eyes darting between their son, and the blade in the Thoranian woman's hand.

"Not that she would care," Claudette said, her eyes slightly wild. "Not now that she's a princess in a fancy castle. She probably never thought twice about us lowly *servants* when she called down dragon fire on our home."

"You were one of Rasad's servants," said Jocelyn slowly, naming the Thoranian advisor who had dabbled in dragon magic, with the intent to use it to annex both the South and North Lands and turn his kingdom into an empire. "You were there when the dragons destroyed his experiments."

Claudette snorted. "They destroyed a lot more than his experiments. They burned the whole place to the ground, never mind who was inside it!"

"Lucy never intended to have your home destroyed," said Jocelyn carefully. "All she did was to tell the dragons what she'd discovered about your master's experiments. Their decisions were their own. No human can control what the dragons do, not royalty, not anyone."

Claudette scoffed. "If you say so, Princess Jocelyn *Dragonfriend*. But it doesn't matter. I don't care about any of that. Do you think I'm avenging my old home? I was a servant there, with no future." Her eyes were glinting, and she looked slightly crazed. "The others might care about revenge, but as far as I'm concerned, the dragons' attack was an opportunity. I was always destined for greater things."

Henrik acted on the instinct of the moment. He had only been half listening to Claudette's rant, his attention on her weapon. She was clearly not experienced with the blade, from the way she was waving it around. And her attention was focused on her words, not her hostage.

He was much closer to her than the guards King Malcolm had summoned. He lunged forward without warning, making no attempt to draw his blade, just seizing Claudette's arm.

She let out a cry, and for a brief moment they scuffled. But Henrik was much stronger, and he soon wrested the dagger from her hand. The weapon fell to the floor with a clatter, and Kincaid raced forward to pick it up and to shepherd his son to safety. Claudette continued to struggle as the guards also surged forward, seizing her arms. A loud ripping sound cut across the tussle, followed by a strange clinking.

Everyone stared down at the item that was bouncing on the stone floor, torn from a pocket in Claudette's gown. Lavinia stepped forward, leaning down to pick it up, but paused at her sister-in-law's voice, unusually sharp.

"Stop! Don't touch it, Lavinia. It's dangerous."

Jocelyn strode forward, kneeling down. Claudette—now fully restrained by two of the guards—let out a cry of fury, but Jocelyn ignored it as she examined the object more closely. Henrik leaned forward to see. It was some kind of crystal, shaped like a hexagonal prism. Its sides were smooth, but the top of the cylinder was jagged. It was a faint purple, and it glowed with an unnatural light.

Jocelyn looked up, her expression grim as she met her husband's eye.

"This is a crystal from the Dragon Realm on Wyvern Islands."

"From Wyvern Islands?" Kincaid came forward, still holding Norik protectively. "I don't remember seeing crystals there."

"I only caught a brief glimpse," said Jocelyn. "I didn't think anything of it at the time. But Lucy described them to me in detail. Rasad had a whole collection of them at his fortress, in his secret room full of experiments."

"But..." Kincaid frowned. "But all of Rasad's experiments were destroyed."

Jocelyn shook her head. "The dragons destroyed everything at his home, and everything he was carrying. But he didn't have this crystal at the time he died. He'd entrusted it to someone else." Her expression darkened. "Don't you recognize its signature? There's a reason it feels so familiar to me."

Kincaid drew in a sharp breath, his expression stormy. "Are you telling me," he started, his voice angrier than Henrik had ever heard it, "that this..." he glanced at Claudette, "this *snake* has been using the same crystal on Ormond that scum in Thirl tried to use on you?"

Jocelyn nodded thoughtfully. "When Rasad was trying to interfere with our marriage, in order to break the alliance between Valoria and Kyona, yes. I think its magic must be something to do with attraction, or some manipulation of it." Her voice turned rueful. "But extremely potent."

Henrik looked at the small talisman thoughtfully. It made sense. When he looked at Claudette, he had seen what he found attractive. Not just the physical beauty, but the characteristics he so admired in Lavinia. The determination, the courage. And Ormond, meanwhile, had seen the demure grace he admired. Qualities that the real Claudette was entirely lacking, and that Lady Brielle had in abundance.

He glanced at Kincaid, and saw that his friend was glaring at Claudette, looking like he wanted to murder someone. Henrik fidgeted uncomfortably. His friend had told him only very briefly about the scheme that had been carried out against the then newlywed couple during their trip to Thorania. Henrik hadn't pressed for details—it had been clear that it was a sensitive topic.

And Henrik could understand why. He knew that Rasad had given one of his underlings the task of beguiling Jocelyn, although he hadn't known the man had used a magic crystal to do it. He wasn't sure if Kincaid and Jocelyn had even known about the crystal specifically. From what Kincaid had told him, all they knew was what Lucy had discovered from Rasad. Namely, that magic of some kind was involved in the man's—thankfully unsuccessful—attempts to divert Jocelyn's affection from her husband.

Henrik grimaced. If Jocelyn had experienced for that stranger even a fraction of the attraction Ormond had been feeling toward Claudette, it must have been agony for Kincaid to watch. No wonder the usually placid prince had been livid when he saw it all happening again. He may not have recognized the source of the emotion, but he must have sensed something familiar in Claudette's power. Something he didn't like to remember.

"So clever, putting all the pieces together," said Claudette, her voice snide. Henrik looked up at her, noting as he did so the horror with which poor Ormond was watching her. The prince wouldn't recover from his disillusionment in a hurry.

The Thoranian woman tossed her head defiantly. "It was most convenient, that Rasad had entrusted a crystal to that fool in his attempt to get between you. At first, when the dragons destroyed everything, I thought that all my observations, my years of clandestine research into Rasad's discoveries, had been wasted. Not even my secret stash of dragon scales survived the inferno. But in the end it didn't matter. The crystals," her eyes lingered greedily on the talisman still resting on the stone floor, "are infinitely more powerful."

She gave a dark laugh. "It wasn't even hard to track it down. That short-sighted fool was using it without discretion, making quite a reputation for himself with the ladies of the Thoranian court."

Her eyes lingered maliciously on Henrik, and he met her gaze steadily, his own expression hard. He didn't care what she thought of him. He knew he was nothing like the type of man she was describing, one who would try to come between a woman and her husband for gold.

"Not that they knew why they found him so appealing, of course," Claudette went on. "But I knew at once what he had. And I knew it could be put to much better use than that."

"You deserve to be hung," growled Kincaid.

Claudette's eyes glittered strangely as she met his gaze. "I'd rather gamble everything for the chance of greatness than spend my life safe in obscurity."

"A gamble indeed, and you lost," said King Malcolm in a grim voice. He strode forward, his presence impressive despite his torn robes and blood-soaked bandage. "We welcomed you graciously, and in return you and your henchmen have caused great harm with your schemes. Men died today. Why have you done this? We had no hand in the destruction of your home."

Claudette's eyes lingered on Jocelyn and Kincaid. "Didn't you?" she said dryly. "Some of my fellow survivors wouldn't see it that way. All you North Landers are the same to them, and everyone knows that the dragons come and go across Valoria as they please. They even crossed the sea to Thorania for the sake of their Valorian friends. Men died that day, too. Some people lost their whole families." Her face stretched into a sneer. "Not that I had anyone to lose. That's not why I spent years planning this, or why so many of the others sailed here with me to see it through."

"Then why?" the king pressed. "Why Valoria?"

Claudette shrugged. "Well, obviously I had to get away from Thorania. I was always going to be a servant there. And we'd heard Valoria was a rich and prosperous land." Her voice turned rueful. "I didn't realize it was so peaceful that one staged bandit attack outside the city would raise so much suspicion."

Her smirk returned. "But I had to be 'robbed' on my way to Bryford—how else could I explain arriving without all the trappings of a wealthy noblewoman? We used all our resources to get ourselves passage across the ocean—there was nothing left to buy fancy dresses and jewelry. The necessity of staging a few more attacks to make the one against me seem less suspicious was nothing in the scheme of things."

Even in the midst of her failure, her expression was maddeningly smug. "It was worth it to introduce myself to the Valorian court as a noblewoman. What simpler way to gain such easy access to the wealth and power of the North Lands?" She threw a mocking glance at Ormond. "You see, Kyona's prince is already spoken for."

Ormond turned his face away, as if unable to bear the sight of her. Remembering the prince's conduct over the last couple of days, Henrik didn't blame him.

"What do we do with the crystal?" Lavinia asked curiously, moving forward to stand beside Jocelyn for a closer look.

"If you don't object," said Jocelyn, looking up at her parents-in-law, "I think I should give it to Elddreki. The dragons will want to know about this, and may want to examine it."

The king nodded slowly at the mention of Jocelyn's dragon friend. "I will be glad to have it out of my kingdom," he said darkly.

Jocelyn pulled a handkerchief out of a fold of her gown, wrapping the crystal up carefully without touching it. "I'm sure the dragons will destroy it," she said reassuringly. "Once they've learned what they can from it."

"Destroy it?" cried Claudette, surging forward without warning. The men holding her were caught off guard, and she broke free, lunging toward Jocelyn. "Don't you know how powerful it is?"

Her eyes were wild, and she looked almost mad as she fell upon the princess. Jocelyn gave a cry, yanking the bundle away from Claudette's scrabbling hands. The Thoranian woman scratched at Jocelyn's face, shrieking unnaturally. Kincaid raced forward with a cry of fury, but the guards beat him to it. They pulled Claudette off the princess, still spitting and shrieking.

"Take them both to the dungeons!" commanded King Malcolm, sounding furious at this fresh attack by the Thoranian impostor.

The guards hastened to obey, dragging both Claudette and her servant toward the door. The man submitted quietly, his eyes wide and shocked, but Claudette continued to fight all the way out of the room.

For a moment, a ringing silence gripped the group, as every eye stared blankly at the doorway through which the pair had disappeared.

"Was she sad?"

Norik's innocent question broke whatever spell held them all in thrall. Kincaid shook his head slightly, looking down at his son, still held in his arms.

"Yes, Norik, I think she was very sad."

"Why?"

"Uh..." Kincaid looked helplessly to his wife for assistance, but Jocelyn was clearly still trying to collect herself after her recent scuffle. Kincaid strode forward to meet her, and she slipped the crystal into a pocket before reaching out shaking arms to take her son.

"Are you all right?" Kincaid asked, his eyes lingering on her face in concern. Red scratch marks were appearing from Claudette's fingernails, down one cheek and along her neck.

"I'll be fine," said Jocelyn, although she still looked unusually pale. She grimaced, putting a hand to her stomach. "Honestly, a few scratches are the least of my concerns."

Kincaid gave her a sympathetic look, reaching out a hand. "Do you want me to take—?"

But Jocelyn shook her head, holding her son more tightly. She had shown great poise, but Henrik had no doubt that seeing the crazed impostor holding Norik at knife point must have been one of the most terrifying moments of her life.

The princess looked to her parents-in-law, her expression suddenly penitent. "I'm sorry that I've been absent so much. I should have realized much earlier what was happening. I don't know how I missed it before." She patted the fold in her gown where she'd put the crystal. "The signature of the magic is strong."

"I do," said Henrik suddenly, and everyone looked at him in surprise. "I know how you missed it." He glanced at Kincaid. "Remember how I told you that Claudette and her guard were saying it was unlucky that you two had returned early from Kynton?" He gestured toward Jocelyn. "That's why. They knew Jocelyn would recognize the dragon magic. I don't think Claudette used the crystal when she was around at all."

He frowned, remembering the strange fluctuations he had experienced, one moment full of admiration for the visiting noblewoman, the next unable to remember why. Had that always been when Kincaid was present?

"I think she was even wary of using it around you, Kincaid," he guessed. "She must have been nervous that you'd recognize it, knowing it had been used on you before, in Thirl. But she got bolder as time started running out, I think, and once she knew Jocelyn was out of the picture."

Kincaid nodded slowly. "And unfortunately I wasn't as quick to recognize it as Joss," he said ruefully. "And if I'm honest, it did work on me, a little." He threw an apologetic glance at his wife.

"Not that she tried to use it on me very strongly, I think. But I remember thinking she was beautiful."

"She used it a lot on me," said Henrik grimly. "I've never been more confused in my life."

"But you saw through her eventually," said Ormond, speaking up for the first time. He looked strained, his eyes haunted. "Much sooner than I did. How did you do it?"

Henrik frowned, shaking his head slowly. "I don't know." He met Ormond's eye. "You seemed to finally see her for what she was, Your Highness. Any idea how you broke free?"

Ormond shrugged. "No. Right up until just now, I thought she was...well, I won't go into what I thought of her." He looked faintly nauseated. He took a deep breath, turning to his parents with a stricken expression. "I'm so sorry."

"I'm just relieved you were under an enchantment," said King Malcolm frankly.

"Don't be too hard on yourself, Ormond," said Jocelyn kindly. "Dragon magic is powerful." She shook her head. "You should talk it over with Eamon sometime," she added, naming her twin brother. "I think you'd find him very understanding."

"But what changed?" Lavinia pressed, her eyes on her oldest brother. "You saw through her before the end, didn't you?"

"I did," said Ormond slowly. "I don't know how. It was when Norik said that she was mean." He glanced at his nephew. "I don't know...it just suddenly hit me. I looked at her, and it was like I was seeing her for the first time. And I didn't like what I saw."

"It was Norik at the gala, too," said Henrik slowly, looking at the toddler, still in his mother's arms. "Remember, Kincaid? He said she wasn't beautiful, and all of a sudden, she just wasn't."

"Yes," said Kincaid slowly, looking at his son with an unnerved expression. "That's how it was for me, too."

"I remember," said Lavinia brightly. "I believe his exact

words were, 'her face is mean, and she looks silly.'" She grinned. "I've never been prouder as an aunt."

"Yes..." Henrik stared at the toddler in awe. "And I never admired her again."

It was true. He could mark it from that moment. He had thought it might have been his realization of his love for Lavinia that made him suddenly immune to Claudette's charms. But that was when he had assumed that the Thoranian was simply using normal methods of attraction. Learning the state of his own heart wouldn't have protected him from magical interference.

"Neither did I," said Kincaid, still looking unnerved. "It's like Norik broke the crystal."

"Just like he did for Ormond just now," said Jocelyn slowly. She was clutching her son more tightly than ever, and her expression was hard to read as her gaze passed to her husband. "What was it Elddreki said about my power passing to our children, Kincaid?"

The prince shrugged, his eyes on his son. "Just that it might. He said he couldn't know for sure." He looked up, an incredulous laugh breaking out. "I think we have our answer."

Henrik followed Kincaid's gaze toward the king and queen, who were both looking stunned—and a little uncomfortable— at the discovery that their grandson had some undefined magical ability in his blood.

"Well, well," Lavinia chimed in, with a chuckle that was much more cheerful than her brother's. In fact, she was the only one who didn't look unsettled. She was just grinning at her nephew with affection. "You're a handy chap to have around, it seems, Norik."

The toddler looked between the various adults, confused, but clearly enjoying all the attention. "Am I the hero?" he asked, his eyes wide and excited.

That broke the tension, and a nervous chuckle passed around the group.

"Yes, little man," said Henrik, grinning. "You're definitely the hero."

"I'm the hero!" crowed Norik, squirming delightedly in his mother's arms.

"Not the only one," said Lavinia, smiling at Henrik in a way that made his ears go red.

"Indeed," said King Malcolm, his eyes on the knight. "Dragon magic aside, I haven't forgotten that I was attacked by very real, very human enemies today."

"And wounded by a very real blade, from what I can see," said Queen Marguerite, anxiety still lurking in her eyes. "Will you see the physician now?"

"Yes," said King Malcolm briskly. "I should. But first," his eyes still rested on Henrik, "there is the matter of the service Lord Henrik has rendered me. He should be properly rewarded."

Henrik started, his eyes flying to the king's. He bowed quickly under both monarchs' unwavering scrutiny, hiding a wince at the pain in his leg as he did so. His quick movements in rushing on Claudette had been enough to undo his rough bindings, and he could feel that the wound was bleeding again.

"Your Majesty, it is my duty and my honor to protect you," he said steadily. "I only wish I had done so more effectively."

"We have already discussed that," said King Malcolm austerely, his gaze flicking to Lavinia and back. "We will not do so again."

Everyone else looked confused, but the king made no attempt to explain his comment.

"You are not responsible for my injury," he said instead. "I am well aware that my escort and I would have been taken entirely by surprise without your warning. And even that wasn't taken very seriously by most of my guards. As far as I'm concerned, you saved my life, not only in alerting us to the intended ambush, but in defending me against the attacker who injured me."

Henrik bowed again, overwhelmed by the strength of the king's praise, and unsure what to say.

"Henrik, thank you," said Kincaid earnestly, clapping his friend on the shoulder. "I'm not surprised, of course, but I'm extremely grateful that you figured out what they were planning, and acted quickly enough to stop them." He paused. "And I guess we should all be grateful that Lavvy had more success than I did in busting you out of the dungeon." He turned to his sister, his brow furrowed in confusion. "How did you manage that?"

Lavinia grinned, tossing her hair. "I'd rather not say."

The queen's sigh was audible, but for once no one chastised the princess.

"I'm grateful, too," said Ormond, his tone stiff and uncomfortable as he turned from Lavinia to Henrik. "And I'm sorry I had you locked up, Lord Henrik."

"You weren't yourself, Your Highness," said Henrik quickly, taking pity on the crown prince's evident misery. "That was obvious to anyone who knows you."

"It seems we all have cause to be grateful to you, Lord Henrik," interjected Queen Marguerite, her expression softer than Henrik had ever seen it before. Her gaze flicked down to his leg, and he winced as he realized that blood was trickling down onto the stone floor. "And it seems that you also are injured."

"It's nothing, Your Majesty," said Henrik hastily.

"Nonsense," said King Malcolm. "My physician will see to your wound as well, Lord Henrik. But first, as I said, you should be rewarded for your service."

"No reward is necessary, Your Majesty," said Henrik uncomfortably. "I did no more than my duty."

"It's not every day a knight is called upon to risk his own life to save his king's," King Malcolm insisted. "Even a member of my elite. And I am aware that your reputation as well as your body has suffered injury today as a result of your attempts to unmask those conspiring against me. I wish to reward you, so let's have no more argument. Come, there must be something I can grant you."

"I...that is..." Henrik faltered. There was only one thing he wanted, and he was unable to prevent his eyes from straying to Lavinia. She was watching him intently, her head cocked slightly to one side, and her eyes sparkling more mischievously than ever.

"There is..." Henrik tried, finding his throat strangely dry.

"Yes?" prompted the king. "Don't be afraid to speak your mind. Some advancement, perhaps? I understand from your commander that you have great ambitions."

Henrik blinked, surprised that the king had spoken to his commander about him. But he pushed the thought aside in favor of more pressing concerns.

"No, Your Majesty," he said steadily. "Advancement will come with hard work and time, and I can be patient. The only request I want to make is too much to ask."

"What is it?" asked King Malcolm, sounding intrigued.

Henrik glanced around the group, and saw that while Kincaid looked utterly bewildered, Jocelyn was barely concealing a grin that could only be described as smug. He didn't dare to look at Lavinia again, sure he would lose his nerve at the reminder of her sheer perfection and unattainability. Could he really be so bold?

"I want to marry your daughter," Henrik blurted out, color rushing up his neck.

CHAPTER TWENTY-FIVE

There was a moment of silence, during which it was all Henrik could do to keep his head raised.

"You want to marry Lavinia?" King Malcolm asked blankly. Henrik noticed that the queen, while looking a little surprised at the forthright declaration, didn't seem as bemused as her husband.

"I do, Your Majesty," Henrik said as evenly as he could. "But as I said, I know it's too much to...that is..."

"And what do you want, Lavinia?" the king asked, mercifully cutting off Henrik's stuttering as he turned to his daughter.

Henrik looked around at Lavinia at last, a hot prickle of embarrassment running over him at his presumption in publicly making such a declaration without actually asking her opinion first. In spite of the king's question, the princess was looking not at her father, but at Henrik, one eyebrow pointedly raised.

"Lavinia, I—" Henrik took a step toward her, stopping abruptly as he remembered all the royal eyes on them. "I'm sorry, I should have—that is, I didn't mean to..." He paused, taking a deep breath as he attempted to pull himself together.

"You're a stuttering mess, My Lord," grinned Lavinia, apparently not sharing his embarrassment. "And I thought the gossip was that Lord Henrik was the smoothest flirt in the court."

"Not quite the smoothest," he retorted, before he could stop himself.

He almost rolled his eyes as Lavinia's grin broadened. Trust the incorrigible princess to make an outrageous joke even out of his attempt to propose to her.

"Your Majesties," he tried again, looking up at the king and queen. "I know I have no position that would justify such a request, and that it's presumptuous even to ask. But I'd never forgive myself if I didn't at least try." He returned his gaze to the princess. "Princess Lavinia, I may not have any right to, but I love you, as I think you know. And I'd very much like to know your answer to your father's question just now."

"Henrik, you idiot," said Lavinia, laughter dancing in her eyes, "I've loved you since I can remember. I'm just glad you finally caught up, because nothing I was doing seemed to work, and I've tried every trick I know."

Henrik laughed, taking another step toward her before again remembering their audience. He turned apprehensively to the king and queen, and Lavinia followed his gaze, a sigh escaping her.

"But Mother won't like it," she said. "My feelings aren't exactly a secret to her. Why do you think she wouldn't let me go to Kyona this summer after you accepted Kincaid's invitation?"

"Lavinia," frowned the queen, clearly uncomfortable at her daughter's plain speaking.

"It is a traditional reward for service to a king," said King Malcolm, the hint of a laugh in his voice. His eyes were unexpectedly warm as they rested on Henrik. "And I, for one, have good reason to believe that Lord Henrik's love for our daughter is genuine, and that he would do all in his power to take care of her."

"I would, Your Majesty," said Henrik, hardly daring to acknowledge the bubble of hope growing inside him.

"For what it's worth," chipped in Jocelyn, still grinning, "I've been convinced he was in love with her for months. You should have seen him in Kynton. He could barely be brought to flirt with anyone!"

Henrik shot the princess a dry look, not sure whether to be grateful or annoyed at her intervention.

"Really?" asked Lavinia, looking Henrik over with great interest. "And here I was as cross as a bear all summer, picturing him taking all the Kyonan girls by storm."

Henrik shot her a long-suffering look, trying to ignore the astonishment on Kincaid's face as he stared at his best friend.

The king, meanwhile, was looking at his wife, one eyebrow raised inquiringly.

"Well," sighed Queen Marguerite, her eyes on her daughter, "it would certainly be a relief to have you settled." Her tone turned hopeful. "Are you absolutely sure you won't take Rodney?"

"Ugh, Mother," said Lavinia, a pained look crossing her face. "Not if he was the last man in the North Lands." She looked at Henrik, her dimple appearing again. "The truth is I'm terribly picky, and I've been holding out for Henrik for years."

The look in her eyes made Henrik's heart beat so quickly he could barely draw breath. He couldn't tear his gaze away from her face, even as the king spoke to him.

"It seems the matter is already decided. You may not hold the most elevated position in my court, Lord Henrik, but you have shown your loyalty in a way that deserves the highest of rewards. You have my blessing."

Henrik ignored Kincaid's laughter and Jocelyn's cheers. He

didn't spare a glance for the queen's reaction to gaining him as a son-in-law, or to Norik's excited stream of questions. All he could see was Lavinia, the laughter in her eyes, the invitation in her smile, and just the very warmth of her. Could it be possible she was really going to be his?

He closed the distance between them with three short strides. The pain in his leg was forgotten as he swept her up in his arms, relishing her delighted laugh as he spun her around, before setting her down and pressing his lips to hers.

It was a quick kiss, given the setting, but the fire of her lips still sent sparks shooting into every inch of him. And it was filled with the promise of a future where he would incredibly, impossibly, have the right to call her his.

"Are you going to be my real uncle?"

The shrill, excited voice, and the insistent tugging on his leggings made Henrik pull his eyes from his princess at last, grinning down at his interrogator.

"Yes, Norik, I suppose I am. I guess I'm in your family after all."

"I said so," the toddler agreed smugly, to general laughter.

Henrik chuckled too, his eyes already back on Lavinia, who was laughing with the rest of them. But before he could respond, a shout from the corridor made them all turn their heads toward the doorway, apprehension on every face.

A royal guard hurried into the room, and King Malcolm strode forward to meet him.

"What is it?"

"Your Majesty," the guard said nervously. "It's the prisoner. I'm afraid she broke free on the way to the dungeons, and—"

"You're telling me she's escaped?" the king demanded, and the guard flinched slightly at his tone.

"Not exactly, Your Majesty," he said, swallowing hard. "That is, she attempted to run from the castle. We would have caught her without too much difficulty, I think, except—"

"What's that?" Kincaid interrupted sharply, and Henrik could tell what had distracted the prince. Screams, muffled by distance, but increasing in volume, could be heard echoing down the corridor.

"Well, she made it outside the castle, but she was intercepted by—"

A particularly loud scream caused the guard to break off again. This time it was Jocelyn who strode forward, her son still perched on her hip.

"There's a dragon here, isn't there?" she asked eagerly. The guard nodded mutely, and Jocelyn turned to her husband. "I think it's Elddreki. I can sense him even from here. My word, his signature seems to get stronger every time I see him."

"Your dragon friend is here?" Lavinia demanded, every bit as eager as Jocelyn. "What are we waiting for?"

Henrik felt a hint of trepidation as the young princess started toward the door, and he hastened to follow her. He knew that Kincaid and Jocelyn trusted Elddreki, but the creature was still a dragon, after all. If Lavinia was going to be anywhere near the beast, Henrik wanted to be close by.

"Gather two squadrons," King Malcolm instructed the guard curtly. "Have them stand by, but not show themselves unless called."

The guard bowed, hurrying from the room, and the king turned to his son and daughter-in-law.

"I mean no disrespect to the creature, but until we can confirm that he comes in peace..."

"Don't worry, Father," said Kincaid lightly. "Elddreki won't be offended." He grinned. "He's used to getting quite a reaction wherever he goes."

"Come on," said Lavinia impatiently from the doorway. The

whole group hurried from the room, Queen Marguerite falling behind due to her determination to maintain a stately stride.

When they reached the entrance to the castle, Henrik had to fight hard to resist the urge to draw his sword. He had heard Kincaid describe dragons on more than one occasion, but seeing one in the flesh was something else altogether.

The monstrous reptile was as tall as several men, the scales that covered every inch of his body glistening in the orange light of early evening. The dragon was more colorful than Henrik had expected, his green, purple, and blue tones sparkling with a vibrancy that seemed unnatural.

The gleaming teeth, and the alarmingly long talons Henrik had expected, however. He looked around instinctively for Lavinia, unsurprised to see that excitement was eclipsing trepidation in her expression.

"Ah, Jocelyn, Kincaid," the dragon said, his eyes passing over the rest of the group curiously. He inclined his head to the king. "Well met, again, king of men."

King Malcolm matched the posture, his voice impressively steady as he responded. "Well met, indeed, Mighty Dragon. Do you come to us in peace?"

"Naturally," said the dragon, who could only be Elddreki. His tail flicked casually against the flagstones, causing a few stifled screams to sound from the growing audience who were gathered around the edge of the courtyard.

The dragon ignored them, his eyes settling on Jocelyn. "I came immediately. Did you intend to call me?"

Jocelyn shook her head, looking stunned. "No. I didn't even realize I could."

"Nor did I, in honesty," said Elddreki cheerfully. "It seems our connection is growing. It is a most fascinating phenomenon."

"Yes, yes," interjected Kincaid hastily, as a musing expression came over the dragon's face. "But why did you come? How did you know there was dragon magic at work here?"

"I didn't," said Elddreki simply. "I only knew that Jocelyn had discovered something greatly distressing, something of relevance to me."

"It must have been when I saw the crystal," Jocelyn breathed. "I thought of the dragons immediately, and that they would want to know."

"Once I arrived, of course, I knew there had been dragon magic at work," Elddreki continued placidly. "I assume this is the culprit? She still reeks of it."

He raised one clawed front foot, shaking it casually. Henrik gave an involuntarily gasp. Until that moment he hadn't even noticed the human clutched in the dragon's talons. Claudette was wide eyed but silent, clearly too terrified to make a noise.

Jocelyn's eyes also grew wide as she took in the woman being held captive by the dragon.

"Yes, that's her," she said quietly. "She was using this to ensnare Prince Ormond—it's a crystal from Wyvern Islands. She got it from Rasad, back in Thorania." She dug into a fold of her gown with her free hand, pulling out the handkerchief.

"That's mine," Claudette hissed, breaking her silence the moment the talisman appeared.

"It is not," said the dragon. His voice was no louder than it had been before, but somehow his tone was so awful that the entire courtyard fell instantly into a nervous silence.

Elddreki leaned forward, snaking his head down to Jocelyn's level and inhaling deeply. "Yes, it is from Wyvern Islands, as you say." He raised his head again, his gaze passing to Claudette, who trembled slightly under his unwavering scrutiny. "You have done great wrong even to have this item, let alone to use it in malice against another human."

Claudette was still a little pale, but she held her head up

defiantly, refusing to acknowledge her fault. Henrik shook his head.

"She's certainly bold," he muttered.

Lavinia, standing beside him, made a quiet scoffing noise. "There's a point where boldness becomes idiocy," she said dryly. "Even I know that."

"And that point is when you're being held captive by a sharp-taloned dragon?" Henrik asked, smiling slightly in spite of the situation.

Lavinia grinned. "I'd say by then, you're well past that point."

"It's a dragon!" Norik's belated whisper—loud enough to carry audibly across the group—drew the dragon's attention to the small boy.

"Ah," he said, tilting his head to the side. "Is this your son, Jocelyn?" He leaned forward again. "He smells like you, a little. But also...something different."

"Wow," breathed Norik, showing none of the fear that was gripping most of the adults in the vicinity. He turned to his father, his eyes wide and excited. "I like dragons!"

Kincaid chuckled, an edge to the sound. "This one's all right, yes."

"Thank you, Kincaid," said Elddreki solemnly, no hint of humor in his voice. "I believe you intend to compliment me." He turned his attention back to Jocelyn. "But to return to the matter of this artifact. It is troubling. The elders of my colony will be concerned to know that one of the crystals survived the destruction of the stronghold in Thorania."

"I'm fairly confident this is the only one that survived," said Jocelyn quickly. "I can explain it all to you. I assume you'll want to take the crystal back to Wyvern Islands, for examination by the elders."

"You are correct," said Elddreki. He looked down at his captive. "But there is still the question of the perpetrator. There are others more suited than I to decide her fate, but the colony would not welcome her presence on our islands, I do not think. Not even simply to face justice."

To Henrik's disbelief, instead of looking more terrified, Claudette had a calculating look growing on her face.

"How will you know if you don't try?" she asked, apparently attempting to be sly. "Perhaps they would be angry with you if you didn't take me there, to let them decide."

Kincaid shook his head, his expression contemptuous. "She's hoping to get more crystals," he said.

Elddreki made a noise of disgust, again shaking Claudette slightly. Of course, slightly to the dragon was still enough to make the human's teeth rattle audibly.

"You are beneath contempt," the dragon said simply. He dropped her onto the flagstones with a thump that made Henrik wince, little as the victim deserved his sympathy. "And I will certainly not be taking you to my colony." Elddreki looked at Jocelyn. "But I will take that crystal, as you suggested."

A sudden cry from Lavinia made Henrik whip his head around, his hand going to the hilt of his sword. It took him a moment to realize that the princess was unharmed, her shout intended as a warning for the dragon. Following her gaze, Henrik saw that Claudette had made the most of Elddreki's distraction, using her sudden freedom to attempt an escape. She had already ducked beneath the dragon's scaled front legs, and was running toward the edge of the courtyard.

"Stop her!" shouted King Malcolm authoritatively.

A number of guards surged forward, but they never reached her. They all drew up in alarm as Elddreki's tail swung out with unexpected force. It slid across the flagstones with a sound like metal scraping on stone, gathering speed by the second. Claudette was still running, but the reach of the dragon's tail was considerable. It hit her with full force, sharp triangular plates and all, just before she reached the start of the gathered crowd.

The Thoranian woman was lifted briefly into the air, before falling with a sickening thud. Henrik tensed, waiting for her next move. But as the long seconds ticked by, he realized all at once that she wasn't going to move. Ever again.

"Is she...dead?" Lavinia asked, her voice hushed.

"What's happening?"

Norik's shrill voice made Henrik turn quickly, and he was relieved to see that Jocelyn was covering the small boy's eyes. He let out a long breath. It was probably the end Claudette deserved, but the toddler didn't need to see it.

Elddreki had also turned at the small boy's question, tilting his head inquiringly to the side as he looked from one member of the group to the next. Their stunned expressions matched those of the crowd. The dragon's eyes settled on the king.

"You said stop her, didn't you?"

"I...I did," King Malcolm acknowledged. He opened his mouth, as if to say more, then seemed unable to think of what to say. After a moment, he shook his head, directing his next words to the nearest guards. "Remove her."

They nodded, hurrying to do as instructed. Within a couple of minutes, all evidence of the grisly incident was gone, and Jocelyn withdrew her hand from the face of the still protesting Norik.

"It seems there is nothing further for me to do here," said Elddreki placidly, apparently unaffected by the grim mood that had gripped all the humans present. "I should take the crystal back to my elders, and alert them to this incident." His eyes lingered on Jocelyn. "Will you accompany me, to explain what has occurred?"

"I can go," said Kincaid quickly, stepping forward. "Jocelyn isn't well."

"I didn't invite you," said Elddreki patiently. "I wish to take Jocelyn."

"It's all right," Jocelyn said quietly to Kincaid. She stepped forward, adding something too quiet for Henrik to catch. Kincaid hesitated for a moment before giving a curt nod. He didn't look happy, but he made no more protest.

"Be careful," he said, his eyes passing between his wife and his son.

Jocelyn stepped up to Elddreki, and Henrik raised his eyebrows at the realization that Norik was still in her arms.

"You wish to bring your son?" Elddreki asked, inclining his head.

"If you're willing," said Jocelyn, holding her son more tightly.

"Certainly."

Without another word, the dragon seized Jocelyn with both front feet, his claws wrapping around the small boy as well. He shot suddenly into the air, and everyone on the ground covered their faces at the sudden rush of wind. Henrik blinked into the sky, trying to follow the dragon's flight with his eyes. In seconds, Elddreki and his human burdens were nothing more than a speck.

"Was it wise, for Norik to go as well?" King Malcolm asked his son, alarm clear in his voice.

"Jocelyn knows what she's doing," said Kincaid firmly. "And we can trust Elddreki."

The king didn't look entirely convinced, but a chuckle from beside Henrik suggested that not everyone in the royal family shared the grandfather's concern.

"I think it's amazing," Lavinia chimed in. "I'm wild with jealousy. Not even three years old yet, and he'll be able to say he's been to a dragon colony!"

Henrik laughed in spite of himself. "Some people get all the luck, hey?"

Lavinia stepped closer, smiling up at him. "Not all the luck," she said warmly, placing a hand on his chest. "Norik may have me beaten when it comes to dragons, but I won a pretty good prize today, too."

Henrik smiled down at her, his heart too full for words. She was glorious in her happiness—no hint of the doubt or frustration, the fear or the hurt that had haunted her eyes too often in the last few days. Her face was made to smile, and he vowed silently to do everything in his power to ensure she had reason to do so for the rest of her life.

EPILOGUE

"Henrik! There you are."

Henrik looked up at the familiar voice. A smile spread over his face at the sight of the spirited princess skipping across the entrance hall with unladylike haste.

"Have you been waiting for me?" he asked, striding forward to meet her partway. There were plenty of others milling around the space, so he resisted the urge to draw her into his arms.

"Of course," said Lavinia brightly. "Now that we're officially betrothed, we should arrive to formal functions together, don't you think?"

"Absolutely," said Henrik solemnly, tucking her arm into his. "It's very important to observe the formalities."

Lavinia snorted, and Henrik couldn't help the grin that broke through his falsely serious expression. It had been a couple of weeks since their betrothal had been publicly announced, but he still felt at times like he must be trapped in a dream. A very pleasant dream.

"I don't think the delegation have emerged yet, so we can still beat them to the dining hall. Even if you are late."

Henrik rolled his eyes as he allowed Lavinia to lead him

down a corridor. "I'm not late. I just had to walk here from home. We can't all live in the castle, you know."

"Oh, I'm not complaining," said Lavinia cheerfully. "I don't mind having you all to myself for a minute."

Henrik smiled warmly down at her, reveling in her vibrancy. He agreed with the sentiment wholeheartedly—it was frustratingly difficult to get a moment alone together, betrothed or not.

He hadn't been paying much attention to where they were walking, but a cold draft made him look up, and he frowned in confusion as he glanced around the poorly lit corridor.

"I may not live in the castle, but I do know that this isn't the way to the dining hall."

"Of course it is," Lavinia contradicted.

Henrik raised an eyebrow, and Lavinia grinned, her dimple appearing.

"I didn't say it was the most direct way to get there."

"Where are you taking me, Princess?" Henrik laughed.

"Nowhere," said Lavinia innocently. "It's just that sometimes, when I wander down little-used corridors with you following me, nice things happen."

"Is that right?" Henrik said, a smile slowly growing.

He glanced around. A solitary servant hurried past, a distracted look on her face as she ducked her head respectfully to the princess. Once she rounded the corner, no one was in sight.

"What kind of things?" Henrik asked his betrothed, drawing her into an alcove behind a particularly formidable suit of armor. "Things like this?"

Without giving her a chance to respond, he enfolded her in his arms, pressing his lips recklessly against hers. His behavior had generally been circumspect, in an effort to reassure the king and queen that they hadn't been rash in bestowing their only daughter's hand on his irresponsible self. But this opportunity was too good to miss.

Lavinia snaked her arms up behind his back, clutching onto his tunic in a way that was sure to disarrange the smooth fabric. He didn't mind. The feel of her so close to him, her warmth, the eagerness of her response as she kissed him back with all her characteristic enthusiasm, made his head spin deliciously.

After a delightfully prolonged moment, he pulled away, his breathing uneven.

"Sometimes," he whispered, pressing his face into her unruly hair, "it's hard to believe you're real."

Lavinia's breaths were a little unsteady too, but he could feel her grin where her face was pressed against his shoulder.

"Of course I'm real. You could never dream me up, you're not nearly inventive enough."

Henrik stepped back, laughing. They had pushed their luck far enough, and he didn't particularly want to be caught by some gossiping servant kissing behind a suit of armor.

"True. You're much too vibrant to have come out of my imagination." He ran a hand through his hair, trying to smooth the disordered mess before offering her his arm. "Ready to go?"

Lavinia sighed, but she put her hand on his arm. "I suppose so. But the welcome gala won't be nearly as fun as being here with you."

Henrik smiled, glancing around at the dark, drafty corridor. "It is a nice spot, no denying it." He started to walk, raising an eyebrow as he looked down at her. "Do you enjoy galas less now that you can't spend them flirting with every courtier who looks your way?"

"Not at all," said Lavinia promptly. She grinned up at him. "Because now I can flirt with you. I've been carefully holding off doing that for years, so I think it will be a long time before the novelty of it wears off."

"Forever, if I can help it," said Henrik, his eyes twinkling.

They reached the dining hall all too soon, and Henrik resigned himself to an evening of scrutiny as he took his seat beside Lavinia. He had never felt unnoticed before, exactly, but it was incredible how many eyes seemed to be on him all the time since the announcement of his betrothal to the princess.

"Congratulations, Your Highness, My Lord."

"Thank you." Henrik smiled warmly at the woman taking her seat on his other side. He'd heard she was back in Bryford, but hadn't yet seen her. "I hear we can expect to offer you similar congratulations later this evening."

"Yes," said Lady Brielle, blushing faintly. "I didn't expect the announcement to be made tonight—I hope it won't distract too much from welcoming the delegation. But Their Majesties, and Prince Ormond for that matter," she glanced up at the crown prince, who was speaking to his father nearby and had yet to take his seat on her other side, "didn't wish to delay."

Lavinia snorted. "I can imagine. I'm sure my parents want to formalize it before some other impostor can attempt a plot against my unattached brother. And as for Ormond," she glared at her brother, "it's no wonder he wants to lock you down before you realize you've forgiven him far too quickly."

The impulsive young princess leaned around Henrik, clasping Lady Brielle's hand with an expression of concern. "I couldn't be more delighted at the prospect of having you for a sister, Brielle, but are you sure you can't do better than Ormond?"

Lady Brielle laughed self-consciously, blushing again as she threw a glance toward the crown prince. "You're too hard on him, Your Highness," she said gently, the softness in her eyes warming Henrik to her even more. "He didn't know what he was doing. When he visited me on our estate all those times, before...before all the mess started...he was so kind, and so wise..." She ducked her head, attempting unsuccessfully to hide both her smile and her blush. "I'm just glad to know that I wasn't mistaken in him, that it was his later behavior, not his earlier, that was out of character."

"Please, Brielle," said Lavinia, sounding pained. "You have to stop calling me 'Your Highness' now we're going to be sisters." She sighed. "And I can see that you really like him, strange as it is." She shook her head. "I can't comprehend your taste in men, but since I like everything else about you, I think I can overlook it."

"Thank you, Your—Lavinia," said Lady Brielle, smiling in amusement.

"Yes, he can be a bit dull, but he's got a good heart, really," said Kincaid casually from Lavinia's other side. "A bit of a humbling is good for us all, but he didn't deserve to be made such a fool of, poor fellow."

Henrik shook his head. "Claudette was certainly ruthless. And the magic she was using was alarmingly powerful." He looked from Kincaid to Jocelyn. "I assume the dragons destroyed the crystal?"

"They did," Jocelyn confirmed, leaning forward in her place on Kincaid's other side. "After a very close examination of it."

"I heard about the dragon coming to Bryford," said Lady Brielle, sounding awed. "I'm not sure whether to be glad or sorry that I'd already left the city by then. Did your son really go to the Dragon Realm?"

Kincaid chuckled. "He certainly did. He'll tell you about it in extreme—if largely incomprehensible—detail if you give him half a chance."

"Weren't you nervous?" Lady Brielle asked, looking at Jocelyn.

The princess smiled. "Not really. I trust Elddreki implicitly.

He would never let harm befall Norik. And I wanted to see what we could find out about his...abilities."

"I didn't know you investigated that whole question while you were gone," said Henrik, interested. "What did Elddreki say?"

"It was Raqisa, actually," said Jocelyn, naming Elddreki's mate. "She's very good at identifying these things. That's why I took Norik to Wyvern Islands instead of just asking Elddreki to have a look at him while he was in Bryford."

"And?" Henrik prompted.

Jocelyn and Kincaid exchanged a look. "She could tell at once that he had magic," said Jocelyn. "And she said it hasn't gotten weaker with being passed down a generation. She thought it was at least as strong as mine. Honestly, she sensed it so instantly that it was a little embarrassing that I hadn't realized it before, being his mother and all. But I suppose since it's always been there, I didn't really know what I was looking for."

"I thought his power might be change, like Joss's," Kincaid interjected. "That maybe he just changed our minds about Claudette. But apparently Raqisa didn't think so."

"No, she thinks it's truth, or something along those lines," said Jocelyn. "She thinks he has the power to expose deception, probably in any form. But in the case of Claudette and her manipulation of the crystal from the Dragon Realm, his magic had the effect of canceling the crystal's power. Since its function was deception."

"How...how incredible," said Lady Brielle, looking like she was trying very hard to keep her calm.

Henrik smiled to himself. Personally, although he'd been astonished when he first learned of the innate magic that Jocelyn and her twin brother were born with, he'd never found it unnerving. But he knew that lots of people were still uncomfortable with the princess's power. Including the king and queen, to some extent, if he wasn't mistaken.

But his smile turned into a frown as he looked at Jocelyn's face. He would have thought she'd be happy to have answers about her son's power, but she didn't look happy. She looked weary, and a little tense.

"What's the problem?" he muttered to Lavinia. "I thought Jocelyn accepted that her power was a good thing a long time ago."

"Oh, she did," Lavinia whispered back. "I don't think she minds that Norik has magic, in a general sense." She chuckled. "Poor Joss."

"What?" asked Henrik, confused.

"Well," Lavinia reasoned, "even the most confident of parents might feel daunted by the prospect of raising a toddler with an innate—and currently undeveloped—power to detect and expose deception."

"Ah," said Henrik, thinking the matter over. He couldn't help the grin that spread across his face as he looked at Kincaid, and saw that he, too, looked a little overwhelmed. "I see." It was possible for a toddler to be too honest, after all.

"Anyway," Jocelyn said, clearly trying to turn the topic away from her absent son, "the dragons destroyed the crystal, so we don't need to be afraid of a repeat of what happened."

"Well, that's something," said Henrik briskly. He looked at Kincaid. "You've already spoken to the real Thoranian delegation, haven't you? What did they have to say about it all?"

"Yes, we were there to greet them when they arrived this morning," Kincaid confirmed. He chuckled. "Norik is already thick as thieves with Cody and Yasmin's little girl. They're going to cause trouble while the delegation is here, if I'm not mistaken."

"Especially for the poor kitchen staff," interjected Jocelyn dryly. "Allow me to apologize in advance on my son's behalf for the absence of the elaborate cake that was supposed to be the centerpiece of tonight's dessert."

Everyone chuckled, but Kincaid's next words sobered the group. "Cody and Yasmin were horrified when they heard what had happened. Especially Yasmin, when she learned how Claudette had used her family's name to claim a welcome into our castle. Apparently neither of them even knew of her, although Yasmin recognized a few of the others as former servants of Rasad's."

He shrugged. "She said that, since her parents' estate is right next to Rasad's former land, they received most of the survivors who fled the dragon attack on Rasad's Bastion, tended to their wounds and such. She thinks it would have been easy for Claudette to steal the family's seal then."

Jocelyn shook her head. "She certainly planned it all a long time before. She must have been very young when the Bastion was destroyed."

"I doubt she had this specific plan in mind back then," mused Henrik. "I got the impression that she was an extremely resourceful and determined person. I suspect she often took the opportunity of acquiring anything that she thought might be useful to her, and then figured out how best to turn it to her purposes later."

"Like she attempted to acquire you," said Lavinia darkly.

Henrik smiled at her, and her expression softened at the warmth in his eyes. "She never had a hope of competing with you."

"All right, all right," interjected Kincaid hastily. "I can deal with you marrying my little sister, Henrik, but not mooning over her in public."

Henrik laughed, unrepentant. "I'll save my mooning for

private, then." He exchanged a glance with Lavinia, the memory of their recent stolen kiss dancing in each of their eyes.

Kincaid looked slightly ill. "That doesn't make me feel better, somehow."

Lavinia grinned at her brother, clearly enjoying his discomfiture. "You can't talk, Kincaid. Henrik's told me how lovesick you were when you thought Jocelyn wasn't going to marry you. Sounds like you were an utter mess. At least Henrik held himself together when he thought he'd never get Mother and Father's blessing."

"Traitor!" accused Kincaid, throwing a dark look at his best friend.

"Ah, yes, I remember when you were suffering from the anguish of frustrated love," Jocelyn said reminiscently. "It was really very endearing."

"You weren't exactly skipping around yourself," muttered Kincaid mutinously, as Lavinia and Henrik laughed at him.

"I'm glad to see you able to join us again, by the way," Henrik said, smiling at Jocelyn. "We missed you while you were so ill." He paused. "And not just because you were the only one who could probably have recognized Claudette's stolen magic right away."

Jocelyn sighed. "Yes, the timing was unfortunate. But I'm feeling much better now. Not quite back to normal, but well enough. The physician dug up an old remedy, some kind of tea made from ginger root." She shrugged. "Who knows if it's that, or just time passing, but it seems to have helped."

"I just wish I knew why it was so much worse this time, and so much earlier," said Kincaid, still looking a touch anxious as he examined his wife.

"Maybe this baby has the magic power of sucking the life from everyone he touches," suggested Lavinia brightly.

Jocelyn shuddered. "Don't even joke about such things, Lavinia."

"Have you asked your mother?" Lady Brielle suggested delicately. "Did she have similar sickness when she was pregnant?"

"Well, yes, she did, actually," said Jocelyn. "But since I didn't have it nearly so bad with Norik, I wasn't expecting it. I imagine my mother's experience was different from normal, anyway. She was probably extra sick because she was having..."

The princess trailed off, her eyes going wide. She looked at her husband. For a moment Kincaid was silent, an eyebrow raised inquiringly. Then the implication seemed to dawn on him, and his mouth fell open.

"Twins," he finished for her. "Your mother was having twins."

There was a prolonged moment of silence, as everyone around the group blinked in surprise. Then Lavinia went off into a peal of laughter loud enough to draw a censuring look from the queen, seated further down the table.

"You're going to have twins," she gasped. "Two magical babies, combined with Norik, the truth-exposing three-year-old. Oh Joss, you poor thing!"

Jocelyn turned to her sister-in-law, still looking stunned. "I don't know why I didn't realize it before," she said blankly. "It should have been obvious, since I'm a twin. But after Norik, I just assumed..."

She trailed off again, looking helplessly at Kincaid. He had been staring at her as she spoke, but all at once his look of shock gave way to a growing smile, and he started to laugh as well.

"We don't do things by halves, do we?" he said.

Jocelyn laughed weakly, putting a hand over her eyes. "Apparently not."

"I think we should take these ones to the dragons earlier," said Kincaid firmly. "Find out what we're dealing with in terms of their powers, before they can figure out how to team up against us."

Lavinia was still laughing. "I'll definitely be on their side, just to give you fair warning."

Henrik grinned. "At this rate, you'll have Valoria peppered with magic-carrying children in no time. Just imagine how many there might be in a few generations, especially if the power really does get stronger each time it's passed down."

"We're not going to have *that* many children, Henrik," Jocelyn said dryly. She shook her head, looking thoughtful. "But you have a point. I wonder what that will really mean for the kingdom. Even the dragons can't predict what will happen, because they never thought humans could carry magic at all until Eamon and I came along."

She glanced at Kincaid. "And I can only assume Kyona will be in the same situation. We should really warn Eamon and Lucy. They should be looking out for any signs in Violet, while she's still a baby. Our poor parents had absolutely no idea what was happening with us, and keeping it a secret didn't do anyone any favors in the end."

Henrik turned his attention away from the conversation between Jocelyn and Kincaid, looking down at Lavinia with a smile playing around his lips.

"What?" she asked, glancing up and catching him looking.

"I was just thinking about the future," he said, reaching up to touch one of the perpetually unruly strands of her auburn hair, which had escaped its pins.

Lavinia grinned. "If I'm honest, I'm a little sad that our children won't have their ability to wreak havoc enhanced by magic."

Henrik chuckled, warmth roaring through him at the idea of children that were a combination of him and the impossibly desirable woman sitting next to him.

"I don't know," he said. "I think they'll have fire enough without magic."

Lavinia rested her hand on his on top of the table, letting out a contented sigh. "At least they won't have to grow up as princes and princesses," she said. "They'll have as much freedom as I can possibly give them."

Henrik smiled. "Speaking of freedom, I spoke to your father this afternoon. He doesn't object to me starting your training straight away."

"Really?" Lavinia asked, sitting up straight in her seat, an excited light in her eyes. "Can we start tomorrow? I can be at the training yard at dawn, if you like! What do you think we should do first? Sword fighting? Archery? Those long pole things?"

Henrik laughed. "Slow down. Firstly, there's no way I'm letting you loose on the training yard at dawn. You'd be far too distracting for the poor knights trying to train."

Lavinia raised an eyebrow, her lips curving mischievously. "You mean you don't want me watching them spar shirtless," she accused. "You're as bad as my mother."

"Your mother isn't wrong about everything," said Henrik ruefully.

She laughed again, clearly taking his expression as confirmation of her guess.

"And secondly," Henrik pushed on, unable to help smiling himself, "there's no rush to cover everything at once. I promised to teach you to fight, and I will, but it takes time to master these things."

"Time is something we have," said Lavinia, her face softening from its habitual laughter into the more intimate smile that was only for him.

"Exactly," Henrik agreed, his heart full. "We have the rest of our lives."

NOTE FROM THE AUTHOR

Thank you for reading *Downfall's Echo*. I hope you enjoyed hearing a little more about the aftermath of the events of *Downfall of the Curse*, and getting to share the adventure of Henrik and Lavinia, now that the irrepressible young princess is all grown up. I would be so grateful if you would consider leaving a review on Amazon—it would really make a difference!

If you, like Jocelyn, are wondering what the impact will be of magic becoming more common in Valoria's and Kyona's human populations, stay tuned for my next series, The Vazula Chronicles, planned for release in 2022. More adventure, fantasy, mystery, and romance to come!

This series will be its own story, rather than a sequel to The Kyona Chronicles, but it will be set in the same world, with some familiar names and places. And some features that are entirely new, as the cover for Book One—*A Kingdom Submerged*—suggests!

Join up to my mailing list at deborahgracewhite.com to be kept up to date on new releases, specials, and giveaways, such as bonus chapters. You will also receive *Dragon's Sight*, an 8,000 word prequel to *The Kyona Chronicles*, told from Elddreki's perspective.

Again, thanks for entering the world of *The Kyona Chronicles*! I hope to see you back again.

ACKNOWLEDGMENTS

Downfall's Echo was initially intended to be a novella which would act as a postscript of sorts to the second generation of Kyona adventures. The plan was for it to match *Captive's Return*, the novella which forms Book Three, and closes out the first generation.

But, as always, I wrote more than I planned, and it turned into a novel! Henrik's story is shorter than Cal's, Jo's, Jocelyn's, or Lucy's. But as I got into his head, I found that it was a full story of its own.

The extra length meant an extra effort from my wonderful team of supporters. As always, my husband Ray deserves the first mention, being my alpha reader (or listener!) and my cheer squad. Thanks for seeing the series through with me!

A huge thank you to my beta readers, Andrew, Dad, Cherilyn, Adrian, Mum, and Tamara. You should all get a medal for making it through the entire series, right to the bitter end. And a massive extra thanks to Dad for your developmental and copy editing, and to Mum for line editing. Dad, you've been incredible with all the hours you've put in, and all the pressure of meeting the rapid release deadline. I'm more grateful than I can say.

Thank you to Karri for the cover—you never fail to come up with something amazing. And as always, thank you to Rebecca for the exquisite map. I can't wait to work with you again!

To you, the reader, thank you for giving me the privilege of being an author.

And above all, to God. Thank You that You never have and never will give up on me. It's thanks to You that I ever have the perseverance to see things through.

ABOUT THE AUTHOR

I've been a reader since I can remember, growing up on a wide range of books, from classic literature to light-hearted romps. The love of reading has traveled with me unchanged across multiple continents, and carried me from my own childhood all the way to having children of my own.

But if reading is like looking through a window into a magical and beautiful world, beginning to write my own stories was like discovering that I could open that window and climb right out into fantasyland.

I cannot believe how privileged I am to actually be living that childhood dream and publishing my own novels. I do so from my hometown of Adelaide, Australia, where I live with my husband and our three little ones.

I've never outgrown my love of young adult stories, and my first series, The Kyona Chronicles, is a young adult fantasy series of six installments.

Feel free to email me at deborah@deborahgracewhite.com

and introduce yourself! Or subscribe to my mailing list at deborahgracewhite.com for free giveaways, sales, and updates.

www.ingramcontent.com/pod-product-compliance
Lightning Source LLC
Chambersburg PA
CBHW060910190726
48286CB00002B/439